H.H. Holmes
The Devil in Me

By

Colby Van Wagoner

DEDICATION

To my mother; Lynda Van Wagoner, Sister Brandi
Sasheen and Adam Williams. Gill and Julie Van
Wagoner. All my wonderful, supportive Facebook
friends, you know who you are! Thank you to everyone
who supports my writing.

"He who fights monsters should see to it that he himself does not become a monster. And if you gaze for long into an abyss, the abyss gazes also into you."
— Friedrich Nietzsche, Beyond Good and Evil

CONTENTS

i

'Prologue'

Delighted to make your acquaintance, I am Doctor Henry Howard Holmes. I present to you, my prologue. These are the words from the mouth and the mind of a person who received a much better end than the endings provided to the unlucky ones who crossed my path. In the end, I do not expect you to understand me, or my actions, only fear me. In fact, you will more than likely be asking the questions my victims had asked me, in the flesh so to speak, such as; how did you become such a madman, and why did you do this, and why are you doing this to me?

I am born Herman Webster Mudgett; however, soon undertook another guise and transformed into the person you have only heard and read rumors of. The author would have you think his research, and words, has brought you to know what I am truly capable of, or have accomplished in my lifetime.

Like you, the author is sheltered by his surroundings and from the hypnotic gaze which my eyes, in their physical presence, can produce in the weak minded. The control I use to manipulate and fulfill my every wish, want, desire, and need. It is far beyond what the imagination can come close to comprehending, for the sane revel in their comforts and safety.

To think I am the creation of a miserable childhood, or a result of my environment, would be naive and ignorant on your behalf. I would expect more from you, since many are exposed to the same childhood I experienced, and have become something entirely different, something other than the monster before you.

Killers before and after me can only dream to accomplish, and pursue, the extraordinary work I left behind for them, but they will fail. I, H.H. Holmes, confessed to and convicted for killing twenty seven victims, will always be spoken of, in the circles of serial killer experts, as the killer that went above and beyond anyone's expectations.

No one will ever know my secrets, or the amount of carnage I actually left in my wake, for it is more than one could ever suspect any one person capable of achieving. Use your imagination if you will and trust me when I say, look into my eyes. I expect and demand your fear.

Yours truly,

Doctor Henry Howard Holmes

'Home Is Not Where the Heart Is'

It was the year of 1876 in Gilmanton, New
Hampshire. Herman Webster Mudgett was in the living
room, drawing pictures of the human form. His
mother, Page Mudgett, was in the kitchen making
dinner and preparing for his father, Levi Horton
Mudgett, to return from a long day of farm work. His
mother was tall and thin with long brown hair, which
hung down to the middle of her back, usually braided.

The summer air was humid, drawing sweat from
the pores like an unforgiving parasite, sucking the life
from its host. His mother insisted on keeping the
windows open, which meant the humid air would seep
through, making the house feel like an oven. He
stopped drawing and looked over at the table, reaching
for the newspaper. Using his shirt sleeve to wipe the
sweat from his forehead, Herman read the front
headline; 1876, Alexander Graham Bell granted a patent
for his invention called the telephone. This will change
the way communication takes place all over the world.

Technologies were rapidly being introduced to the world, "Mom, someone invented a telephone!" Herman yelled out.

She was too involved with her work in the kitchen to respond, which she usually was when Levi was about to return from work. A glass of water quenched Herman's thirst and scratchy throat. Placing the glass on the table, he adjusted his legs to get more comfortable. The shirt and pants he was wearing were a bit tight. Herman's father always insisted he wear a nice shirt and a pair of pants. The pants were making his legs itch.

Herman turned to the second page and continued reading: The Settle Carlisle Railway, in England, opened to passenger traffic. Meanwhile, The Transcontinental Express arrived in San Francisco, California, via the First Transcontinental Railroad line. The train ride took eighty three hours and thirty nine minutes, after having left New York City.

Herman longed to travel and would often drift off; daydreaming of the day he would have his freedoms as an adult. His mind raced at the thought of climbing onto a train and riding across America. Seeing the different people and cultures, and traveling, would be extremely fascinating. Further, into the paper, he read: The United States will be celebrating its centennial, and Colorado has been admitted as the 38th U.S. state. In the presidential election of 1876, Rutherford Hayes is declared the winner over Samuel Tilden.

Herman always skipped most of the local events, since there was no interest in the town of Gilmanton, or their local news. Extremely interested in travel, Herman always imagined leaving New Hampshire. The news, about the Transcontinental Express, sparked his interest, also Colorado, with its scenic mountains colorful landscapes and the large state of Texas. He planned on traveling to all the places he read about in, both, his encyclopedias and the newspapers, Texas, California, other U.S. States, and eventually Canada.

Usually the most interesting topics, and special interest stories, were towards the end of the paper. One of the smaller headlines caught his eye. It just so happened, this material would shape Herman Mudgett's future. It read: Failed grave robbery of the Lincoln Tomb. However, police have no leads and no suspects, as no one witnessed the event. Licking his finger and turning the page, an impressionable image raced through his mind about the idea of a grave robber, such an intriguing and gruesome thought.

With an extensive collection of encyclopedias for reference, and the vast information discovered in the newspapers, learning and knowledge came quickly. This aided him in obtaining clarification and new ideas. Herman was also becoming deeply intrigued by the numerous subjects; he was learning about, in his science and biology classes. The drawing would have to wait. He jumped to his feet, opening one of his encyclopedias, locating a small section on grave robbing.

Reading further, his mother called out from the kitchen, "Herman, what did you say about a telephone? What is a telephone?"

"I will explain later, mom, after dinner." She did not reply, too focused on her preparations for the evening.

The encyclopedia had some interesting information. He began to read, out loud, "Grave robbery or tomb raiding, is the act of uncovering a grave or crypt, to steal artifacts or personal effects. A related act is body snatching, which is someone exhuming a grave for the purpose of stealing a corpse, rather than stealing other objects." He paused, "Body snatching?"

"Body snatching? Herman Webster Mudgett what are you reading about?" He was startled by his mother, as she walked up behind him, brushing her hand through his hair, "Do not read too much about that, son. You know you will be up late at night, again, having nightmares. You should be reading your bible."

"All right, all right, mother." Herman's mother was always worried about his disturbed sleep patterns.

Too often, he woke in the middle of the night. But, for some odd reason, he found himself reveling in the images his mind would present in his nightmares. There was comfort in the horrific experiences his dreams would present. Fear and uncontrollable feelings, from the drastic emotions, would haunt him when he would wake. There was a sense of exploration in his dreams. The nightmares would allow him to do things; otherwise, unattainable in reality.

Looking at the encyclopedia, Herman returned reading where he left off. This time he would not read aloud, chuckling, because of his mother's response to the words "body snatching". It causes great difficulty in the study of archaeology, art history, and history. Countless grave sites and tombs have been robbed before scholars are able to examine their contents.

Grave robbers are often lower-income individuals, who sell their goods on the black market, "Selling stolen items, on the black market? This is interesting."

New ideas were hatching, which would have to be written in his journal. But first, more reading on grave robbery was called for; though some artifacts may make their way to museums, or to scholars, most end up in private collections instead. Ancient Egyptian tombs are one of the most common examples of tomb, or crypt robbery.

Modern grave robbing, in North America, also involves abandoned or forgotten private grave sites. These sites are often desecrated by grave robbers in search of old and valuable jewelry. Affected sites are typically in rural, forested, areas where once prominent wealthy landowners and their families have been buried.

"Now we are getting to the good stuff." He whispered, under his breath.

Remote and often unmapped locations of defunct private cemeteries make them particularly susceptible to grave robbing. The practice is encouraged upon the discovery of a previously unknown family cemetery by a new landowner. Laws that have been enacted, in the various regions, have been ignored due to extreme poverty. The robbing of graves continues to grow each year.

Pondering over the concept of grave robbery, for jewelry and other valuables, was interesting. However, he was much more interested in the process of body snatching. The strange rush of imagining being in the snatcher's position and what it would feel like, digging up a grave in the middle of the night, pushed him to read further. The intense feeling of unearthing a body, which had been placed in a casket and buried, intended to rest in peace overcame him.

He continued imagining the conditions of the bodies and the various processes of preparing a body for burial. Further into the encyclopedia, he discovered the section on body snatching and read; Body snatching is the secret exhuming of corpses from graveyards. A common purpose of body snatching is to sell the corpses for dissection, or anatomy lectures in medical schools.

Herman closed the encyclopedia, gaining a better understanding of what it was he wanted to pursue in life, attend medical school and become a doctor. He switched to reading the newspaper discovering another fascinating article. The headline reads, "First cremation in the United States took place". The crematory was built by Francis Julius LeMoyne.

The article went into specific details of the new process. Cremation is a new advancement eliminating the increasing lack of space in grave yards. The process allows families to keep the remains of their loved ones in beautiful vases. Cremation also helps to eliminate the spread of disease, which can spread quickly should a virus, or plague, occur within the general populations.

Cremation reduces dead bodies to basic compounds in the form of gas and bone fragments. This is accomplished through burning the deceased at high temperatures. Cremated remains, which are not a health risk, may be buried in memorial sites or cemeteries. They may be legally retained by relatives, or dispersed in a variety of ways and locations.

Herman's eyes were wide open, as his mind digested the material he was reading. It was a new, overwhelming feeling and a sense he had never felt before, "Doctor Herman Webster Mudgett." Inside, saying it out loud, he felt a renewed drive to do improve in school. If he were to get better grades in school, as opposed to his prior grade achievements, he would be well on his way.

Herman was determined to continue reading and researching, in order to impress his teachers. However, there was a new agenda forming in his mind. He continued reading; a body, prepared for cremation, must be placed in a container, which can be a simple cardboard box, a wooden casket, or coffin. Most casket manufacturers will provide a line of caskets specially built for cremation.

After the funeral service, the interior box will be removed from the shell, before cremation, permitting the shell to be reused. Funeral homes are beginning to offer traditional caskets, used only for the duration of the services. After which, the body can be transferred to another container for cremation.

Continuing to explore his thoughts, for a few moments, he was becoming more and more fascinated with the idea of the events leading up to someone dying, and death. He closed the newspaper and returned to drawing the human body, in his sketchbook. It was a way for him to escape the growing and never-ending bickering, and tensions, between his mother and father.

The Mudgett's home was a simple structure, as were many of the other neighborhood houses. Herman's room was in the confined and musty attic space. His father moved him into the attic, after turning his first room into an office space. There were pictures of his grandparents, additional family members, but very few group photos. The pictures captured a sense of tenseness, and the struggles many families were experiencing.

The house was painted a simple white with brown shutters besides each window. The yard was decorated with colorful annuals, perennials, and green bushes, providing the illusion that everything beautiful on the outside, was actually quite different than what was happening on the inside. In the rear of the house, was a medium sized barn where his father kept his carriage and yard tools.

His father was always returning home late, later than usual, nowadays. And, aside from that, the problems between his mother and father seemed to be escalating every evening. Levi was a slightly overweight man, with a receding hairline and an aged rough looking face. Being able to avoid his father's rage and anger, directed towards his mother and him, was becoming an unavoidable routine.

Herman stopped drawing, sat back on the couch remembering a time when his mother and father used to sit in the living room, reading scriptures and praying together. However, that had all changed, since Levi had been frequenting the local pub, more often than usual. It seemed the man he remembered as a caring father, had become a distant memory. In the past, his father was extremely religious, but he had become disconnected.

After arriving home, his father seemed more agitated than usual. He rushed through the front door, up the rickety stairs and into the master bedroom, slamming the bedroom door behind him. He was smoking his usual cigar. The trail of smoke floated from the front door, up the stairs, and into the upstairs bedroom. The scent of his father's cigar smoke made him nauseated. What could he do though, tell his father what the effects of the cigar smoke had on him?

At the time of his father's arrival, rarely any attention was paid to what Page and Herman were doing. Levi simply walked through the door and proceeding straight to his room, where he was no doubt pouring himself a tall glass of bourbon. It was the bourbon and whiskey stealing away the man he once felt comfortable calling pops and poppa.

"Herman put your toys away. Go into the kitchen. Please, prepare the table for dinner." His mother instructed, walking up the stairs and to the bedroom door where her husband had retreated.

Herman put away the drawing paper, pencils, and encyclopedias into their specific places, went into the kitchen and listened through the kitchen's vent to what his mother would say to his father. His mother was always calling his pencils and drawing paper, toys. He was still viewed as a little boy playing in his room. First, he heard his mother knock on the bedroom door. Standing just outside the bedroom she hesitated, then softly spoke, "Honey, how was the farming today?" No response came from the bedroom.

Due to the silence, it was obvious his mother was waiting, for any replies, before entering the room. Herman quietly snuck up the stairs and peeked around the wall. Page was standing at the door, her knees shaking and quivering. It was like she was standing at the edge of a cliff, waiting for someone to push her over. She had become just as terrified of Levi, as Herman. She would tell stories about the days when they would take long carriage rides and have afternoon picnics in the park.

His mother had told Herman, in confidence; about his father's detachment and distance ever since Herman's birth. During the birth, she remembered the look on her husband's face, as he watched her cradle their new child in her arms. In the hospital, an immediate sense of jealousy became obvious in Levi.

Throughout Herman's life, his father's jealousy never subsided. But, his mother would only tell Herman those things in confidence and made sure to promise to never tell or reveal any of it to his father.

"Dear, do you mind if I come in?" The door creaked, as it opened.

His father responded, as she opened the door, "Page, will you please give me a few minutes? I just got home from working all day in the humidity. Do you think I want to hear you drill me about every little thing?"

Herman stood quietly, near the top of the stairs, expecting the worst. After a few minutes of silence, there was some rustling then a few loud footsteps across the wood floor and the crash of glass. There was silence, but only for a few moments, broken by a loud crash and finally the bedroom door slamming shut.

Herman crept back down the stairs and rushed back into the kitchen. Next, came his mother's whimpering from the upstairs hallway. She cried to herself, keeping any fright or terror from overcoming them both. She knew that Herman felt the same fear of his father that she felt.

Footsteps came from the stairs, echoing into the living room, down into the main level of the house. Herman's mother walked into the kitchen wiping her eyes and sniffling, as she began helping him set the table. She walked to the stove, removing a few of the pans and began to dish the food onto the plates. Herman walked over to the table, pulled out a chair and sat quietly at the table.

His mother knew there was no need to say it, but she reminded him, "Honey, please behave tonight. Your father had a bad day." He knew what it meant.

As it was with every other night of his father's evening routine, Levi would descend the stairs and enter the kitchen, grumbling and complaining. Mostly, about the food Page had spent hours making. After a few moments, he heard the bedroom door open and footsteps on the staircase. His mother's body language changed. The tense situation increased, as they waited for Levi to enter the kitchen.

Levi walked into the kitchen indistinctly grumbling, as expected. He had his cigar in his left hand and carried a glass in the other, most likely filled with Bourbon or whiskey. After returning home from work, and coming down from the upstairs bedroom, his father was usually carrying a glass for most of the night.

"What are we having tonight, dear, more overcooked meat and lumpy potatoes?" His speech was already becoming slurred, along with an aggressive tone.

Page responded, "Well, dear, I do the best that I can. It's just, cooking on this stove can be tricky. One can never tell when the gas is going to be working right, or if a good amount of gas will be flowing through the units."

"I suppose you blame me for that?" He exclaimed, walking over to the table, placing his drink in front of him and moving the knife and fork next to the plate. "Well, I'm waiting." He exclaimed, moving the ashtray closer to his plate.

Herman's mother walked to the table and began serving the meatloaf and potatoes. She finished scooping the potatoes onto the plates, returning the pot to the stove. She turned and reached for the last plate, Levi grabbed his wife's arm, violently, just before picking up the plate.

"So, what did you two do today? Did you talk about me and what a wonderful husband and father I am?" His mother, concerned, stopped and looked over. Herman knew better than to respond to his father's questions.

"No, honey, Herman went to school and came home, on time, as usual. I cleaned the house and washed your clothes." His father looked around and then back at his mother.

She began shaking, uncontrollably, as he continued to tighten the grip around her wrist, "Herman, how was school, did the other kids at the academy push you around and treat you like the little weakling you are?" Herman kept quiet, shifting in his chair at the dinner table, visions of the bullies at school flashing through his head.

He thought to himself, if only he had ability to strike fear into someone, or everyone for that matter. He could use that ability to his advantage, just as his father was able to do. Herman thought about one of the older boys at school, John Statham. He was always convincing the other boys into bullying him and the other smaller boys. They would take his school books and throw them across the hallway, or drag him into the bathroom, forcing to drink the toilet water. They took pride in making the weaker boys look foolish in front of the other kids.

Herman quickly responded to his father, "No, father, I stayed away from the other kids, except for Clara. She is nice to me." Levi, finally, released his grip from his wife's arm.

"Sit up, straight, in your chair." He was suddenly showing interested in Herman's new friend, "So, my son has a girlfriend? You like spending your time with the girls, instead of being a man and roughhousing with the other boys? It appears we have a merry for a son!"

"She is not my girlfriend, just a friend from school." His dad turned, seemingly upset that he would get such a response regarding his inquiries.

Levi stood up from the table, picked up the pot of hot potatoes and walked over to Page. He held the pot in his right hand and the cigar in the other, "Maybe, I have to set an example for you, about how women should be treated?" He took the steaming pot of potatoes, emptying the entire contents over his wife's head, scalding her scalp and skin.

Page screamed out in pain falling from her chair, to the floor, reaching for the closest dish towel. Levi slammed the empty pot on the table, walked over to Herman, grabbing him by the back of the neck, placing his cigar back into the ashtray.

"Herman needs more discipline, more pain, to show him how to interact with the other boys at school!" He pushed Herman down, spreading him across the kitchen table. With his free hand, he pulled up Herman's shirt revealing the skin of his back. "Here, boy, let me rough up the skin on that pretty little back of yours!" Levi reached for his cigar, took a long drag and lowered it towards Herman's skin. Herman felt the heat of the cigar against his skin. He pressed the cigar slowly into the skin. Herman winced and cried out in pain, as the cigar burnt deep into the skin of his back.

"James 5; verse 20 Herman, He must know that he who causes a sinner to be converted, from the error of his way, shall save his soul from death and shall cover a multitude of sins." Herman knew his father was slipping into an insanity he had only read about in his books. But, now, Herman was experiencing it first hand. The books spoke of sanitariums and the places they put people who lose their minds, or commit violent acts against other members of society.

Rage boiled inside Herman. He was no naive little ferry boy, but knew his father belonged in one of those places, "Does that feel good son, and are you getting the point? You little ferry." Levi threw him across the room and returned to the table. Page was still sitting near the stove, sobbing, as Herman lay on the hallway's floor.

Levi returned to the table and continued to eat dinner, not showing the least concern for his actions. After he finished his dinner, he left the room. Page and Herman quietly cleaned the mess in the kitchen, caused by his father's outburst. She cleaned the cigar burn on Herman's back with a wet rag; afterwards, putting all the dishes back into the cupboards.

"Herman, you go on up to bed. I'm going to make sure that your father has gone to bed for the night." Herman could not get up to his room fast enough. Opening the door to the attic, he stood in the doorway listening to his mother crying. His breathing and heartbeat were rapid.

After closing the door to his room, he walked over to the small window. Herman leaned against the wall. His unfinished room had exposed red brick. The wooden floorboards creaked when he would walk across them. It was important to walk as slowly and quietly as possible, as to not attract any unwanted attention from his father. The room required candles and a small rusted lantern to provide a very dim light.

Standing at the window, the only view was the quiet dirt road below. A slight wind was blowing a thick fog through the trees. A cold front had moved in and the temperature had dropped, drastically. A small alley cat wandered down the center of the dirt road, sniffing the ground and then walked off, disappearing into the night. Herman went over to the end of his bed and sat on the floor tired and frustrated with his father's lack of compassion and lack of love for his family. Someone needed to do something, but who could he trust?

Reaching down to the floorboard, Herman pulled up one of the wood panels revealing a secret hiding spot. Inside was a shoebox, decorated with drawings of bugs and birds. He removed the shoebox from the floorboards, placing it on the floor next to his small bed. Opening the lid, the box revealed a collection of carefully arranged insects, consisting of bees, wasps, butterflies, and dragonflies.

Feeling a sense of pride in his bug collection, Herman would spend the majority of his weekends running through the fields, climbing trees, and looking for better specimens for his collection. Once a more colorful, unique, bug was found he would collect it, seal it in a jar, and watch it slowly flutter until it was motionless. After that, he would take the specimen and compare its beauty to the other bugs in the collection.

Herman's favorite was the colorful wasps, and hornets he had discovered, along with the large yellow bumble bees. Slowly running his fingers across them, one by one, he replaced the box's lid and returned it to its secret hiding place. The piece of the floorboard was carefully placed back into its position. Herman crawled into his bed.

Once in bed, strange noises would come from his mother and father's room. It was a continuous and repetitive noise, the bed hitting and knocking against the wall. Later, he would hear his mother crying again, most likely, after his father had passed out. Each night, Herman would keep the pillow over his head, until he was asleep.

'Just Another Day in the Life'

The next morning Herman woke, shivering in his cold attic bedroom, yawning and wiping the crusty buildup from the corners of his eyes. Once he had dressed, and walked down into the main living room, he discovered his father had already left for work. A sense of relief overcame him, as he shrugged it off and sighed. His mother was arranging some of the mantle decorations, running a feather duster over each ornament. She looked over at Herman, revealing a bruise under her eye.

He never inquired about the bruises she had on her body. Why would he? It was obvious where they came from and who had done it to her. He returned to his room, after finishing his breakfast, his thoughts on his father's abuse of his mother. His father had become a cruel and violent alcoholic, never likely to change, since he was as selfish as his father before him. Herman was never close with his grandfather, or had ever wanted to get to know him.

The only opportunities for Herman to see his grandfather was at holiday dinners and rare family gatherings. His grandfather was usually scowling at everyone in the room. It was unsure whether it was just his demeanor, or if he was actually wallowing in despise for what he was forced to be a part of. Sitting in his favorite chair, he sipped bourbon from a small glass. His grandfather always had the glass and a whiskey bottle carefully arranged on a table, scowling.

It seemed as though his father was unconsciously following the same path his father led, before him. Anger swelled deep inside him, thinking about his father and his grandfather. Maybe it was his destiny, as well. His mother called out, "Get ready for school. You have a busy day ahead of you!" Interrupting Herman from the thoughts and feelings he was having towards his father.

"All right, mom, I'm almost ready." Herman exclaimed, packing some books in a small book bag and tying the book bag closed. Each book was individually placed into the bag; afterwards, he placed the bag over his shoulder. He walked downstairs and to the front door. His mother stood near the door.

She leaned over, kissing him on the forehead, "Don't let the other boys push you around, or tease you. If they do, promise me you will tell your teacher, all right?" Herman nodded his head and walked out the front door.

His mother waved, as she closed the door. Walking across the front yard, Herman picked up a stick and continued down the street. Birds were chirping and flying from tree to tree. Small insects were swarming about. The morning air was crisp, indicative of the New England area. In the distance, other boys and girls were approaching. There was a taller boy walking with a group of three other smaller boys. It was the Statham boy. Herman swung the stick at some bushes, whacking away at some of the branches and leaves.

The group of boys was walking just ahead of him, jabbing and pushing each other. Slowing his pace, he hoped to avoid them at any cost. Herman whispered under his breath, "Please, do not let them turn around." If he could just make it to the academy, the teachers would spot him. The teachers were usually standing in front of the academy.

There were always at least two teachers supervising the students, as they arrived at the school. They would stand watch, making sure each of the students made it into the school, on time. Some of the teachers were more lackadaisical than others, but two of the regular observers were vigilant with their observations. The student's safety and best interests were always a high priority.

Herman walked farther and saw the Statham boy turn and spot him. He poked at the other boys and then pointing back towards Herman's direction. The Statham boy walked from the group of boys, who was following closely behind, "Hey everyone, look, it's the ferry!" The Statham boy exclaimed. The past week, he had pushed Herman into the bathroom, knocked him to the floor and splashed the water from the sink into his face.

The boys approached, pushing Herman to the ground, knocking the book bag from his shoulder. The bag hit the ground and his books scattered across the dirt. He reached down and started to pick up the books. The other kids surrounded him, each of them kicking the books from reach and pressing Herman's face back into the dirt.

"Cry baby, ferry boy! Ferry boy!" They repeated and called out, continuing their taunting. The bully walked forward, kicked Herman in the face knocking him to the ground, face first.

After the direct blow to his face, all Herman saw was a flash of light and stars. They all were laughing, turned and quickly ran towards the school. Lying on the ground and crying, a young girl approached. She saw what the boys had done, walked up and began picking up books from the ground. Herman was beginning to regain his bearings, and shake off the effects of the attack.

"Are you all right?" Clara asked.

He did not respond, only wiped away the tears and dirt from his face. They finished placing the schoolbooks in the book bag bag. Clara helped Herman to his feet, "Herman, you should stand up for yourself. If you continue to allow them to treat you that way, they will never stop."

"I know, but there are too many of them." Clara was a year older than him. She rubbed his back and they walked off towards the school. Clara reached down and took hold of Herman's hand.

As Clara and Herman reached the school grounds, a teacher approached, "You two are going to be late for class. The first bell has already rung!" As the teacher approached, she discovered the red mark on Herman's face. "What happened to you Herman, who did this to you?"

"It is nothing; I tripped and fell into the dirt, Mrs. Gentry." He attempted to provide a believable response, while still looking down at the ground. The teacher was aware the other boys would frequently pick on the other, weaker, boys. She reached down and firmly took Herman by the arm, leading him into the school. The school's hallway was made of thin wood, which creaked in certain spots when walked upon.

The school's windows were usually kept open, during the cooler times of the year, and the smell of the flowers and fresh air blew inside. They arrived at the principal's office. Herman was assigned the "waiting chair", just outside his door. Mrs. Gentry knocked on the door and a voice called out from inside, "Come in."

She opened the door. "Sir, I have a young boy here, Herman Mudgett. I think you need to have a word with him."

He waved his arm, as Mrs. Gentry reached over and led Herman into the office. Upon seeing Herman, the principal exclaimed, "Why it is, Herman Mudgett, my favorite student!" He would say that to all the students. All the students were his favorites and Herman did not really care for the principal's happy go lucky attitude. It seemed so insincere, almost like an act. Herman hesitated, as he walked into the office.

The teacher placed her hand on his back, leading him to another chair, facing the principal. He felt a sharp pain shoot up his back from the cigar burn his father had given him the night before. The principal looked up at Herman, discovering the red mark across his face. He placed his pen on the desk, with a concerned look. Mrs. Gentry slowly stepped back and stood behind the chair.

The principal looked him in the eyes, "Herman, I am concerned. I know that you do well in class and you have never been called to my office for causing problems. What is happening?"

Looking down at the floor, then over at the wall at some of the pictures, Herman replied, "I was walking to school and tripped over a rock." Principal Jeffrey and Mrs. Gentry knew he was not being honest.

Both of them were showing considerable concern towards the situation, "Herman, you need to tell me the truth. If you do not let me help you, it is just going to continue." The principal stood, walked from behind his desk and crouched down.

He placed his hand on Herman's chin, examining the red mark, turning his head to the side to get a better look at the bruise, "This is bad Herman. It does not look like you fell in the dirt, because there are no scratch marks, indicating to me that someone did this to you. This is a deep bruise, from a hard blow."

"I do not want to cause any problems. I tripped on a rock and fell, that is all." The principal stood up and walked back to his desk. He sat in his chair and sighed sliding forward. Herman thought, if only he could manipulate and control conversations and situations like his father was able to do. He was becoming more determined to do so. Something his father seemed to do, with ease.

Mrs. Gentry took a small bottle, dabbing liquid on a small rag. A stinging sensation shot through Herman's cheek, as she cleaned the wound. The principal continued, "Herman, I want you to tell your parents to come see me, tomorrow. I want to discuss this with them." Herman knew, telling his parents about the incident would mean his father was not going to be happy. Missing work meant discipline.

"All right sir, I will tell them when I get home, this afternoon."

"You are a smart boy. I just do not want to continue seeing you get hurt."

The teacher helped him from the chair, leading him out of the office, "Herman, I want you to go to class and continue to focus on your studies." He walked out of the office, down the hall, towards the first classroom. His spirits were crushed and he moped just before entering the class. Mrs. Gentry returned to Principal Jeffrey's office, closing the door behind her.

Opening the classroom door, the students and the teacher looked over at Herman, "You are late, Herman."

"I was in the principle's office, talking with Principal Jeffrey and Mrs. Gentry."

"Well, then, please take your seat." The teacher looked back down at his desk, arranging some books and papers.

Herman was preparing for his science class, looking towards the side of the room, as the teacher sat at his desk and began reading from the textbook. A skeleton hung from a steel frame in the corner, always capturing his attention. He was unable to think or focus on anything other than the human body, death, and decomposition.

The teacher stopped his reading, stood from his desk, and began passing around small mason jars containing frogs. "Now, class, we are going to be learning about the dissection process." Herman's attention swiftly shifted from the skeleton to the mason jars the teacher was distributing to the rest of the class. His anticipation became uncontrollable. His heart was beating faster, as the teacher finally placed a small jar on his desk. The liquid in the jar swirled, causing the frog to sway from side to side.

"The frogs that you see before you have been preserved in formaldehyde. It is a colorless gas with a pungent odor. It is an important liquid to many other chemical compounds, especially for polymers. Solutions of formaldehyde are used as disinfectants and for preservation of biological specimens. Take a moment to open the jars and smell the liquid, but be careful not to spill any of it, get it on your skin, or in your eyes."

The teacher walked back to the front of the classroom and pulled down a large screen, revealing two drawings of a frog. One was a frog in its regular state. Next to it was another frog, after being dissected.

The teacher continued, "Formaldehyde tends to fix the tissue that produces the firmness of flesh, in an embalmed body. In post mortem examinations, a procedure known as a sink test involves placing the lungs of an animal in a solution of formaldehyde. If the lungs float, the animal was probably breathing, or able to breath, at the time of death. And, since the frogs are floating, they were obviously breathing at the time of death, only being killed a few hours ago."

Herman opened the jar and smelled the liquid. It was a strong smell and he was overcome, almost immediately. Looking at the frog bobbing in the liquid, he began reaching into the jar to touch it, "Please, Herman, not yet," the teacher instructing him to wait.

The teacher passed out the remaining dissection kits and some printed instructions. The instructions were basic and the teacher walked around the classroom, carefully showing each student the dissection process. The printed diagram read as follows: First, make an incision on both of the lymph nodes of your frog. The lymph nodes are found under the jaw on either side of the frogs.

Next, cut through the abdominal muscles and bones. Make a thin vertical cut from the throat to the

hind legs. The sternum will be freed by cutting the
bones connected to the shoulders. If your frog is a
female, you will have to remove any black eggs that sit
in her abdomen. The heart is located in the center,
behind the frog's forelegs. The thin tissue surrounding
the heart is the pericardium.

The brown colored area, below the heart, is the
liver. Between two of the lobes you will find a small,
green, organ which is the gall bladder. The coils are its
small intestine and found in front of the, long, curved
white structure of the stomach. The pancreas is easy to
spot. It is the white, thin, string of tissue between the
stomach and the first coil of the small intestine.

Next, the fat bodies are the yellow wormy looking
parts surrounding the heart, liver, and stomach. Fat
bodies are important for frogs, because they store fat
and allow the frog to thrive during its winter
hibernation. The spleen is similar to the gall bladder, in
terms of appearance. It is found below and to the left
of the stomach and its purpose is to store blood cells.

If you push the other organs to the side you will
see the red kidneys found on the back wall of your frog.
Lastly, the lungs are found in the thorax and are also
hidden by other organs. The lungs are found on either
side of the liver. The lungs are quite small, because the
frog additionally breathes through another organ, its
skin.

Herman carefully read through the instructions and
looked over the instruments intended to be used for the
dissection. He slowly ran his fingers over each
instrument, feeling the cold steel of the scalpel, the
clamps, and other instruments. They were arranged in a
metal pan, doused in a strong smelling alcohol. The kit

contained a scalpel, pins, tweezers, scissors, seekers, which were a pin like probe.

The teacher continued, "Now, take the frog from the container using the long tweezers and place the frog on the metal tray, next to your dissection pans." Herman removed the frog from its container and placed it on the piece of metal. The rest of the students followed the teacher's instructions.

"Following the instructions, take your dissection instruments and begin the dissection. I will be walking around the classroom and assisting each of you. If necessary, just raise your hand." Walking in between the rows of desks, the teacher was carefully watching over each student, ensuring they were following the process correctly.

Herman took his time, cutting through the frog, removing the thick layers of skin. Continuing to follow the instructions, closely, Herman identified each of the internal organs. The teacher walked up from behind, stopping just behind his desk. Looking over Herman's shoulder, the teacher observed how slowly he was using the instruments and precisely discovering new sections of the frog's internal organs.

"Excellent work Herman. Continue to take your time, slowly working through the instructions." Herman smiled and continued the dissection.

The teacher walked ahead to the next student, sitting just in front of Herman. The class finished up the remaining parts of their dissections and cleaned up their areas. Herman walked to the front of the class, removing the pins from the frog, letting the frog slide into the trash container. A sudden sense of loss overcame him, since he had become, in a way, connected to the frog, after cutting it open and discovering the internal organs.

"Class, you all did very well. Herman, can you see me at my desk? Class is dismissed." The teacher called out, excusing the class for the day.

Just in front of the teacher's desk, Herman patiently waited. The teacher removed his thick eye glasses, "Herman, I think you have a talent for this. You should look into a medical school, after high school. See the school adviser. I am sure he can show you some reputable schools." The teacher placed his glasses on some papers.

"Thanks, I will." Herman returned to his desk with a renewed enthusiasm and finished cleaning the dissection instruments. He wanted to get his hands on one of those kits. The morning's events, and the bruise on his face, were a distant memory.

"Herman, you can leave the kit with the others, over on that table." His teacher pointed towards a desk.

"All right and thanks for the advice." His teacher smiled. He was a very stern, but knowledgeable man.

After school, Herman walked through the schoolyard and towards a field, next to the school, climbed through a fence and walked into a field. There was a large grove of trees in the center of the field. He slowly approached the trees and sat just below them. After placing his book bag next to one of the tree trunks, he heard a rustling noise. In the dirt, to the right of the tree, was a small bird struggling and crawling in the dirt.

Herman stood up, walked over to the bird and crouched down. The bird was injured. Looking up, he assumed it must have fallen from the nest he discovered on one of the tree limbs. Reaching down and picking up the bird, Herman cupped it gently in his palms. The bird's mouth was open and it was making a continuous chirping noise.

"Are you hungry? You must be if you have been away from your mother for too long." Herman turned and walked back to his bag, picked it up and threw it over his shoulder.

Running from the field, he climbed back through the fence and ran down the path leading to his house. When he arrived home, his mother was hanging sheets and laundry on the backyard clothesline. The sheets were swaying in the wind and the sun was reflecting his mother's shadow. He ran to his mother, the book bag swinging against his back. Page saw that Herman had something, cupped in his hands.

"What have you found, Herman?" She stopped hanging the laundry and walked towards him.

"It is an injured bird. Can I keep him and feed him till he gets better?" His enthusiasm was soaring, as he waited for her reply. Even though he knew what the answer would be.

"You know that your father will not approve of that! Now take it back to where you found it." She looked at Herman's face and saw the red mark on his cheek, "What happened to your face?" She put the remaining clothes pins in the laundry basket and reached for the bruise on his face. She turned his head to the side revealing a dark red bruise on the side of Herman's cheek, "Who did this to you?"

"I tripped on a rock and hit my face on the ground."

"It was the Statham boy, from school, wasn't it?" She knew the Statham boy was bullying him, along with the other boys. She was fed up with it.

She walked Herman to the back door, opened it, and took him inside, "Take the bird up to your room and I'll bring up a small box from the cellar." He ran up the stairs and grabbed a small towel from the bathroom closet, turned, and went into his room.

Later, his mother walked into the room handing him a small box. Herman took the small towel and tucked it snugly in the box. Page helped him gently place the bird in the box and next to the window seat. She turned to Herman, "Now, let me take care of that bruise."

She reached over and began wiping the bruise with a wet rag. The water was warm. She continued soothing the swollen bruise. She turned and walked out of the room. Herman checked on the bird and looked down, as it chirped. The bird looked hungry. He rushed from the house, out to the back yard, and began digging in the dirt hoping to find some worms in the soil.

After a few moments of digging, Herman discovered a large juicy worm, pulled it from the soil and cleaned off the dirt. Returning inside the house and climbing the stairs to his room, he quickly closed the door. Inside the box, the bird was looking up with its mouth open. Herman began dangling the worm just in front of its mouth. The bird took the worm and choked it down, quickly swallowing it.

Happy to see the bird eating, it was a good sign it might survive. After seeing the bird eat the worm, Herman began wondering what his father would say and how he was going to react after returning home. He took the box in the closet, put it inside, closed the door and walked over to the doorway. He opened the rickety door, walked down the stairs and into the living room.

His mother was sitting on the couch and looked up, as he came into the room, "Your father," she paused, looking down at the floor, "He is not going to let you keep it. You have to be ready to accept that, Herman."

"I know mother, but maybe he will see me feed it and change his mind." She shook her head in disagreement and returned to folding the laundry, pulling each article from the basket, draping them across her lap.

"I'm going to go outside for a while. Is that all right?"

"Yes, but come back inside within the hour. I'm going to start making dinner and preparing for your father to come home from work."

Herman ran down the hall, through the kitchen and out the back door. He was climbing in the backyard tree and tying a rope to a branch, as the Statham boy approached carrying a small puppy. Herman looked down, watching, as the Statham boy walked underneath the tree, cradling the puppy in his arms. He looked so happy and content with his dog. So, Herman thought of the bird and how his father would not let him keep it. Why should the Statham boy get to have an animal and not him? It was just not fair.

'Shifting Realities'

Fall had arrived. The town's bountiful trees were becoming a colorful blend of bright orange and red leaves. The trees surrounding the Mudgett residence were still turning fall colors, but provided cover for when Herman wanted to become invisible to the outside world around him. He had remained in the backyard tree for the better part of the evening.

Later, in the distance, he heard familiar mumbling and groaning approaching. Herman quickly climbed down the tree and rushed into the back door of the house. "Wash up and get the plates ready for dinner, honey. Your father should be home any time now."

In the wash basin, Herman carefully cleaned his hands with extra detail, scrubbing the brush's bristles under his trimmed nails, removing the dirt which had accumulated throughout the day. When finished, he dried them on a cloth, making sure there was no leftover mess. His father would not stand for a messy wash basin.

Herman approached the cupboard, opened it, and began removing dinner plates. As he was setting the table, his father opened the front door slamming it behind him. He walked into the kitchen repeating the same actions, as he did every other night. Every night, he would return home from work mumbling and complaining about the smell of dinner, what went wrong throughout the day, and other indistinct rumblings. There were also complaints about the shortcomings of his wife and son.

"Dry food again? Every night, I come home; there is always the smell of that disgusting meat cooking. Will you ever make something more appetizing?" Flailing his arms and motioning towards the stove.

Page and Herman kept quiet, attempting to avoid a repeat of the events that occurred the prior evening. Sometimes, Herman wished his mother would be able to find the right recipe to appease his father's taste buds. Even then, he would most likely find something to complain about.

Levi walked out of the kitchen and up to the bedroom. Herman and his mother heard the drawers opening and closing. The closet door opened and immediately slammed shut. The sound of his father walking down the upstairs hallway echoed throughout the house. Suddenly, the sound of the footsteps on the wooden floorboards stopped. The house was silent.

Herman was frozen with fear, at the kitchen table, knowing his father would discover his bird. If the bird was found, it would result in serious repercussions. A door opened, and for a few moments the eerie silence remained throughout the house, "What the hell is this?" His father's voice called out from upstairs. "What the hell is in your closet, boy?" Herman sensed the rage in his voice and knew what was coming.

Levi stomped down the stairs, holding the box with Herman's bird inside. He stormed into the kitchen and slammed the box onto the table, "Just what in the hell do you think you are doing?" He looked down and Herman, his face red with rage and anger.

He turned to Page, "Do you think I'm going to let him keep some, sick, animal in his room? And you sit back, in my house, and let him do anything he wants."

Herman's father turned and looked into his eyes, "What the hell happened to you, why is there a bruise on the side of your face?"

Herman's mother stepped towards the table, "He tripped, on his way to . . ." Levi swung his arm towards her, striking her across the jaw. She screamed and stepped back, holding her hand up to her face, staring vacantly in a state of shock.

"I wasn't talking to you, you worthless piece of shit, I was talking to my ferry son." He reached into the box and pulled out the bird. It was squirming and struggling to break free of his father's grip.

Levi raised the bird in front of Herman's face holding it tightly in his hand. The bird's eyes were looking at Herman, innocent, confused, and terrified. Levi looked back into his son's eyes and began to squeeze tighter and tighter. The chirping became louder and louder. There was a crunch and the helpless bird went silent in his father's grip.

"No, father, it was just a bird. I was going to tell you." He exclaimed with some hesitance. Herman's voice was shaky and his hands trembled. As he removed his hands from the table, the sweat formed handprints below. He placed his hands into his lap. Levi reached for one of the plates and slid it in front of him.

He turned and picked up a knife from the table, never taking his eyes off his son.

The stare increased the tension beyond anything Herman and his mother had experienced from Levi, in the past. Levi raised the knife and released his grip, allowing the bird fall onto the plate. He took the knife and pressed it against the bird's neck, slowly pressing down, sliding the knife back and forth. He cut through the bird's neck, separating its head from the body.

His mother stood, sobbing in front of the stove, tears running down her cheeks. Levi placed the knife back on the table and reached for the plate, picking up the bird's body. He swung his arm around, gripping the back of Herman's neck, raising the bird above his head. Squeezing the bird as tight as he could, blood began to drip down Herman's face.

Herman's mother screamed, "No!"

"You, shut up!" Levi barked at his wife. Herman felt the blood pour down his face and the taste of blood entered his mouth. His father threw the bird down onto the plate and ordered, "Eat it."

"What?" Herman replied with his eyes wide open and a confused look on his face.

"You heard me, eat it, now!" Herman sat in his chair unable to move. Suddenly, Herman grabbed one of the knives on the table. Lunging at his father, he grabbed him around the waist attempting to tackle him to the ground, intent on stabbing him with the knife. Levi thrust his elbow into his son's back, knocking him to the floor. Herman choked and coughed unable to breath, the wind knocked out of him.

Picking his son up from the ground with one arm, he threw Herman back into the chair. Back at the table, he ripped the knife from Herman's hand, "I should shove this knife into your chest, you ungrateful little shit!" After throwing the knife to the floor, he reached down to the plate and grabbed the bird's head, shoving it into his son's mouth. Herman gagged, attempting to spit out the bird's head.

Levi kept Herman's mouth closed with his hands, forcing Herman to swallow. He choked down the head, gagging, as his father released his head. Herman proceeded to throw up on the kitchen floor, the bird's head mixed in with the vomit. He ran from the table rushing up the stairs and into his attic bedroom, slamming the door behind him. Herman walked over to the bed.

Page was on the kitchen floor, sobbing, as Levi reached down to the plate and picked up the body of the bird, "I have a family of imbeciles."

He turned and crouched over his wife, reached down, clutching the back of her hair and forced the body of the bird in her mouth, "You stupid bitch, what is wrong with you? This is my house and you will live by my rules, or you and Herman will suffer the consequences. Clean up this vomit. I should make you lick it off the floor!"

She squirmed, on the floor, gagging and attempting to push her husband's hands away from her mouth. He continued pushing the bird into her mouth and then, finally, stopped. She spit the bird back into his face. Infuriated, he began striking her repeatedly across the face, harder and harder. He struck her, until she was motionless on the kitchen floor.

Herman could hear his father leave the kitchen, knowing he was not through with him, yet. He walked up the stairs and barged through Herman's bedroom door. Pulling the belt from his waist, he walked across the room and began swinging the belt, beating his son repeatedly, leaving welts and cuts across his back. This was nothing new and something Herman had become accustomed to. He began losing consciousness, as he heard his father began spouting off indistinct scripture.

The words faded, as he continued his beating. Then, the words became clear. Herman's father, again, angrily began quoting scripture, "John 3, verse 19; and this is the judgment: Because the light has come into the world and men loved darkness rather than the light: for their works were evil." Blood slowly trickled from Herman's wounds. He began shaking and convulsing, fading in and out of consciousness. The stars were swirling in his eyes. Next, came a bright flash and Herman was paralyzed on the bedroom floor.

His father left the room, slamming the door behind him. Down in the kitchen, Page lay on the floor. Levi walked into the room. He reached down and grabbed her wrists, lifting her over his shoulder. He carried her up the stairs to Herman's room and kicked open the door.

"John 8: verse 44; you are of your father, the devil: and the desires of your father you will do. He was a murderer from the beginning: and he stood not in the truth, because truth is not in him. When he speaks a lie, he speaks of his own: for he is a liar and the father thereof, your father Herman."

He turned to see his father carrying his mother into the room. A voice called out to Herman, "Do not fear, or have any cause for worry, my son. For I am with you and am here to provide you comfort. This will all be over soon and if I can, I will make it a distant memory." The voice, in his head, faded.

Walking over to Herman, Levi threw his wife to the floor without any hesitation. Leaving the room, rushing into the hallway and down into the bedroom, he yelled, "This is going to be our little bonding moment, Herman. Let's have a little fun, shall we?" Herman couldn't make out what was going through his father's head. He could not even tell if any of it was real. What was his father talking about?

Reaching down to his mother, Herman gently ran his hand across her face. His father returned to the room, carrying a bottle of liquor. Drinking from the bottle, he exclaimed, "Now, boy, I am going to show you how to command respect." He took long swigs from the bottle of bourbon.

His father continued his rants of scripture, "O death, where is your victory? O death, where is your sting? Now the sting of death is me: and my power is the law, thanks be to God, who has given us the victory through our Lord Jesus Christ." Levi took the liquor bottle and held open Herman's mouth, pouring the bourbon inside. The liquor's strength burned his throat, as he swallowed and spit up the alcohol. His father laughed and stood up.

"Do you like that, son?" He exclaimed, looking down, "Herman, you have a red face and bloodshot, red, eyes!" The room began spinning, "Herman you are shaking uncontrollably. Are you going to pass out and lose consciousness, again?"

Herman blacked out. A shadowy figure stepped forward from the darkness. His face was blurry, but his voice was crystal clear, "My son, fear not. This will all be over soon."

The figure's voice was deep, and ominous, but familiar and comforting. Herman replied, "Who are you?"

"I will tell you Herman, in time." The figure was hazy and blurry. The vision faded and his father's silhouette came into view. Herman's eyes adjusted to the dim lighting the candles, and lantern hanging from the ceiling, provided. Herman's father placed the liquor bottle on the floor, next to his wife, and picked up the belt from the bed tying it around her neck.

Herman continued to question the reality of the situation, "Why are you doing this?" His mother began choking, as Levi tightened his grip. Her eyes opened wide and she began gasping for air. His father continued tightening his grip, pulling harder and harder, until she lost consciousness.

Levi, breathing heavily, continued to mutter scripture, as though trying to justify his actions, "Revelation 21: verse 4; And God shall wipe away all tears from their eyes: and death shall be no more. Nor mourning, nor crying, nor sorrow shall be any more, for the former things are passed away." After a few minutes, his mother stopped breathing. Levi released the belt and mother's body fell to the floor, just in front of Herman.

Herman reached down to her and laid his head on her back. Had he just watched his father murder his mother? Everything was moving in slow motion. He was unable to move, or react to any of the occurring events. He began crying, as his father stood up walked from the room, slowly closing the door behind him. Herman crawled next to his mother, lifted her arm and placed it around his neck, continuing to cry. The darkness overtook him.

That night, Herman continued to drift in and out of consciousness, unable to determine what was real and what had been a dream. In the cellar, standing over a large hole in the ground, Levi was sweating and holding a shovel. There was a lantern hanging on the cellar wall, its light flickering, creating an eerie glow against the cement wall. After finishing the hole he turned, placed the shovel against the wall, and walked up the stairs. From the cellar, into the living room, Herman heard him walk up the stairs and stumble into his room.

Levi discovered Herman, lying next to Page's lifeless body, asleep in her arms. He walked over to her body, grabbed her by the ankles, dragging her lifeless body across the floor. He pulled the body down the stairs. Herman could hear his mother's head bouncing on the wooden staircase. The noise was so loud he stirred on the bedroom floor.

Sweat was pouring down Herman's face and his clothes were drenched. He stood up, struggling to reach the doorway. His vision was blurry and his head, spinning. He walked down the stairs, around the banister, and towards the hallway. Struggling to maintain his balance and footing, he used his hands to reach for the wall and anything else that would help him to make it to the cellar.

Reaching the door to the cellar, his father arranged his wife's body into an upright position, and then shoved her down the stairs and into the cellar below. Herman rubbed his eyes, attempting to get a better perspective of the event unfolding before him. He heard the body tumble and roll down the stairs into the cellar.

Herman's father descended into the darkness. He stumbled to the cellar door and looked, below. Herman's mind was still foggy and his vision more blurry than before. Was he really experiencing this? Vaguely, he saw his father pick up a shovel, using it to fill a hole with dirt.

After covering the hole, he reached over and picked up his whiskey bottle. He was sweating and continued drinking from the bottle. His breathing slowed, until he finally passed out. The lantern flickering above his head dimmed and finally burned out. Herman's head became unusually warm and a ringing sound filled his ears and his surroundings faded.

The next morning, Herman woke up on the floor of his room. Severe pains shot through his head. His thoughts were clouded as to what actually happened the night before. Thoughts of his mother and father raced through his head. Did what he remembers really happen, or was he dreaming the whole thing?

He stood from the floor and walked out of the bedroom, down the hallway, and into his parent's bedroom. There was no one in the room and he could not hear anyone down in the kitchen. Herman turned and walked down the hallway, descending the stairs, "Mother," He called out and continued, "Father?" Herman walked into the living room. There was a torn up note on the table.

He placed the pieces together and read, "Herman, I have decided to take a little time away from your father and left, late last night, to visit my parents. There is food in the oven and enough food in the cabinets for you to last a week, or so. I have placed some money under your mattress, should you need to go to the grocer, for more food. I love you, and will be home soon. Love, your mother." Maybe this is what caused his father's murderous rampage.

Walking towards the kitchen, Herman passed the cellar door, noticing it was open. Descending the staircase, and down the cellar, he reached the lantern at the bottom. Reaching towards a shelf, he picked up a match and struck it against the wall and lit the lantern, which slowly illuminated the room. Herman was losing the strength in his legs and fell to the floor. The lantern struck the ground and went out. As the lantern went out, everything around him faded to darkness.

When he began regaining consciousness, he discovered his father, lying in the dirt, holding his liquor bottle. Everything was still fuzzy and confusing. What was happening to him? He had never felt this way before. He looked around at the dirt and fell to his knees.

Had his father strangled his mother, in front of him? Was her body buried in the cellar? Was it all just an elaborate act his father played out while in a drunken state? Herman stood up, examining the cellar ground, noticing nothing out of the ordinary. No freshly disturbed dirt. So why the shovel and why did he believe what he saw the prior evening? Things were just not adding up.

He left the cellar, walked into the kitchen and out the back door. In the backyard, he crouched over throwing up into the dirt. The events of the prior evening would forever change his life. He felt his mind separating from his body, but could not explain why. It was as though he was watching the events, happening around him, from outside his body.

Later in the afternoon, Herman woke to his father standing over his bed. Levi reached down and restrained his arms, tying them to the bed frame. Next, he proceeded to finish tying Herman's legs to the end of the bed. After securing the ropes, he turned and closed the door behind him, "Father please let me go, I will be good, and I promise not to tell anyone!" He frantically pleaded, but his father never returned to the room.

Herman lay in bed with his arms and legs bound to the bed frame. His stomach was constantly growling, and he began to struggle with the ropes. They were tied so tightly, they were cutting off the circulation. His wrists and ankles had red marks from the constant rubbing against the skin. Finally he stopped, and lay back, wondering how long he would be tied to the bed. Would his father come back and let him loose, or would he come back drunk and decide to kill him?

That evening, the front door of the house opened and voices echoed from downstairs. Herman did not recognize the second voice. However, he did recognize his father's voice. Footsteps echoed from the staircase, stopping as they reached the top. After a few moments of silence, the noise continued down the hallway.

He could hear stumbling and banging against the walls; afterwards, boisterous laughter erupting from a woman. The footsteps went down into the master bedroom and stopped. Moments later, the door slammed shut. After about an hour of loud moans, and low pitched mumbling, the bedroom door opened and footsteps came down the hallway.

Herman's father opened the door to the room and leaned in his head, "Well, boy, are you having a good night?" His words were slurred and Herman did not respond. Hopefully, his father would leave the room,

"Well, then, when you are ready to speak, I will be ready to untie you and let you get something to eat."

"Wait! I am having a good night and I am hungry." His father returned inside the room, walked over to the bed and untied the ropes.

"Now go get something to eat, before I whip you again." His father swayed, struggling to maintain his balance.

Herman rushed down the stairs and into the kitchen contemplating escape, but was not prepared. There were more preparations and arrangements that needed to be made and careful thought to be done about the situation. He reached up, opened the cupboard, and pulled out two mason jars of beans. Herman reached into the drawer and pulled out a spoon. He opened the can and with his hands, shoveling the beans into his mouth.

He looked back up and grabbed another jar, turned, and took the extra food up to the attic bedroom. He hid the food in his secret hiding spot, underneath the floorboards. He replaced the floor boards back over his hiding spot. Quickly jumping back into his bed, he pulled the covers over his head.

Herman's mind was racing. He remained as still as possible, breathing as little as he could, in hopes that his father would not return and just pass out for the night. Hours passed, until the door to Herman's bedroom opened. His father walked in first, followed by the strange shadow of a tall woman.

He was still in a slight daze and could not make out any details in the dark, "So, this is your son?" The woman's raspy voice broke the silence, causing an immediate increase in Herman's breathing, and the pace of his heart.

"Yes, that is my little shit. Go ahead and do whatever you want with him." Drinking straight from a bottle, he then handed it to the woman, wobbling in his position at the door.

She walked over to the bed and lay down. The woman reeked of sweat and liquor. She reached under the blankets and began touching and rubbing Herman's leg. She rubbed her hand up to his crotch and started pulling at the belt of his pants, while pouring liquor into his mouth. She continued removing his clothing.

Feeling Herman's body tremble, she whispered, "Don't worry sweetie, I promise, you will like this."

Levi watched as the unfamiliar woman became intimate with his son. He smiled, "Son, you are now a man." Herman cried, as the woman continued her advances.

After the woman finished, Levi walked back over to the bed and tied the ropes back around his son's wrists and ankle's. He began to black out; again, from the amount of liquor the woman forced him to drink. Out of nowhere, Herman was blindsided with a blow to the face from his father. The force of the blow split Herman's lip, followed by a loud ringing in his ears.

Blood pooled on the bed sheets. His father and the strange woman left the room, closing the door behind them, walked down the hallway and into his father's bedroom. Throughout the night, Herman could hear his father and the woman continuously laughing and making love. As Herman slept, a voice spoke to him in a dream, "Herman? It is me. You know what you need to do and what needs to be done?"

The next morning Herman woke, discovering he was still tied to the bed. His jaw and lip was swollen and sore. While looking down at his legs, a large spider crawled from the end of the bed. It slowly made its way along the edge of the bed, turned, and crawled onto one of his legs.

He felt the spider's legs tickle against his skin. Anxiety overcame him. His heart rate increased. The spider scurried all the way up his neck, around the side of his face, and onto his nose. He sneezed and wriggled his wrists, jerking his legs, attempting to free them from the restraints.

After an hour, Herman was able to free one of his ankles. He quickly pulled the other leg free and soon had the ropes untied from his wrists. Jumping from the bed, frantically rubbing his hands all over his body to make sure the spider was gone. After removing the floor boards, Herman removed the jars of beans he took from the kitchen twisting the lid off the jar. He was so hungry he shoveled them into his mouth using his hand.

Clothes were spread on the floor of his bedroom. He quickly gathered them up and dressed. After dressing and straightening his shirt, he walked out the back door and climbed up into the backyard tree. He waited, watching, for the Statham boy to routinely walk his dog under the tree.

Herman climbed as high up into the tree as he possibly could and saw that the boy was playing in his front yard. Herman climbed down from the tree and walked to the field, next to the school. The rusty fence was easy to climb through. He waited quietly behind a large grove of trees. Light headed and weak from lack of food, a voice entered his head, "It has to be done my son. You know it in your heart." What was this voice, motivating him to think these thoughts and do such things?

The Statham boy's mother called from a window, "Honey it is time for lunch. I need you to tie up the puppy and come inside." The Statham boy tied the puppy to a rope, opened the front door, and went inside the house closing the door behind him. Herman walked from the field, climbed through the fence and walked across the street towards the Statham's front yard.

He slowly approached the puppy, which was sitting quietly near the tree. Cautiously looking around the neighborhood, he wanted to ensure no-one was out, who could be a witness to him in the yard. The rope, around the puppy's neck, was tied to the trunk of the tree. The small puppy wagged its tail, excited by an approaching person. Herman reached down, softly stroking the puppy on the back of the head and picked it up. He bounced the puppy in his arms and arranged the puppy, holding it in both hands and cooing to it.

He lowered the puppy between his legs, hoisted it up and over a hanging tree branch. The puppy flew over the tree branch and dropped towards the ground. The rope snapped tight and the puppy jerked in mid air hanging from the tree branch. The rope held the puppy, which was dangling in mid air and turned, as Herman ran down the street towards his house.

Returning to the cover of his back yard, Herman quickly climbed up to the highest point in the tree. The puppy swung back and forth, motionless. The Statham boy walked from the front door discovered his puppy hanging from the tree. He ran to the puppy and then back into the house. Moments later, his mom came running from the house followed by her son. Her son was crying, as she consoled him. Herman watched from the tree, as the Statham boy's mother untied the rope around the puppy's neck. Herman smiled and returned inside his house.

Two days later, Herman woke in his room. His father was none the wiser about him being able to untie the ropes. After all, Levi had been gone for the past three days. There was blood covering his hands, "Where did all this blood come from?" He thought to himself, it must have been from the Statham's puppy. Did he go back to their house, later that night? Was the dog buried in the back yard? And, did he dig it up?

He stood up from the floor, walked out of his room and down the stairs into the cellar. Walking over to the wall, he retrieved the shovel and began to dig into the mound of dirt where he thought his mother was buried. He dug into the dirt, until he discovered a face. He brushed away the dirt to reveal the facial features. The skin and muscles were disfigured and there was the distinct appearance of lye in the shallow grave. The expression was vacant and the eyes grey, sunken, and lifeless. He took the shovel, lined it up with the neck, and pushed his foot down with all the strength he could muster.

Herman continued pushing the shovel down with his foot, until the head separated from the body. He reached down and picked up the head, lifting it up, just in front of him. If it was his mother, she was his life, always there when his father would hurt him or the kids from school would bully him. She understood what he was going through and feeling.

He poured more lye into the hole and then covered it back over, making sure to level out the hole and make it look as undisturbed as possible. From the cellar, he walked up the stairs and left the house, carrying the head out into the backyard barn. His father rarely used the barn, aside from the carriage parked inside, some various yard and garden tools and a push mower. His lazy father never had any reason to have a barn in the backyard.

He removed a few large wooden boards from the ground and lowered the head in a bucket, just inside the pit. He walked over to a shelf of chemicals, grabbed a smaller bag of the lye, opened the lid and poured it into the bucket. He had learned the chemical would remove the flesh, leaving a perfectly preserved skull.

Leaving the rickety shed, he returned to the house and the cellar, retrieving the shovel, planning on ambushing his father upon his return. Herman lay in his bed, smiling, prepared to wait all night or until he heard the front door open. He began shaking and convulsing out of nowhere and soon blacked out. He could not remember how long the blackout had lasted.

He heard his father walk into the kitchen, stumbling against the walls and then up the stairs. As he reached the top of the stairs, Herman rushed from around the corner swinging the shovel at his father's head. The shovel struck his father directly between the eyes. The force from the shovel struck deep into his father's face.

Levi fell backwards and down the stairs, the shovel dislodging from his face, as his body crashed to the floor below. Herman walked down the stairs to see if the woman was with him. She was nowhere to be found, so he walked to the cellar door and opened it. He pulled his father's body across the hallway floor to the cellar door, leaving a long blood stain on the floor.

After lifting the body, he pushed it through the cellar's doorway. The body slammed against the stairs and down into the cellar, landing in the dirt. Herman walked into the cellar and began digging. It took him most the evening to finish burying his father. After finishing, he returned back upstairs to his room stopping at the bedroom door. Something caused him to stop, turn, and walk down the hallway into his parent's room.

The spinning interrupted his footsteps, a pain shot through his head. His hands were covering his eyes, attempting to block the light. Once he regained his bearing, he searched through their drawers, taking all the valuable jewelry and watches, looking at each piece, "This should fetch me a good price."

He walked over to the closet, opened it, and looked inside. After rummaging through all the boxes and suitcases, he discovered a wood panel in the floor, removed it and discovered a shoe box. He opened the shoe box, discovering a large amount of money. It was his father's life's savings.

Removing the money from the shoebox, "It's a good thing you do not believe in banks, you stupid son of a bitch." He removed all the money and one of the smaller suitcases from the closet, retreating to his room.

He removed the wood panel from the floor and pulled out his other shoebox. He prepared all the items in the suitcase, closed it and walked from the upstairs. With the suitcase, and one of his father's bags, he retrieved some wax paper wraps from the kitchen and walked out of the back door and into the farm.

The wax paper was prepared in the barn, dropping it on the floor; he reached down and removed the wooden boards from the ground. Herman retrieved the treated skull and carefully wrapped the wax paper wrap around it, placing it in one of his father's bags. Returning inside the house and up to his parent's room, he pulled out a bottle of liquor his father had stashed and returned to the living room.

Herman sat on the couch, looking at the bag thinking of the woman his father brought into the house and what she had done to him. His father would never be able to hurt him again. Sitting on the couch for most of the evening, Herman reached over to the bottle. He twisted off the top, leaned back, took a long drink and then lowered the bottle back on the table. After a few drinks, the rage inside him grew when his thoughts returned to the woman. He wished she would be naive enough to return to the house.

The following morning, Herman woke with another hazy memory of a horrible night. Things were not connecting. He didn't know what was real. All of it could be just an illusion, a hallucination from all the alcohol consumption. As far as he was concerned, he could be dreaming now. At this point, he was so confused; he didn't know when he was experiencing reality. Either way, he would need to get out of the house and out of town, fast.

But first, final arrangements needed to be made. Leaving the house for a final stroll through town, he was carrying a suitcase and the bag containing the skull. His teachers had always told him he should follow his heart and decide what it was he wanted to do, later in life. He was always fascinated with collecting and dissecting animals. But his father and mother strongly discouraged the strange behavior, discovering their son cutting animals.

Herman stopped, standing in the center of town and saw the paper. Picking up the paper, the cover portrayed the image of a prominent man's picture. It was a doctor, working on an experimental operation that would forever change the medical field. The doctor was in Michigan at one of the medical universities.

Looking at the picture on the cover of the newspaper he quickly made the decision to, one day, attend medical school in Michigan. He walked across the street to one of the local diners, opened the door, and stepped inside. Making his way to the back of the diner, Herman chose the most inconspicuous spot in the place.

As he slid his bags under the table, a young girl walked over and spoke with a gentle voice, "Can I take your order?" It was Clara Lovering, from school. She immediately recognized him and exclaimed, "Herman, what are you doing? You look awful, are you all right?"

He began playing on her emotions, "My mother and father disappeared and I do not know where they are, or if they will ever be back."

"Oh my, that's terrible, have you reported this to the police?" She replied.

"What can they do? If my parents are gone, then it is just me."

She sat across from Herman, dressed in a white button up shirt, revealing just enough cleavage to cause his mind to wander. He thought about what she would look like with her clothes off, her naked body glimmering in the sunlight shining through the window. Herman looked up into her blue eyes, "I'll have a plate of steak bits with potatoes."

Clara smiled back at him and walked to the kitchen window, placing the order with the cook and then checked on two other customers to see if they needed anything. A little while later, Clara returned to the table and carefully placed a large plate of food just in front of

Herman, "There's some water, can I get you anything else?"

He shook his head, "No, thank you, Clara." Herman slowly ate his meal, eating each bite, savoring the taste in his mouth. His senses were becoming clearer, as the amount of liquor he had drunk the prior evening was wearing off. He finished the meal and laid down some money on the table.

Clara saw that Herman was finished and walked over to the table, "I get off in a few hours. Can I meet you back at your house?" She looked at his wrists, "What happened to your wrists?"

"I can explain more, back at my house. It would be nice, if you came over, Clara. I'll be waiting there." He smiled; looking deep into her eyes and was now beginning to understand how charisma and charm could gain advantage over people. As long as he was polite, respectful, and charming, it seemed that gaining someone's trust was an easy task to accomplish.

Reaching under the table, he retrieved his suitcase, the other bag, and walked out of the diner. On the road before him, horses, and carriages passed. People rushed across the street to get to the other side. Herman walked down the road with thoughts of selling the house and what it would take to have the house put under his name. It would require too much work and might even get him caught in a lie, or even fraudulent activity.

He arrived back at his house and sat out the deed to the house and his father's will. The will was already made out and signed, but the deed to the house would be another thing, "Forget it." Herman would have to write in a clause, which would pass the house to him should anything happen to his mother or father.

The handwriting would have to be exact. He knew that he would have to file a missing persons report and take the matter to an attorney to finalize the deed of the house over to him and then sell the home, "This would take too much time." He spoke out. Herman walked around the house cleaning some of the dirt off the floor, and near the entrance of the cellar. The house seemed spotless and there were no signs of anything suspicious.

A few hours later, there was a soft knock at the door. He stood up, from the couch, and walked over to the door. Opening the door, Clara stood wearing her casual work uniform, revealing the soft skin of her neck. Her hair was hanging, just below her shoulders. There was a medium-sized ladies bag, hanging from her shoulder.

"Please come in, Clara. Can I get you anything to drink, maybe some lemonade?" He asked, politely.

"Sure, that would be great, Herman." She shifted, seemingly a bit uncomfortable being alone with Herman.

"Please have a seat, let me take your bag." He took her bag and hung it on the coat rack, just beside the door. Clara walked over to the couch and sat down. Herman walked into the kitchen, picked out two glasses and some lemonade from the kitchen. Returning to the living room, he placed the glasses on the table and looked into Clara's eyes, while slowly pouring the lemonade into the glasses, "Clara, what are your plans now that summer is here and we are through with school?"

She looked up at him, "I am not sure what I'm going to do. My parents are poor and can barely afford the mortgage payments. I may travel to Alton, to stay with my grandparents, and help lift some of the financial burden from my parents."

"I'm sure it would be nice to see your grandparents, as well. However, I am going to be leaving for medical school. I plan on getting my degree and medical license, then opening up a practice, somewhere. I have not decided where I would like to start." Herman could see Clara's eyes, suddenly, become fixated on his ideas and ambitions.

She was listening intently, as he continued talking about his plans and ideas and what he wanted to accomplish. Herman had her complete attention and continued to expand and embellish his stories, taking pride in his charm and ability to lead her right along.

"Oh, Herman, I have not been able to tell you this, but I have feelings for you. I believe that you have those same feelings for me!" Jumping up from the couch and throwing her arms around him. Herman smiled and returned the embrace.

They talked, late into the evening, sharing their thoughts and feelings for each other. He discussed his plans for the week and how he needed to make some arrangements. Also, he shared his plans on becoming financially stable in order to complete, and achieve a medical degree.

"I should be going, Herman."

"It is getting late." They both said their goodbyes. Clara kissed him, before leaving, and politely stopped his further advances towards her. In no time at all, he knew that she would be his. She left and closed the door behind her.

Herman returned to finishing up some final details in the coming week. His plans were now in motion. His ambitions, future achievements, and planned accomplishments would never be stopped. Clara and Herman were spending more and more time together. They spoke about marriage and moving to Alton, New Hampshire, to live near her grandparents.

He would be close to the Dover Asylum for the insane and mentally ill. His fascination with human anatomy, and the levels of pain and stress the body could handle, was growing. He would spend hours reading about current events and advancements in the medical industry and the process of attaining a medical education and a degree in medicine.

'A New Life'

Herman had acquired a Malmaison style carriage from a local carriage retailer. Herman and Clara packed their belongings into the carriage. They were prepared to set out on the scenic journey, from Gilmanton, to Alton, New Hampshire. Once the carriage had been packed and serviced, Herman led a horse to the front of the carriage, securing it to the tug, girth, bit and reins, "Are you ready Clara?"

"I am, dear. Do you have everything you need from the house?"

"There is nothing there for me now. I removed everything I need." He carefully arranged his luggage, and the bag concealing the skull, taking care to conceal the bag as inconspicuous as possible. The discovery of a human skull might be difficult to explain, should it be found.

Herman climbed onto the carriage seat, sitting next to Clara, "Let's go."

He used the reins to direct the carriage onto the main road leading through town. Herman guided the horses behind two other carriages, "Looks like we are going to have a slight delay making our way out of town."

"I do not mind. This may be the last chance we get to see Gilmanton." Herman held tightly to the reins, directing the horse around a large puddle in the road.

Clara held tightly to the side of the seat, as the carriage bounced over the rougher parts of the road, "Your house is coming up, on the right."

"I know." Herman's response was aggressive.

She recognized the change in Herman's tone and demeanor, "Look, Herman, is that your mother and father?"

Herman did a double take, opening and closing his eyes, "It can't be."

His head began to spin and he turned to Clara, "You take the reins. Please don't stop for my sake, or theirs." He climbed into the rear of the carriage, peering through a small window.

Herman looked across the street, as his parents were pointing towards the Statham's home. The last thing Herman saw, before passing out, was two police wagons and policemen walking around the Statham home. One of the officers was speaking with the Statham boy's mother. Herman blacked out in the back of the carriage falling to his side.

Unconscious, the voice in his head returned, "Son, you must remember that there is nothing to incriminate you. I made sure to aid you in your tasks and will continue to assist you throughout your life's journey."

Herman recognized the voice and found a solace, knowing that he was receiving guidance and assistance, "You will have to reveal your identity, soon. I need to know who is helping me, so I can seek you out when I need your help and advice."

"Very soon, Herman, be patient." The ominous voice faded.

On the road to Alton, Herman stirred in the back of the carriage and regained consciousness. Clara was leading the carriage past rivers, over bridges, and through the colorful forests filled with thick trees and a variety of wildlife. Birds flew through the air, passing from tree to tree, chirping and calling out to each other. Various insects were buzzing just in front of the carriage, as the horse made its way down the dirt trail.

"Oh, Herman, you are awake. Do we need to seek out a doctor?"

"I am fine. Clara you need to know, from time to time, I have strange episodes."

"Well, if you know anything about me, I am going to insist you see a doctor, because these episodes could be serious and require treatment."

Herman climbed up onto the carriage's seat, next to Clara, changing the subject, "There is nothing more beautiful than the open forest and watching all the wildlife running free." He stretched and took in a deep breath, "Ah, fresh, forest air!"

Herman's mind was unable to focus on anything but Alton and getting started at any position available at the Dover asylum.

"Herman, what are you thinking about?" Clara inquired, noticing Herman's vacant stare.

"I'm looking forward to getting settled in, starting work at the asylum, and earning some extra money for medical school." He smiled and looked over at Clara, taking his finger and brushing a strand of hair from her face, carefully arranging it behind her ear, "There, now, that's better." Herman kissed her on the cheek, taking the reins from her hands.

The couple continued their long ride through the groves of trees and along the rough stretches of road. Clara smiled knowing that Herman was becoming a driven man. She wanted a long and happy marriage with Herman and to become Clara Lovering Mudgett. Something that she was now becoming driven to do. To please Herman and become the wife he would always cherish.

They arrived at the edge of the town of Alton, after a long day and a half ride. The small town was quiet, with groups of people walking along the side of the town's roads. There were a number of men and women working in their yards and gardens. Alton was a farming town comprised mainly of religious churchgoers and self sustaining cotton, vegetable, and fruit growers. Their products were grown, cultivated and sold throughout the surrounding smaller towns and cities.

"I haven't visited Alton for years. Nothing has changed." Clara looked around the town, recognizing many of the areas she frequented as a child.

Herman and Clara rode into the center of town. Herman stopped the carriage just in front of the town's market, which had postings of land and homes for sale. Herman quickly eyed a flyer displaying a quaint cottage on the outskirts of town and pulled the advertisement from the board. Clara had purchased a small amount of groceries for the couple's first evening together. They decided to stay the night in a small hotel, near the market.

In the distance, an ominous storm was approaching the town. A steady wind had picked up. Trees swayed from side to side, their leaves falling to the ground and sweeping across the road. Within moments, the rain began falling steadily and large flashed of lightning streaked across the sky, followed by extraordinary rumbles of thunder claps. The town's people quickly rushed indoors. Herman and Clara checked in with the hotel manager, paid for their stay, and made their way to their hotel room for the evening.

The following morning, Herman was arranging his clothes, "I am going to set out towards the cottage and meet with the owner, inspect the dwelling, and discuss the asking price."

"This is so exciting, please hurry back, Herman." Claire was still in bed looking at the town through the window.

After a short carriage ride, and arriving at the cottage, Herman was surprised to see the cottage's condition was better than expected. Clara left the purchase of the cottage up to Herman's judgment of the property and knew that he would be able to pick out a beautiful home for them. She was excited to live with Herman, marry, and start a family of her own.

The owner had yet to arrive, allowing Herman the opportunity to look around and inspect the condition of the home and property. The home had an acre of land, plenty of fruit trees, a large garden, and a pleasant little path leading up to the entrance of the cottage. Large trees surrounded the perimeter of the property providing plenty of shade.

In the rear corner of the property was a wooden gazebo. The prior night's rain had dissipated earlier in the morning; however, it left deep puddles spread across the property. Herman knew Clara was going to love this place. After a short time, the owner of the property arrived. He parked his carriage and climbed onto the muddy surface, "Hello there, my name is

Anthony . . . Anthony Wilson. I hope you have had a
chance to look around, despite the muddy conditions."

"I am Herman Mudgett." He replied, shaking
Anthony's hand with enthusiasm.

The two discussed the land and details of the
purchase, "I feel the asking price is quite reasonable.
For the amount of acreage and the condition of the
home, the price is something one might say, a steal?"
He chuckled, patting Herman on the shoulder.

"I was slightly surprised at your asking price, after
having a chance to peruse the property and very
surprised at the price of the land." It was well below
what the land was worth. Herman inquired about the
low price and the owner explained, "I just lost my wife.
I am going to travel west and live in the southwest
territories, near my parent's property. I am just looking
to sell the property, and home, as quickly as I can."

"I am sorry for your loss, Mr. Wilson. I will take
the property and be able to pay you in two days time, as
my money is still being transferred by armored carriage
from Gilmanton." Even though Herman had all the
money in his possession, there was an interest in telling
the man he was having his money transferred via armed
carriage. The idea seemed to make more of an
impression on the owner.

"Very well, where are you staying?"

"I am staying at the hotel, in town, just near the
local market."

The two agreed to meet in two days and finalize
transferring the deed to Herman's name. Herman was
pleased the property was in such good shape. A quick
agreement to the purchase would allow him to take a
carriage ride out the asylum and seek employment with
the supervisor.

The owner climbed into his carriage, "Have a good day, Herman."

"And you as well, Mr. Wilson." He replied.

Mr. Wilson tugged at the reins, "Please, call me Anthony." He tipped his hat and directed the carriage from his property. Herman followed suit and rode his carriage back to the hotel, where Clara was waiting.

The following day, in the hotel's restaurant, Herman and Clara were eating breakfast, "I would like to travel to the asylum this afternoon."

"I am excited to see the house."

"I will take you the following morning." After breakfast, Herman prepared to leave for the asylum. "Hurry back Herman, I want to spend a quiet evening with you. And, I have a surprise planned for you. I love you!" Clara waved excitedly.

"I love you too, Clara. The ride may take the remainder of the afternoon." Herman replied whipping the reins of the horse, setting out towards the asylum, which was about a three hour trip by carriage. He learned that the name of the supervising doctor was Dr. Caswell, a well known doctor and psychologist in the New England area. He learned more about the asylum itself from a resident who had lived in the area since birth.

The asylum was built to house forty nine to one hundred patients, but was quickly filled beyond its capacity just years after it was built. The remaining, more dangerous, patients were kept in the tunnel cells on the basement level. Visitors were discouraged from being in the basement level. Even friends and family were not allowed visitation in the basement level, due to the amount of incidents and attacks from the inmates who were uncomfortable seeing unfamiliar faces. The asylum was a two-story building with a large attic.

The first floor was occupied by the supervising physician and psychiatrist, and his family, along with seventeen inmates. The second floor was usually occupied by nineteen inmates; however, was soon filled to capacity and beyond and the attic by eight inmates. There were fifty six cells and apartments in all, twenty one cells, on the first floor, twenty three on the second, and twelve in the attic.

The asylum was constructed in 1871, repaired and enlarged with wooden materials, floorings, partitions, sheathings and furnishings to all the cells of pine lumber, so portions of the building enabled staff and guards to see each other between the floors and cells. It was heated throughout by steam from the boiler, pipes hung overhead. The outdoor enclosure was surrounded by a wooden fence, about twelve feet high.

The windows of the asylum were barred and some of the windows had heavy wire screening on the inside. The building had four doors, one in the main building, one in the cell, one leading into the outdoor enclosure for women and one leading into an enclosure for men. The building was supplied with two hundred feet of rubber hose, a hundred feet of which were coupled onto pipes leading to a tank in the attic. A twenty thousand gallon tank was always kept filled from a nearby pumping station.

Herman arrived at the asylum earlier that afternoon, in awe at the building's architecture and construction. There was an eerie feeling about the grounds, the building itself, and the surrounding landscape. Herman rode the carriage to the front gates and was greeted by the security officer, who immediately opened the gate after Herman introduced himself, "Hello, sir, my name is Allen."

"Good day to you, Allen. I am Herman Mudgett, here to see Dr. Caswell." He tipped his hat.

"The supervisor is waiting for you and has received your written letter of employment request. Everyone here gets excited when they hear about a new face arriving." The man closed the gate, after Herman had pulled his carriage past the security fence.

"It was very nice to meet you, Allen."

"It was a pleasure to meet you, Mr. Mudgett." Allen replied, as he closed and secured the main gates of the asylum.

Herman rode up the path to the front entrance and was greeted by another security officer, "I'll keep watch on your carriage, sir." Herman thanked the man and opened the large door of the asylum's entrance.

The supervisor's office was near the front lobby. Herman walked to the opened door and tapped on the wooden doorframe. The supervising doctor looked up from his paperwork, "Please come in and have a seat. My name is Dr. Caswell." He extended his hand towards Herman.

"Herman Mudgett, I'm very pleased to meet you, Doctor." Herman wanted so much to be called doctor. How prestigious and respectable would it be to have the title? The doctor was dressed in a fine tailored suit, and a pair of carefully buffed dress shoes. He put on a pair of reading glasses, looking over Herman's letter of employment request.

Herman and the supervisor discussed the job opening as an assistant, "The job includes assisting me, the other doctors and the patients, in my absence. There would of course be extensive training sessions, which I would personally oversee, should I take you on as an assistant."

"I wish to fill the position, Dr. Caswell."

"As the asylum's supervising doctor, I am required to fill out final paperwork and the employment forms, just as a formality. You have a unique sense of charisma Mr. Mudgett. Can I show you around the grounds?"

"I would appreciate that, very much, doctor," responding enthusiastically.

"Herman, what do you know about the mentally ill and psychology?" The doctor asked, as he stood up and looked at Herman's overall condition and appearance.

"I have read some details in my medical encyclopedias and journals. Only an average amount, at best."

"Herman, if you have some time, I will give you the introduction training I give to all the new assistants. Here are a notebook and a pencil for you to take notes. Please follow me."

Herman discussed the conversation he had with the man back in town about the asylum's history and construction. The doctor was impressed with his knowledge of the building.

"So, I will begin with explaining the patients I have experienced and those of which are now residing in the building. There is a variety of disturbed patients, here at the asylum. Their conditions span from the many different categories of mental disorders and many different facets of human behaviors and personalities that can become disordered." The doctor was very animated and waving his arms about the hallway.

He continued, "Anxiety or fear which interferes with normal functioning, may be classified as a simple anxiety disorder. Commonly recognized categories include specific phobias, generalized anxiety disorder, social anxiety disorder, panic disorder, agoraphobia, obsessive compulsive disorder and post-traumatic stress disorder. These can occur from various family situations, traumatic events, and severe abuse."

"Can that just be a normal disorder someone develops and can be successfully treated, by a regular physician, or does it always require a patient to be committed to an asylum?" Herman was continuing with his notes, making detailed notations about the disorders, which he planned to study further.

"Not all cases require psychiatric treatment; however, if left untreated by a physician can result in catastrophic outcomes. Other affective processes can also be classified as a disorder. Mood disorders involve unusually intense and sustained sadness, melancholia, or despair, is known as major depression, or clinical depression." The doctor paused as Herman continued his notations.

He paused from taking notes, "So, not to sound inexperienced, a person who is sad can slip further into another disorder and fall deeper into a depressive state?"

"Yes, Herman, they can even become manic and unstable. This is when their physician would recommend a psychiatric evaluation by a psychiatrist. You would be surprised at the advanced state a human being can reach, in such a short amount of time."

Herman thought of his father and replied, "My father would most likely be a candidate for an evaluation, but he is no longer with us." Herman thought to add the lie to the conversation to avoid any blow back from mentioning his father.

"I am, truly, sorry for your loss." The doctor patted Herman on the shoulder and continued, "A manic patient involves abnormally high or pressured mood states known as mania, or hypomania, alternating with normal or depressed moods. Patterns of belief, language use, and perception can become disordered, ergo; delusions, thought disorder, hallucinations. Do you have all that, or should I talk slower?"

Herman replied while writing vigorously in his notebook, "I'm getting all of this, it is very fascinating."

"Now, the extreme patients are kept in the attic and basement, for obvious reasons and the assistants and I must be accompanied by guards in these rooms at all times. Psychotic disorders in this domain include schizophrenia and delusional disorder. Schizoaffective disorder is a category used for individuals showing aspects of both schizophrenia and affective disorders, such as these patients." Dr. Caswell was pointing to different patients, as they walked down the hallway, and some sitting in their cells.

"Schizotypy is a category used for individuals showing some of the characteristics associated with schizophrenia but without meeting certain criteria. Personality, the fundamental characteristics of a person that influence his or her thoughts and behaviors across situations and time, may be considered disordered if judged to be abnormally rigid and maladaptive."

"A list of a number of different disorders such personality disorders, including those sometimes classed as eccentric, ergo; paranoid, schizoid, and schizotypal personality disorders. Sometimes individuals can be classed as dramatic, or emotional, or those seen as fear related. If an inability to adjust to life circumstances begins within three months of a

particular event or situation, and ends within six
months after the stressor stops, or is eliminated, it may
instead be classed as an adjustment disorder."

Herman continued writing down the doctor's
words in his notebook. The doctor walked down a
large, metal staircase to the main level and turned to
Herman, "The first level houses the less extreme
patients like eating disorders, which involve
disproportionate concern in matters of food and
weight. Sexual and gender identity disorders may be
diagnosed, including dyspareunia."

"Various kinds of paraphilia are considered mental
disorders, sexual arousal to objects, situations, or
individuals that are considered abnormal or harmful to
their person or to others. Sometimes, like in the cases
you see here, it is required to bind the patient's hands to
prevent them from following through on their
compulsions." Two male patients had restraints keeping
their hands, restricted, behind their backs, as they
wandered aimlessly around the asylum's first floor.

"Are these patients medicated?" Herman inquired.

Dr. Caswell turned, "The administration of
medication is essential during their treatment at the
facility. Each patient is administered the medication that
best matches their disorder. Sometimes it is necessary
to change and even increase the dosages."

"Have there ever been cases where a psychiatrist
develops one of these disorders?"

"Indeed, these disorders can affect and appear in
any individual because we are all faced with the same
emotions, experiences, and our brains can easily fall to
any level of the fore mentioned disorders."

"That makes perfect sense to me." Herman made
a notation.

"People who are abnormally unable to resist certain urges or impulses that could be harmful to themselves or others, may be classed as having an impulse control disorder, and disorders such as kleptomania or pyromania. Various behavioral addictions, such as gambling addiction, may be classed as a disorder should it interfere with the individual's finances, the families and even friends finances, by the gambling addiction becoming a threat to another's well being and the person with the disorder well being."

"Obsessive compulsive disorder can sometimes involve an inability to resist certain acts but is classed separately as being primarily an anxiety disorder." The supervising doctor was walking Herman through the groups of patients on the first floor, pointing out each one and continuing his explanations.

Some of the patients were leaning against the walls, others were sitting calmly in chairs, staring vacantly in front of them in no particular direction, "The use of drugs, when it persists despite significant problems related to use, may be defined as a mental disorder termed substance dependence, or substance abuse. Disordered substance use may be due to a pattern of compulsive and repetitive use of the drug that results in tolerance to its effects and withdrawal symptoms when use is reduced or stopped."

"People who suffer severe disturbances of their self identity, memory and general awareness of themselves and their surroundings, may be classed as having a dissociative identity disorder, such as depersonalization disorder or dissociative identity disorder itself, which has also been called multiple personality disorder. Other memory or cognitive disorders include amnesia or various kinds of dementia.

Conduct disorder, if continuing into adulthood, may be diagnosed as antisocial personality disorder. That's about all for today. That should give you plenty to study up on."

"Thank you for the opportunity. And, yes, there is a lot of information to digest and study. I will see you the following week." They shook hands and Herman left through the doors of the main entrance. He thanked the security officer for watching his carriage and left to return to the hotel. The ride was pleasant and he arrived at the outskirts of Alton after the three hour carriage ride.

Clara was waiting for him in the hotel lobby and rushed to greet him. "Herman, I was waiting for so long. How was your ride, was the asylum an eerie place?"

"On the contrary, the asylum was fascinating. I was offered the assistant's job, a tour of the facility, and the first introductory training, which is why it took me so long to return." He hugged Clara.

"Wonderful Herman, it is just what you wanted. I knew that you would be offered a position, because you are a brilliant, charming, and smart man." She hugged him and took his hand, leading him down the hallway to their room.

When she opened the door to their hotel room, Herman discovered a large table near the window with an assortment of trays filled with vegetables, potatoes, and steak cuts. It was just what Herman needed, after the long ride and the extended tour of the asylum. Upon finishing their dinner, Clara led Herman into the bedroom, stopping him at the bedside and softly whispered in his ear, "I want you, and I want to be your wife, Herman."

Herman paused and looked into her eyes, "Will you marry me, Clara?"

"Yes!" She screamed out loud and threw her arms around Herman's neck. Herman returned the embrace. Clara passionately kissed Herman. The two slowly moved to the bed, removing their clothes.

Sunday morning, Herman and Clara ate breakfast. Afterwards, they took a carriage ride out to the property Herman was preparing to purchase as their first home. Clara was amazed when she gazed upon the land and the cottage, "I love it, Herman!"

She jumped from the carriage and ran to the backyard. Herman smiled and followed closely behind. Clara was already at the end of the property, looking over the gazebo and the garden, "Let's look inside. It's just beautiful Herman, it is perfect!" They finished touring the inside of the cottage, walked out to the front of the yard and stood, holding each other, gazing at their future home.

The following morning, Herman finished the deed transfer and paid the owner the agreed price for the property. He proceeded to the asylum to start his first day of work. At the asylum's entrance he was greeted by the doctor, who led him inside and proceeded to continue his training and the daily duties of the assistant, "This is a short list of your job description. You will also be assisting the doctor in the autopsy procedures of the deceased patients. This will be your first big step in achieving a medical degree and becoming a doctor."

The following months, Herman continued working at the asylum gaining the trust and receiving additional training from the doctor. Night had come and Clara walked from the kitchen, after finishing up some cleaning, "Herman, I need to tell you something. I am pregnant with your child. You are going to be a father."

Herman, sitting at a desk, studying his medical journals was taken by surprise with the unexpected news. He shut one of the books and stood, "I . . . I am shocked. This is wonderful news!" He hugged Clara and knew that it was time to prepare for the arrival of their first child. The following Sunday, Herman and Clara were married. Their son was born seven months later and it was decided to name the child Robert Mudgett.

In one of the smaller rooms of their cottage, Herman and Clara had set up the baby's room. There was a small crib, cloth diapers, and other baby supplies, toys and the walls had been painted light blue, "He is just . . . he is so beautiful, Herman. He looks just like you, well, he has my eyes."

"He has the eyes of a little angel." Herman carefully placed their child into the crib, wrapping it with a small blanket, "Perfect, let's get some sleep. I have a feeling he will be hungry in a few hours." Clara took Herman by the hand, and after turning out a small light, they retired to the master bedroom.

At the asylum, Herman began gaining the trust of the patients, as well as the other resident workers in the building. Dr. Caswell presented Herman his first dissection kit. "Herman this dissection kit was presented to me, by the doctor I received my training from. I, now, present it to you." Dr. Caswell reached down to his desk and lifted a suede covered box, handing it to Herman. Herman placed his hands on the kit and began to feel a strange energy flow through his body, as his hands rested on the box.

Herman took the box and opened it, gazing at the contents inside. His eyes widened and reflected off the steel of each instrument, "Thank you for this kind and thoughtful gift. I swear that from this moment on, I will use the kit for the betterment of the medical community and relieve the poor and unfortunate of the ailments and illnesses which overcome them." It just so happened, Herman's ambitions for the future was quite the opposite. He remembered the kit he had used to dissect the frog, back in his days at the academy, and saw the similarities of the instruments. The kit contained a scalpel, pins, tweezers, scissors, seekers, and other instruments.

The doctor explained to Herman the additional surgical knife in the kit, "The kits that you may have been using in your earlier classes were much simpler. This kit is for more advanced surgeries including, this, the Liston knife. A type of knife used in surgical amputation."

"The knife was named after Robert Liston a Scottish surgeon noted for his skill and speed in an era prior to anesthetics, when speed made a difference in terms of pain and survival. The knife is made out of high quality metal and has a typical blade length of six to eight inches. Surgical amputation knives come in many styles and have been slightly modified between 1840 and our present time. These changes reflect changes in techniques used by the surgeons, and makers of surgical knives."

Herman lifted the knife and inspected the long slender blade and the jagged ridges along the top of the blade itself. The doctor continued, "Amputation blades, from the eighteenth century to the present day, are generally known for their distinctive 'down' curving blades.

By 1870, amputation blades had become straighter and more closely resembled the, Liston, European style. Since the Crimean War ended in 1856, it is likely the American Civil War had a greater impact on long slender blade style, than Dr. Liston. The task of amputation may be more responsible for the Liston title than any specific design."

The following months, Herman performed his responsibilities as the doctor's assistant, also taking on many of the doctor's personal procedures and other tasks. He looked after the major care and administration of medications to patients, also assisting the doctor in some of the major autopsies and dissections of two deceased patients.

Dr. Caswell supervised Herman, as he performed the functions of his first autopsy, "You are doing very well, Herman. Soon, you will be working unsupervised and collecting organs to be preserved as experimental tissue for use in some of the medical schools in the area. I will run over the details of the process, when you are ready." Over the following week, Herman began transporting preserved organs to the surrounding universities, discovering the universities were paying a good price for the samples they were receiving from the asylum.

Collecting specimens and organ samples was providing Herman additional finances, aside from the pay he was receiving from the asylum, as an assistant. He would take the specimens from the cadavers and sell them to the universities, even if Dr. Caswell did not instruct Herman to remove the organ samples from the cadavers. Spending more and more time at the asylum was putting a strain on the relationship between Herman and his new bride, Clara.

One afternoon, Herman found himself treating a catatonic woman named Rose. She was placed in the attic of the asylum, with the rest of the extreme patients, because she had become a threat to her own physical safety. A male nurse was assisting Herman and explained, "The prior month, Rose attempted to throw herself out the second story window of the asylum, however, the window did not break and she ended up with some cuts and bruises on her body." The male nurse watched, as Herman prepared his examinations.

Standing over the woman, and preparing to administer a mixture of medications, he prepped her arm with a tourniquet tied just above her elbow. The security officer stepped back and, for a moment, was distracted by a high pitched scream from a patient in the next room. Rose's straight jacket had been removed, leaving her arms freely hanging and resting beside her on the bed.

Just as Herman pressed the needle into her skin, Rose threw her arms upwards, placing her hands on each side of Herman's head. The security officer rushed to restrain Rose. However, Herman lifted his arm and stopped him, "Wait Joseph, let her go, there should be no reason why Rose would break from a complete catatonic state. I want to see what she will do."

Joseph, the security officer, slowly stood back and watched closely, as Herman turned and looked into her eyes. He lifted each eyelid to check her pupils. They were dilated and showing response to light. She looked up at him and inhaled deeply, "You have been touched." Herman was in a state of disbelief at her words, "What, Rose, what are you saying?"

"You have been broken and reacted against the one who broke you. I see it in your eyes." Herman was now in a state of panic and began breathing heavily, "Herman, you did it didn't you?"

She held her hands tightly against the side of Herman's face, her grip became tighter and tighter, she began moving slowly towards Herman and whispered in his ear, "You will do it again and again. Your eyes reveal it." She licked Herman's face and then bit him on the neck. Herman screamed in pain. Joseph, the security officer, jumped towards Rose pinning her to the bed. Herman reached up to his neck and placed pressure on the bite.

"Rose, what the hell are you doing?" Herman shouted, taking the syringe of medication, quickly administering a larger dose into her vein. Rose slowly relaxed, onto her back, into a sedated state. Joseph quickly placed the straight jacket back around Rose's arms. "Herman, you need to be more careful with these patients. They cannot be trusted under any circumstance," laughing nervously, "Are you all right?" He laughed.

"Yes, Joseph, I was just surprised that she spoke at all. I will have to get your statement for the report, which will need to be filed with Dr. Caswell."

"No problem, Herman, but this is not the first time, or the last, that Rose has bitten someone. Just ask the doctor about his own experiences with her."

Herman took out his handkerchief and placed it over the wound on his neck. Joseph finished securing Rose to the bed, double checking the restraints. Herman and Joseph walked from Rose's cell. Joseph closed and locked the metal door, "I always double check the patients' doors to ensure it is secured and

locked. We don't want any more mistakes, right?"
Joseph smiled and laughed.

Herman looked back into the room and gazed at
Rose, who slowly turned her head to the side, slightly
opened her eyes and smiled at Herman. A chill went up
his spine from the words Rose spoke to him. She knew
what he had done. Somehow, she saw it in his eyes and
knew exactly what he had done.

Herman returned to the doctor's office and wrote
up the reports about the day's events. Joseph had done
the same and given Herman his report, "I'll leave out
what Rose said and just say that she attacked you. I
have never heard anything like that from any of the
patients, before." He looked at Herman, giving him a
concerned look, "You understand about being more
careful around the patients in the attic and basement. I
need to make sure that you understand that."

"Thanks Joseph, I am, but I am also a little
surprised about the conversation, as well." Herman
finished the report, leaving it on Dr. Caswell's desk.
The doctor was out for the day, so Herman finished up
a few unfinished tasks and informed the night security
officer, Jack, he was leaving.

"Have a good evening, Herman." Jack helped
Herman open the door, "Do you need any help to your
carriage?"

"I can manage, Jack, thanks for the offer." He
carried his coat and suitcase in one hand, pressing his
other hand against the door.

Herman walked from the front door of the asylum,
placed his belongings into his carriage, turned and
looked up at an attic window. The sun had just passed
below the tree line and the light from the dusk sky
reflected upon the window to Rose's room. As Herman

looked up at the window, he could have sworn that a shadow passed in front of the window. He shook his head and climbed into his carriage, jerking the reins forward and riding off on the trail home.

The following day, Herman arrived at the asylum to find Dr. Caswell in his office. "Herman I am offering you a training session, in a psychological medical conference located at the State Hospital in Danvers, Massachusetts. I would attend; however, I have already been the last few years, as a doctor. This conference is designed for students and future students. This is your letter of acceptance into the conference."

Herman stood at the door of the office and looked at the desk, "Doctor Caswell, did you read the report about what happened with Rose, yesterday?"

"Yes, Herman, but you have read her file and know that it is not the first time she has attacked a doctor, or a security officer for that matter."

"Well, then, I will be honored to attend the conference, thank you doctor."

"I know you have been spending endless hours and days at the asylum and that you would jump at the opportunity to attend this conference. Take the rest of the day off. Tomorrow, I will give you more details. This is the brochure for the asylum in Danvers, Massachusetts." Herman took the pamphlet, thanked the doctor again and walked back to his carriage.

He quickly rode home to inform Clara of the opportunity the supervisor had offered to him. He informed Clara, who was less than excited to have Herman out of town for the month, "Herman, we have just had a baby. I know this is important to you, but I want you to stay here with me. You need to spend more time with me and the baby." She insisted.

Herman was becoming upset and frustrated at the lack of support coming from his wife, "Clara, you know how important this is for me. This will open doors for me. I will be able to attend a medical university. Dr. Caswell has already written my referral letter. After this conference, I will only have to decide what school to choose."

"So, that is it, you have already made your decision without even asking me?" Herman looked back at Clara, after standing up from the bed, and knew that something had changed between them, ever since the birth of their son. He almost passed out standing at the bedroom door when, suddenly, a vision of his mother and father flashed through his mind.

The vision was of his mother and father and how they had grown distant from each other, after his birth. The vision continued up to the point of Herman suddenly recalling killing the Statham boy. That was the skull he had possession of, not his mother's, but his first victim.

The next flashback was of Rose telling him that he would do it again. Herman rushed from the room, out of the front door of the house falling into the dirt. He was holding his head in his hands, sweating, as thoughts of killing Clara ran through his head. The mysterious voice in his head returned, "I told you, I would take care of everything. Right up until the very end, my son. I will show you the way." The voice faded.

He knew at that point, he was leaving and that after the medical conference, he would not be coming back and there was no other choice. He could either stay or go nowhere, which might lead to the murder of his wife and child, or attend the conference and go straight to medical school. It was an easy decision for him to make.

All the necessary information for the medical conference was in the brochure of the hospital, all the treatments, patient care, and details of the facility. Herman read into the night as Clara slept in the bedroom. The brochure read as follows:

It was built in 1874 and opened in 1878 under the supervision of prominent Boston architect Nathaniel Jeremiah Bradlee, on a secluded site in Danvers, Massachusetts. It is a multi acre and self sufficient, psychiatric hospital designed and built according to the Kirkbride Plan. The final construction reached a cost of one and a half million dollars, with the estimated yearly per capita cost of patients being three thousand dollars.

The administration building measures ninety by sixty feet, with a one hundred thirty five foot high tower. The kitchens, laundries, chapel, and dormitories for the attendants are in a connecting one hundred eighty, by sixty foot building, in the rear. In the rear is the boiler house of seventy square feet, with four hundred fifty horsepower boilers, used for heating and ventilation. Middleton Pond supplies the hospital's water.

On each side of the main building, are the wings for male and female patients respectively, connected by smaller square towers, with the exception of the last ones, on each side, which are joined by octagon towers. The former measures ten feet square and are used to separate the buildings. The outermost wards are reserved for extreme patients. The west side is male wing and the east is female.

Most of the buildings on the campus are connected by a confusing labyrinth of underground tunnels, also constructed over the years. Many of the Commonwealth institutions for the developmentally delayed and the mentally ill are designed with tunnel systems to be self sufficient in wintertime. There is a tunnel that runs from a steam powered generating plant, located at the bottom of the hill running up to the hospital, along with tunnels that connect the male and female nurses' homes, the Bonner Medical Building, machine shops, pump house, and a few others.

The system of tunnels branches off like spokes from a central hub behind the Kirkbride building, leading to different wards of the hospital and emerging up into the basements. This hub is an underground maintenance area of sorts. The original plan is designed to house five hundred patients, with one hundred more possible to accommodate in the attic.

The asylum is established to provide residential treatment and care to the mentally ill. Its functions are now expanding to include a training program for nurses and a pathological research laboratory to expand shock therapies, lobotomies, drugs, and straitjackets, being used to keep a crowded hospital under control.

Over the next few days, Herman prepared for his trip. He removed all the money from his bank account, packed some of his clothes, including a shirt he had kept from his father's belongings. After finishing his packing, he walked into the bedroom upstairs and provided Clara some false reassurance, "After the conference, I will return and not be leaving for any length of time, in the future, without you. I love you." Clara was distant and did not respond.

That evening he gathered all his belongings, carefully packing them in the carriage and prepared the horse to leave in the morning. His money was hidden in a small leather satchel, underneath the back porch. All his preparations were made in order to leave in the morning. Standing near the back porch of the house, he looked up observing the light of the full moon and the stars which blanketed the black canvas of the night sky. He knew this chapter of his life had come to an end.

'Crazy Train'

The following morning arrived. The sun was slowly rising above the horizon, its rays beaming through the trees of the thick forest. Herman finished harnessing the horse to the carriage and walked over to Clara and the baby. He kissed his son and looked up at Clara, "I will write you and tell you all about the conference. I will miss you and the baby."

He kissed Clara and turned, she stopped him, "Herman, be careful and come back as soon as you can, I love you." Herman turned and kissed her one last time, walking off and climbing onto the carriage. He directed the carriage from the front of the house and into the distance. Clara watched, holding their son and was waving to Herman, as he left.

Arriving at the center of town, where the sales and purchases of carriages were made, Herman parked his carriage. The owner of the store was standing out front. Herman approached him, "Hello."

"Hello to you." The owner replied, "How can I help you?"

They shook hands, "I am looking to sell my horse and carriage." Herman walked the owner to the carriage.

The owner looked over the carriage and the horse's condition, "Well, the horse is in a healthy condition. However, the carriage is another story."

"I agree." Herman replied. After making arrangements with the owner, for the sale of his horse and carriage, Herman then made his way over to the train station and purchased a one way ticket to Danvers, Massachusetts.

The train pulled into the station. Herman boarded the train and chose his seat in the rear of the first car, carefully sliding his luggage under the seat holding another bag on his lap. Looking around and noticing all the other passengers had settled into their seats, he slowly unzipped the other bag, revealing the human skull. Slowly turning the skull, and looking deep into the shadow of its hollow eyes, there was no turning his attention from the fascination which overtook him.

The train ride took the better part of the day. The train jerked back and forth along the tracks. Train travel was not Herman's favorite means of travel. He would just as much rather take a carriage, as that was what he was accustomed to. Passengers walked up and down the aisles, some entering the dining car, others were sitting in their seats reading and speaking, back and forth, indistinctly.

As the train arrived at the Danvers station, Herman was informed by one of the conductors, "The train has reached its destination sir. I hope you enjoyed the ride."

"I did, thank you." He replied. The train came to a stop, steam blasting from underneath the main engine

and across the platform. Passengers slowly began
exiting the train. Many were well dressed, looking tired
and run down from traveling the long and bumpy train
ride.

Collecting his luggage and bag, Herman stood
from his seat and exited the train. His luggage was
collected from him by an employee, "I'll keep this bag."
Herman held tightly to the bag containing the skull,
"Thank you, sir." and tipped him for his prompt
service.

"Where are you heading?" The employee inquired.

"I am going to the Danvers asylum." He obtained
the information from the railroad employee for the
easiest way to travel to Danvers asylum.

The employee directed Herman to the front of the
station, "I'll hail a carriage for you." A carriage pulled
up to the two and the employee loaded Herman's
luggage onto the carriage. The driver was very
knowledgeable about the town.

On the ride to the hospital, Herman was given an
earful from the carriage driver. It was only an indication
that he would prefer not to live in this town for long.
As the carriage approached the path, leading up to the
hospital, an overwhelming feeling and ominous power
from the asylum overcame Herman.

The building itself was immense and towered over
the approaching carriage, like a bat or bird overtaking
its prey. There were multiple towers stretching into the
sky, the red brick of the building gave the onlooker the
impression there was more taking place inside, then just
regular patient treatment and psychiatric care.

Stepping from the carriage, Herman was greeted by
two gentlemen dressed in white uniforms, introducing
themselves, "Hello sir, we are the orderlies assigned to

show you to your sleeping quarters in the nurses building and to show you around the grounds. We will take your luggage and bags to the male nurses building on the southwest side of the asylum grounds." One of the orderlies pointed out the male and female nurses building. Another orderly explained to Herman the rules of the hospital and that he would be given a tour of the facility, later that afternoon.

As the carriage driver drove from the asylum, and down the dirt road, the orderlies led Herman to the male nurses building. Herman was allowed time to settle in and unpack his clothes. Afterwards, was led to the main dining hall in the nurses building and then into the basement.

One of the orderlies opened a locked gate. A large tunnel system was revealed. Herman and two other men were led into a vast tunnel system. The lighting was dim and the tunnel smelled of damp mold. Rain was obviously leaking through the cracks in the walls, during the typical heavy rainstorms in the New England area.

Towards the end of the nurse's tunnel, leading to the main building, the group arrived at a larger tunnel system and a sign indicating the sections dividing patients and staff. The group entered into the left tunnel, designated for the staff, and walked past numerous patients on the right side of the divided tunnel. At first glance, the patients seemed just as normal as any of the orderlies, except one small detail, their movements were slow and uncoordinated. Their eyes were vacant and it was apparent they were highly medicated.

One of the orderlies turned to Herman and the two other men, "These patients are the less extreme patients. They are allowed to walk the patient grounds, freely, and in certain areas of the hospital. However, they are monitored by orderlies at opposite ends of the tunnel and throughout the hospital." The current of electricity flowing through the lighting system was interrupted. The lights would flicker and become compromised at certain hours of the day, due to the amount of energy being used throughout the hospital. "The amount of electricity used in the asylum must be overwhelming?" Herman inquired.

One of the orderlies turned to the group, "There is a large amount of power being used at peak operating hours. The electricity powers the rooms, halls, and the equipment to run this entire establishment. We like to use the term establishment, instead of asylum. It helps the patients feel more at home and comfortable." The groups were led into the main building and taken through the many wards of the hospital.

After the tour of the main levels, and the male and female wards, the group was led to the extreme patient ward, Ward A. They were reminded of the rules of approaching and speaking with patients and not to address them in any way. Entering Ward A presented an immediate change in mood. The pressure and tension could be felt, as Herman walked through the security gates. The gates were immediately locked behind them.

Patients were not allowed to walk in the hallways, unless accompanied by an orderly and only if they were they were restrained in straight jackets. Some patients were restricted in simple restraints, others in straight jackets and protective metal head shields and masks.

Looking into the cells, Herman was surprised that a person could live in the types of conditions the asylum was in. It was explained, "The patients are kept highly sedated and are criminally insane and violent. Therefore, the seclusion is necessary in order to protect the other patients and patients from hurting themselves." Herman thought of how much pain and suffering the human body and mind could endure, until they ultimately cracked under the conditions. This situation was a slightly less extreme, but he could not help wonder about the pain and suffering torture would bring.

After the tour, the group was led down a winding steel staircase, enclosed in a fence. They were led into the auditorium, where a number of other men and women were sitting, randomly, among the seats. Herman walked to the middle of the auditorium. He took his seat, as a well dressed doctor walked to the front of the stage and began speaking, "Ladies and gentlemen, if you would kindly take your seats, we will begin the presentation. Afterwards, we will break for lunch and meet back in the auditorium for our second meeting."

A doctor approached the podium and began speaking, "Good morning, I will begin with a brief history of psychiatry and then continue with some information about the diagnosis, and the variety of treatments, developed for the mentally and criminally insane. Firstly, the word asylum means shelter, or refuge. This is an institution for the care of the destitute, sick, and especially the insane, some criminally. The first actual mental asylum in America opened in 1769 under the guidance of Benjamin Rush, who became known as America's first psychiatrist."

"Benjamin Rush was known as America's first psychiatrist and a professor at America's first psychiatric hospital. The hospital, located in Williamsburg, Virginia, was the only such institution in the country for fifty years. Rush graduated from Princeton University at the age of fifteen and studied medicine at the University of Edinburgh in his twenties. Soon, after, he began to practice medicine. He realized that his primary interest was in the treatment of the mentally ill." The doctor arranged his papers.

"At first, Rush disapproved of any kind of restraint and for long periods of time outlawed the use of whips, chains, and straitjackets, developing more humane methods of keeping control. Looking at some of his methods, we may feel he was quite harsh. But in his day, his methods were considered exceedingly humane and some continue to be used here at this asylum."

The doctor continued speaking, "The tranquilizing chair is a device intended to heal by lowering the pulse and relaxing the muscles. It is designed to hold the head, body, arms and legs immobile for long periods of time and enable the patients become settled. The treatment is similar to placing the inmates into seclusions."

"A technique that brought about the idea of using trepanation in its place was called the gyrator. As its name suggests is a contraption similar to a spoke on a wheel. The patient was strapped to the board, head outward. The wheel was rotated at a high rate of speed, sending the blood racing to his head and supposedly relieving the congested brain. The circulating swing worked similar to the gyrator with the patient bound in place in a sitting position. Looking back, it is obvious the treatments were primitive but as mentioned, before, the change has been made to trepanation." The doctor paused and sighed.

After taking a drink of water, he looked back down at his notes, "Trepanning, also known as trepanation, is a surgical intervention in which a hole is drilled into the human skull, exposing the dura mater in order to treat health problems related to intracranial diseases. It may also refer to any burr hole created through other body surfaces, including nail beds. It is often used to relieve pressure beneath a surface. A trephine is an instrument used for cutting out a round piece of skull bone."

"Evidence of trepanation has been found in prehistoric human remains from Neolithic times onward, the practice cures epileptic seizures, migraines, and mental disorders. Evidence also suggests that trepanation was primitive emergency surgery after head wounds to remove shattered bits of bone from a fractured skull and clean out the blood that often pools under the skull after a person receives a blow to the head."

"At some point, rumors spread a man had attempted self trepanation. It is a rumor talked about, but obviously never confirmed. His attempt at self trepanation is just that, after some time there was an ominous sounding schlurp and the sound of bubbling. He drew the trepan out and the gurgling continued it sounded like air bubbles running under the skull, as they were pressed out. He looked at the trepan and there was a bit of bone in it."

"He had also attempted to perform a self trepanation with a drill. However, these are rumors and no doctor in his right mind would attempt to perform this procedure on themselves. To attempt a procedure of this type would suggest that a person would most likely require to be committed to this establishment!"

There was some murmuring, followed by a few outbursts of uncomfortable laughter.

The doctor paused, somewhat reveling at his obvious attempt at humor and then continued, "As history progresses, our view of mental illness came to devise the victims are to blame. Explanations such as possession by evil spirits, moral weakness and other such diagnosis create a stigma of mental illness and place the responsibility for a cure on the resulting outcasts themselves." The doctor began pacing back and forth across the stage.

"The most apparently ill and dangerous inmates are chained to the walls. Some inmates are crowded into dark cells, some sleeping two on a mattress on damp floors and chained. If they are placed into seclusions there is no fresh air, no light, very little nutrition and for extreme misbehavior, they soak for long periods in ice water containers. This method settles the patient. No differentiation is made between mentally ill and criminally insane. All are contained, packed together and treated with the same behavior modification treatment."

"Seclusion is used as a control tactic in psychiatric treatment settings. Seclusion of an agitated person in a quiet room, free of stimulation, may help to eliminate an escalated situation which may be dangerous to the agitated person or those around him. In addition to administering medications, seclusion is a tactic devised for those unwilling to follow instructions or the facility's policies and procedures."

"Patients who are secluded, due to aggressive behavior, should not be restrained in seclusion, nor administered medication to calm them, instead non restraint measures should be taken into consideration.

Other measures, such as behavioral therapy, should be considered when assessing the care of the patient. Seclusion must only be used in the best interest of the patient. It must only be used as a last resort and must not be prolonged as a form of punishment on the patient. The act states that a person can only be placed in seclusion, if it prevents them from hurting themselves or others."

"Behavior therapy, or behavior modification, is an approach to psychotherapy based on learning theory which aims to treat psychopathology through techniques designed to reinforce desired and eliminate undesired behaviors. Functional analysis has even been applied to problems that therapists commonly encounter like client resistance, partially engaged and involuntary clients. One way to enhance therapeutic effectiveness is to use positive reinforcement or operant conditioning."

"We will now break for an afternoon lunch, the orderlies will lead you to the cafeteria, then we will meet back in the auditorium for another short conference. There are also some manuscripts and documents near each of the exits. Please take advantage of reading over the material during your lunch, feel free to discuss and explore the topics of the manuscripts. Ladies and gentlemen, I thank you for your time and hope this presentation was informative and helpful on your journey's to becoming doctors."

The group stood and walked towards the rear of the auditorium. Herman picked up a manuscript, the additional documents, and proceeded into the cafeteria. He was served a plate of steak bits, and potatoes, one of his favorite dishes. He sat near the back of the cafeteria, in an area that was slightly less occupied than the other sections.

Herman wanted to take advantage of reading the material, during his lunch break and, hopefully, not be disturbed. The first manuscript was thicker than the other documents, but he began reading intently. After the second presentation, it was clear Herman was not interested in psychiatry.

Remaining in the asylum for another three days, Herman Mudgett attended various trepanations and surgical procedures performed on some of the more extreme inmates, as they were called. The remaining day Herman prepared his belongings and thanked the other members attending the conference. He walked up to the main building and informed the two orderlies he was ready to leave.

After waiting for over an hour, a carriage arrived at the front of the asylum. Herman's bags were loaded onto the carriage. Upon entering the carriage, he looked back one last time at the ominous red brick building, as the carriage pulled away. Part of him was slightly relieved he was able to leave the asylum and was not one of the patients committed to remain.

The carriage approached to the Danvers train station, bouncing along the rough stretch of roads. After the carriage pulled up to the station, Herman unloaded his bags. He walked over to the ticket counter and purchased a one way ticket to Michigan. Sitting and waiting on a bench, he reached into one of his bags and took out his father's shirt. He looked at the shirt, smelled it and began violently gagging, until he finally threw up on the ground behind the bench. He wiped his mouth with his father's shirt and threw it behind the bench.

The conductor called out, "All-a-board!" Passengers began approaching the train and boarding, lifting their suitcases into the train.

Herman stepped to the side of the train and climbed into the passenger cabin, walked down the aisle and found an open seat towards the rear of the train, away from all the rest of the passengers. The steam blew from the side of the lead engine and, slowly, the cars jerked forward. Within moments, the train was slowly making its way down the tracks. Herman looked out the windows of the train, as it passed small towns and over large complex steel bridges.

The scenery was amazing and he paid close attention to every detail of the passing towns and landscapes. He took out his sketch pad and began drafting rough sketches of the scenic landscapes. Feeling drowsy, he laid his head back against the seat closed his eyes and quickly drifted off to sleep. Soon, visions of his father began haunting his dreams. As he slept, he mumbled, his words were incoherent and grew louder as his dream progressed.

A familiar voice entered his mind, "Hello son, I am still with you. You are, now, well on your way to fulfilling your ultimate goal. I am proud of you, son."

After a few moments, he jerked awake and looked around the passenger car. A few of the passengers were staring back at him. He wondered if he said anything strange or peculiar in his sleep. What would it matter?

Herman reached down to his suitcase and pulled out a small bottle of bourbon. Ducking down behind the seat in front of him, he took a few drinks from the bottle. Once he had finished, he placed the bottle back into the suitcase. He looked around and noticed an attendant walking towards him. The attendant arrived at his seat, informing him, "Dinner will be served in the main dining car from eight to ten o'clock."

"Thank you very much." Herman replied.

He stood and walked through the main passenger car, and into the dining car. There were multiple people and families preparing to be served their dinner. A well dressed sever walked to Herman, "May I seat you, sir?"

"Yes please." Herman followed the server to a smaller table and sat.

"The meal for tonight is duck served with a side of potatoes and a small salad." The server placed a set of utensils and a glass of water on the table. Herman took the glass and guzzled down the water. His thirst was quenched and his dry throat relieved. After finishing his meal, he noticed a group of older women looking in his direction. One of the women smiled and licked her lips. Herman stood and returned to the passenger car and took his seat. He was soon asleep, leaning on the window.

The train rode for three days, stopping at various stations, picking up more passengers, and letting others off. Finally, the train arrived at the Ann Arbor, Michigan, train depot slowly coming to a stop. The conductor announced the stop. Herman stood up and retrieved his suitcase and bag.

He stepped off the train and onto the busy platform of the train station, as people walked in different directions, quickly rushing to get to their destinations. Herman made his way to the main lobby of the station, discovering a stand selling papers and maps. He looked at the selection of books and magazines, while a local directory caught his eye. He reached down and picked up the book.

He flipped through the pages and came across the description of the medical classes available through the University of Michigan. He looked at the description of the school, paid the shop keeper, and placed the book into his satchel. Herman quickly left the station making his way down the streets of Michigan stopping in front of a small hotel, walked to the front doors and stepped inside.

Approaching the desk clerk, he reached into his pocket retrieving a small wad of money. The desk clerk finished writing in the registry book and looked up to Herman. "How can I help you, sir?"

"I need a room for the night." Herman replied politely.

"I'll just need five dollars and your name?"

"It's Herman Mudgett." He slid the five dollars across the desk to the clerk. The clerk took the money and slid him a room key.

"That will be room twenty three. It is up the stairs, on the second floor, the third door on the left. Are you here with your parents?"

"No, I'm planning on attending the medical university in the spring semester." Herman was offended from the clerk's remark. He looked up at the clerk with a scowl on his face. The clerk, realizing his remark caused offense, coughed, and replied, "It is a wonderful school and I am sure you will enjoy the teachers. Do you need the registrar's phone number?"

"No, thank you, I have the phone number from the local directory."

Herman picked up his suitcases, turned, and walked up the stairs to his room. He unlocked the door, opened it and stepped inside. After exploring the room and its amenities, he placed his luggage and bag in the closet and opened the window. Looking out to the street below, he watched as people walked by and carriages slowly made their way down the busy street.

Herman spent the remainder of the afternoon walking the streets of Michigan, getting a better feel for the city and looking at the local scenery. He walked through the local park and sat on a neatly painted bench, near a tree. The glistening lake nearby was filled with ducks and geese wading through the water in no particular direction.

His mind wandered to his mother and father standing outside the house, back in Gilmanton. He wondered if anyone noticed his sudden disappearance and if the authorities would eventually seek him out for the death of the Statham boy, since the events coincided. Smiling at the thought of anyone left wondering of the Statham boy's fate, he stood up and walked back to his hotel room.

After resting for a few hours, he stood up from the bed and walked over to the closet, opened his suitcase and pulled out a white dress shirt. His pants were ragged and torn at the bottoms. A shopping trip was in order and to be accomplished the following morning. For now, he was off to see about getting into one of the local pubs near the university. He left the hotel and made his way across the center of town, jumping onto a horse drawn carriage car riding it to the edge of the university campus.

He located a busy pub, walked inside and over to the counter waiting for the bartender to walk over to him, "Hello, youngster, what can I get you?" The barkeep was wearing a modest uniform, his hair combed neatly back with some type of oil.

"I'll take a beer." Herman reached into his shirt pocket.

"Aren't you a little young, kid?"

"I'm planning on attending the medical university this coming semester. I have a little extra for you to forget the age." Herman slid a larger bill to the bartender. The bartender looked down at the bill, smiled and walked to the tap, poured the lager into the glass tipping the handle back up and returned to Herman with the glass.

"Enjoy, what was your name again?" Herman looked at the man and replied, "I did not say, but it is Herman . . . Herman Mudgett."

"It is nice to meet you, Herman. I assume you will be spending some time in here, am I correct?"

"More than likely, if I decide to take the medical exams."

"Herman, you give me a holler if I can get you anything else." Herman sat at the bar and could not believe in such a short amount of time he was now away from his father and on his own. He smiled, as chills ran down his spine. He had also got away with his first murder.

The following morning, the air was chilly and a slight breeze was blowing through the hotel window. Herman rose and sat up in the bed, looking out the window. The sun was shining through, reflecting its rays on the floor. He stood up, walked over to the closet and proceeded to put on his clothes. He reached into the suitcase and pulled out some money from the shoebox he had taken from his father's room. He counted the money, smiled and left his room.

He spent the majority of the morning arranging for an apartment, registering with the medical university, and shopping for some new suits and clothes. Walking past a hat store, he looked inside the window at a neatly brushed, grey, Sebrell Fedora hat. Admiring the look of the hat, he stepped inside and was greeted by the shopkeeper, "Good afternoon, sir, how may I assist you?"

"I would like to be fitted for that, grey, Sebrell Fedora hat in the window."

The shopkeeper stepped into the back of the shop and reached for a box, neatly stacked on the shelves. He pulled out the hat and stepped behind Herman, placing the hat on his head. The man directed Herman to a mirror. As he looked into the mirror, it seemed as though he was immediately transformed into the image reflecting back at him. Charming, cunning, and now more mature looking, certainly someone that could be taken seriously and respected.

"I will take it." Herman turned and quickly paid the shopkeeper. "I will wear it. I do not require the box."

"Thank you for your purchase, sir." The shopkeeper shook Herman's hand.

He accomplished all of his intended tasks in a miraculous amount of time and was now prepared to start a new life in Michigan the coming years. He paid the deposit and first months rent to the landlord of a building, which was right next to the university's campus. He paid the small registration fee to the university and retrieved his bags from the hotel.

He made his way to the apartment building, which was near the university. There was a courtyard, just outside and he walked through the gate to the front door, opened the door and walked into the building. The building was well maintained and a variety of trees, flowers, and shrubs, decorated the landscape's surroundings. He immediately felt at home and was excited to see his new apartment.

His apartment was on the first floor of the building, furthest to the back. He walked his bags to the door, unlocked it with the key and slowly swung the door open. Walking inside, he made his way to the window and opened it. Next to the window, was a small table with an electric lamp, a large couch and a bed.

Smiling and satisfied with the accommodations, he whispered, "This will be perfect", walking over to the closet, opening one of the bags, he lifted out his first victim's skull. He removed part of the wrap, slowly raised the skull to his lips and kissed it, removing the remaining wrapping and sat the skull on some paper. To his left was a bucket filled with rags, reaching into the bucket he removed the rags and placed them on the floor.

Inside his suitcase was a bottle of preservative, he pulled out the small bottle from inside. Placing the bottle on the floor, just near the bucket and carefully raising his first victim's skull above the bucket, he opened the bottle and poured the contents into the bucket, allowing the skull to soak inside.

Using the rags, he carefully wiped down the skull, afterwards, placing it on the window seat, allowing it to air dry in the breeze blowing through the window. Herman removed his gloves and tossed them in the bucket. After some time passed, he removed the bucket and walked it out to the garbage container, just outside the back door of his apartment, then returned to his room.

He returned the skull to the bag, zipped it up and placed it back into the closet. Next, he pulled out some wooden hangers. He carefully placed his clothes on the hangers and arranged them in the closet. He walked back over to the window and closed it.

He retrieved the shoebox of money and counted it on the table, placing the majority back into the box and hiding the box under a panel under the wood floor. After finishing with his arrangements, he pulled the sheets down and climbed into bed, pulling the covers over his head and slowly drifted off to sleep.

'Learning Curve'

Months had passed and as expected, Herman was now attending medical classes at the University of Michigan and excelling in the beginning classes. His professors were amazed at his ability to learn the aspects of human anatomy and the dissection procedures so quickly. His professor exclaimed, "Herman, you must have some prior experience in anatomy and surgical procedures." The professor continued, "I have not had many students excel in such a way, without prior experience."

"The experience from my days in the Gilmanton Academy's science, and biology, classes first sparked my interest." Herman continued in his diligence, dissecting a cadaver, "I also worked as an assistant in an asylum in Dover, New Hampshire, and acquired some clinical experience in the Danvers State Asylum, as well."

His professor looked over Herman's cadaver assignment, smiled, and returned to his office. Little did he know of Herman's true intentions for taking medical courses at the university. Herman spent most of his evenings in the university's autopsy room, working on cadavers and putting in extra time after hours to excel in his courses.

One evening, he was in the autopsy room, standing over a steel table, focused on his work on a recently deceased cadaver. He pressed the scalpel into the cadaver's skin, afterwards cutting open the rib cage with the shears, and a saw, to cut away the rib plate; afterwards spreading it with a retractor.

He looked over the cadaver's shady blue skin, and the facial features. The young man's body was stiff and the muscles rigid. He lowered his head, closer to the internal organs of the body, fascinated and in awe of each of the organs and what their specific functions were. The heart and lungs were exposed.

Herman was careful to ensure that the heart was not damaged or disturbed during the process. He used a scalpel to remove the soft tissue still attached to the chest plate. The lungs and heart exposed, Herman sat aside the chest plate to eventually be replaced at the end of the autopsy.

First, Herman viewed the heart, looking at the overall condition. He proceeded to remove the heart by cutting the pulmonary veins, the aorta and pulmonary artery. The lungs were removed by cutting the bronchus, the veins and arteries. Next, the abdominal organs were removed, one by one, after first examining their conditions. Herman examined each organ, weighed and took tissue samples by extracting small slices. The stomach and intestines were examined and weighed.

What would the organs reactions be, to long procedures of pain, should the human body be dissected alive? Contemplating these thoughts, his professor walked in. "Herman, what are you still doing here?" His professor was carrying his bags preparing to leave for the evening.

"Professor Renzor, I was just finishing up on the intestinal tract."

"Ah yes the intestines? I have always thought them to be the worst part of human anatomy. You should leave for the weekend. I will finish cleaning up here. A young man should invest some of his time being somewhere he can get some relaxation and take his mind off cadavers, at least for a while!" His professor laughed.

"I agree, thank you professor." Herman placed the scalpel on the table, hung his apron on the hook near the wash basin and washed his hands, drying them on a nearby towel. He threw the towel into the laundry basket, opened the swinging doors of the autopsy room, stopped, and turned, "Professor, how long did it take you to achieve your medical degree?"

"It takes about four years, Herman, depending on how much work you put into it. With the amount of time you are working in the lab, I do not think it is going to take you much more time than it did for me."

"Goodnight, Professor Renzor."

"Good evening, Herman."

Herman rushed from the autopsy room and back to his apartment, where he cleaned up and changed his clothes. After getting ready, he made his way across the campus to the town's popular local bar. Looking through the window Herman could see the bar was filled with businessmen. Sitting near the front of the bar were two other medical students from his class, "Why do they have to be here?"

His mind was racing about the two male students, they were such know it alls. He opened the door and quickly walked past his two classmates and to the rear of the bar. He lowered his head and waited for the server.

"Hey honey, what can I get for you tonight?"

"I will have a draft that will be all." He replied with a smile.

The waitress walked towards the main section of the bar and exchanged some words with the bartender, who looked over towards him. After getting a good look at Herman, the bartender waved. Herman kindly returned the wave and smiled. The waitress was probably only concerned about his age.

"Hello, Herman, how are you doing this lovely evening?" Herman turned to see Billy, one of the students from his class, standing near his table. Billy placed his hand on Herman's shoulder, attempting to show some attempt at camaraderie.

"Hello Billy," Herman replied, less than enthusiastically, as the waitress arrived at his table placing a glass of beer in front of him.

"Are you having a little weekend fun, Herman?" Billy exclaimed, sitting down at the table. Herman picked up his glass and took a long drink, "Herman, take it easy, you might want to pace yourself for the weekend ahead." There was a snide tone to his remark. Herman did not appreciate the way Billy had invited himself to sit at the table.

"Billy, did anyone invite you to sit down?" Billy's expression changed, as he realized Herman was not interested in his company.

"That is fine." He pushed Herman from his chair, knocking him to the floor, "See if I ever try to be nice to you!"

Billy stood up and walked back to the table, where the other student was sitting. The two exchanged words, most likely about Herman. The bartender walked over to Herman and helped him up to the chair, "Are you all right, Herman?"

"I am fine. That is a fellow classmate. You can tell by his charm how pleasant it is to attend classes with him." Herman's tone was sarcastic. The bartender picked up on it, right away. The bartender walked over to the front of the bar and stood at Billy's table. He was lifting his arms and pointing at the door. The two students stood up, Billy slammed his hand on the table. The bartender grabbed Billy and led him out the front door. The other student glared back at Herman with a scowl on his face.

The bartender walked back to his table, "I'm sorry about that, Herman. Looks like a sour start to the weekend, for you."

"No problem, I was just not in the mood for his company. It obviously offended him." Herman brushed off his jacket and arranged his hair.

"I'll have the waitress bring you another draft, on the house." Herman smiled back at him, the bartender returned behind the bar. Herman sat at his table and looked over towards the window. His thoughts were now focused on intensifying his ability to defend himself and it would all start with his classmates.

The two classmates stood at the window making obscene gestures with their hands and then left after getting some satisfaction, but little reaction from Herman. Herman paid them no mind and looked up, as the waitress placed another drink on the table. Herman smiled, "Thank you." He spent a few more hours in the bar and was now inebriated.

He stood up from the table, walked over to the bar and settled his bill. The waitress and bartender waved to him, as he walked past the bar and out the front door. Putting on his hat he turned and walked down the street, towards his apartment. Strolling along the empty streets he began kicking a can on the sidewalk, watching, as it tumbled into the road. Walking further along the road, loud voices were echoing from around the corner.

Turning the corner, he came across the two classmates both smoking cigarettes. He walked towards the middle of the street, attempting to cross and avoid any confrontation, "Herman!" Billy called out, throwing his cigarette into the street, running towards Herman. His speed increasing as he continued his approach.

Herman braced for the impact, as Billy crashed into him knocking him to the ground. Herman quickly jumped from the ground and leaped at Billy, overtaking him on the sidewalk. He swung his right fist towards Billy's face, striking him just above the jaw.

After landing the first blow, he continued punching him in the face repeatedly, until he had knocked Billy unconscious. The other classmate, seeing the rage in Herman's eyes, turned and ran down the street. Herman stood up looking down at Billy, "Still think it was a good idea to give me shit, now?" He spit on Billy's face, turned and walked off towards his apartment.

When Herman arrived at his apartment building, he walked into the courtyard and looked up into the front window of the other apartment. A couple walked back and forth, just in front of the window, most likely cleaning. Another man was pacing back and forth looking for something, obviously frustrated. Herman could always read people's body language.

He walked down the cobblestone pathway and to the door of his apartment. There was a note on the door indicating an inspection of his apartment by the landlord. Herman ripped down the note, opened his door and walked inside, throwing the note on the floor. He took off his jacket, hung it in the closet, threw his hat on the table and fell onto his bed, quickly falling asleep.

Over the next two years, Herman continued his hard work in medical school and was spending most of his time, after class, in the autopsy room. The amount of insurance schemes he was running, earned him tens of thousands of dollars. While he was still married to Clara, Holmes was spending his off time traveling, over the weekends, to visit a woman he had met at the bar. Another six months had passed. He married Myrta Belknap in Minneapolis, Minnesota and soon had a daughter, Lucy but he was soon uninterested with the marriage.

He filed for divorce from Clara but the divorce was never finalized. The university was impressed with his work ethic and was allowing him to dissect and dismember bodies for medical research. After he would finish the autopsies, the organs would be sent to hospital labs for further studies. He worked late into the evening, on the last cadaver.

The following day, the professor stood at the front of the class and began addressing them, "The demand for cadavers is growing, as medical schools are established in the United States. Please take note, that between the years of 1757 and 1789 only seventy of the thousands of physicians had studied abroad, mostly in

England. Study of anatomy is essential in the medical field, setting it apart from homeopathic and botanical studies."

Walking to the chalk board, the professor began writing, "In 1847, doctors formed the American Medical Association in an effort to differentiate between the true science of medicine, and the assumptions of ignorance, based on an education without the experience of human dissection."

The professor pointed at a picture hanging on the wall, "In 1762, Dr. William Shippen, Jr. founded the medical department of the University of Pennsylvania. Dr. Shippen put an advertisement in the Pennsylvania Gazette announcing his lectures about the art of dissecting, injections, etc. The cost was just five pistols." Some of the students chuckled.

"Yes, only five pistols, and in 1765, his house was attacked by a mob, claiming the doctor had desecrated a church burial ground. The doctor denied his actions and made it known that he only used the bodies of those who committed suicide and executed felons."

"In Boston, Dr. John C. Warren attempted to set up a cadaver provision system, similar to the systems already set up in New York and Philadelphia. Public officials and cemetery employees were routinely bribed for entrance to Potter's Field to retrieve cadavers." The professor turned to the class.

Adjusting and cleaning his glasses, he continued, "Finally, in New York, the bodies were divided into two groups, one group contained the bodies of those with the utmost respect from society, or most likely to be called for by friends. The other bodies were not exempt from exhumation."

"In Philadelphia's two public cemeteries, doctors have claimed bodies regularly, without consideration. If schools or physicians were in disagreement, over who should get the majority of the cadavers, the dispute was settled by the mayor. A popular conspiracy that resulted in a harvest of over four hundred bodies, per school year."

Herman was wondering if the hospitals and the universities paid for the cadavers and organs the same way the hospitals in New Hampshire did. This could be a lucrative business opportunity, so he raised his hand, "Yes, Herman."

"How is it done, I mean, how do they obtain the cadavers for the universities?"

"Good question, Herman. Class, now the cadavers are donated by the families of the deceased, which is still making difficult for the universities to obtain the cadavers needed. We will be continuing to use the cadavers in the classroom, which we have been working on continuously, due to the shortage of incoming cadavers."

Herman was now thinking about the many ways he could obtain cadavers and, in turn, sell them to the universities and medical schools, not only around the country, worldwide. It would take some time, but he was sure with his mind, and ingenuity, he would be able to come up with something.

Herman was becoming more and more confrontational, after spending long nights at the bar. He would walk the streets looking for couples, men, and even women, traveling alone. He would assault them and take their purses, wallets, jewelry and other valuables. Not because he needed the money, but his growing passion for control over people was consuming him.

After another few months, he soon progressed to attacking a few victims and brutally slashing them with a dissecting knife he had stolen from school. He was now collecting a wide variety of surgical knives, and medical devices, using the dissection tools to dismember his victim's bodies and transport them to the university, late at night.

His schemes and actions were carried out well below the radar of the police and the school authorities. He was well trusted at the university and even had his own set of keys to the autopsy room. He would take the victims to the autopsy room and put them in the storage room, only to dissect them the following day.

After another year at the University of Michigan, Herman achieved his degree and graduated top of his class. He was now a prominent student and was offered numerous practices in the Michigan area. His plan would not work until he was able to purchase his own building and open a medical practice and business. He figured the needs of the medical universities for organs and cadavers would allow him to continue fulfilling his rage and murderous desires. He would also be able to use the university as an alibi, should the police become suspicious about his actions.

Herman walked out of his apartment one afternoon, stopping at a local paper stand. He purchased the morning paper and read the front page. It reads; many local residents are becoming concerned with the increase in missing persons, and mysterious disappearances. Police are investigating the crimes and claim there are a majority of crimes that fit a pattern and involve one person.

Herman flipped open the paper to the foreign news. Just as he turned the page, a section of bold letters reached up and grabbed his attention. It reads; Murder in White Chapel, the mysterious murder of an "unfortunate" working girl. The signs indicate the murderer slashed the victim's throat and it appears parts of the woman were removed and taken from the scene.

Police are not commenting, at this time. Herman looked at the picture of the woman and the police standing around the body. This immediately caught his attention and his curiosity peaked at the opportunity to travel and potentially find, follow, and study another killer. Was this killer just as effective and elusive as he had become? Was this killer established and have a larger body count than he had?

He thought back at his own murders being reported in the paper, his heart rate increased and he was now paranoid about how he was going to continue his excursions, without the police and authorities becoming suspicious. He decided that he was going to take his medical degree, personal valuables, move to a new city and make a fresh start.

Herman walked back to his apartment and began packing. He retrieved his money from under the floorboard, his first victim's skull and placed them in his suitcase. Herman cleaned up the apartment and made sure he was ready to leave the following morning. He had one last thing to attend to.

He walked out of his apartment carrying his medical bag, onto the sidewalk and down the street, towards the bar. After arriving at the bar, he spotted Billy sitting near the front. Herman smiled and walked towards the window. Arriving at the window, just in front of the table Billy was sitting at alone, he tapped the glass catching Billy's attention. He walked from the sidewalk, to the front door and into the bar. Walking directly towards Billy, he reached the table.

Billy stood up, uncomfortable at Herman's arrival. Herman placed his right hand on Billy's shoulder and pushed him back down in his chair, "Let me buy you a drink, Billy," Herman placed his bag under the table, sitting down in the opposite chair, looking up at him with a devious smile, "You will accept my apologies, Billy. I did not want to cause any further confrontations with you."

Billy, apparently uneasy about the situation, fidgeted and replied, "Apology accepted, Herman, but it was I who attacked you, that evening."

"Yes, you did, Billy." The server brought Herman his usual. He thanked her and then returned his attention to Billy, "I thought I would come by, see if I could catch you, before leaving in the morning."

"You are leaving, where are you going to go?" Billy inquired.

Herman had developed a menacing attitude, and an ability to take control of a situation just like his father, "I am not sure, at the moment, maybe Chicago or London. I hear they are both beautiful cities and full of opportunities." Herman reached for his glass, quickly drinking the beer. After finishing, he slammed the glass on the table, the force causing Billy to jump from the table. Herman realized he had a commanding fear over his classmate and achieved what he had set out to accomplish.

A voice echoed in Herman's mind, "That is very good, Herman. You are getting more experienced in striking fear into someone. You are coming along, just fine. Now, do what you have to do. You know it needs to be done." The voice faded.

"Billy, if you will excuse me, I have some things to do before I depart tomorrow." Herman shook Billy's hand, stood up from the table, and retrieved his bag. He walked to the bartender, exchanged a few words, shook his hand and walked out of the bar. As he walked past the bar's window, he looked back at Billy with a sinister grin.

Billy left the bar and stumbled onto the sidewalk, walked towards the university and around the corner mumbling to himself, as he continued down the sidewalk. He walked over to a wall, unzipped his pants and began urinating on the ground below. A figure approached him from behind. The shadow came into view on the ground in front of him. The approaching shadow caused Billy to tremble, as his urination slowed and then stopped. He turned discovering it was Herman, who stood completely still, wearing a long jacket with his hand outstretched to his side.

"Hello, Herman," choking as he finished muttering his name. Herman's arm swung towards Billy, his expression turned to fear as he reached up to his neck. A gash slowly separated the skin of his throat and blood began flowing from his neck, over his fingers and onto the ground in front of him.

He fell to the ground choking and spitting up blood, but was unable to call out for help. After a few moments of choking, and struggling to breath, his body became motionless. Blood flowed on the ground beneath him and Herman crouched down, just above Billy's stomach. He took his knife and began to cut Billy's clothes, opening his shirt and the front of his trousers.

He took the knife and cut deep into the stomach area, spilling the intestines on the ground, a disembowelment. He reached down between Billy's legs, took his sexual organs in his hand, and sliced them from his body. He took Billy's mouth, opened it, and shoved them into his mouth.

He stood up from the body, smiled and turned, walking back to his apartment. He reached his apartment, opened the door and walked inside. He took his bag and cleaned it; afterwards, washing the blood from his hands. Picking up a bottle of whiskey, the several drinks calmed his nerves. Placing the bottle on the table, the view from the window was calming. Staring outside for a few moments, with a vacant gaze, he closed the curtains and went to bed for the evening.

'New Beginnings'

The following morning, Herman woke and retrieved his belongings. He had arranged for a carriage to transport him to the train station. As he walked out the door, he saw the carriage had already arrived and was parked just in front of the building, "Good day to you, sir."

"Good morning. I am headed for the train station."

The driver replied, "That will not be a problem. Climb inside."

He placed his luggage inside, climbing into the carriage, "I am in a rush to get to my train on time."

"Not a problem, sir, I will be as quick as I can." The horse quickly pulled the carriage down the road. When it was close to arriving at the train station, the driver informed him. "Sir, we are arriving at the train station."

Herman retrieved his bags and the carriage came to a stop just in front of the main station. Stepping from the carriage, he handed the driver payment for the ride turned and watched, as people were entering the main section of the station. There were businessmen, married couples carrying children, and a few stragglers who were carrying cups begging for money. Walking into the station, he purchased his ticket and stepped out on the platform, noticing that people were already boarding the train bound for New York. So he walked to the door and handed a conductor his ticket.

"Right this way, sir. I hope you enjoy the ride."

"Thank you very much, sir." Herman turned one last time and looked back at the view of the city. He calmly stepped up into the train and chose a cabin car in the back. The sleeper cabins were now Herman's first choice in travel, since it was secluded, private, and had a nice view of the country. The train's whistle blew and large plumes of steam shot from the top of the steam engine.

Herman began keeping a diary of his travels and was writing frequently about his experiences from the Dover asylum, Danvers asylum, and during his tenure at medical school. He was very detail oriented in his ability to describe the very emotional experiences, to the simple way a tree's autumn leaves fell, as the wind's breeze blew through its branches.

Herman peered out his stateroom's window, as the train left the station and slowly moved forward along the tracks. As the train gained speed, the carriages and people walking along the streets of Michigan slowly faded into the distance. Herman was, again, starting another chapter of his life.

Herman's luggage had increased from the amount of possessions he acquired during his time at medical school. His extensive book collection allowed him to improve his knowledge of the world, etiquette, and people skills. The lack of moral responsibility and social conscience was something to overcome, and tackling this was something to be accomplished during the five day train journey to New York.

Herman entered one of the main dining cars and was greeted by a group of enthusiastic travelers, "Greetings, sir."

"Good evening to you all." Herman tipped his head and was surprised at the immediate recognition from the distinguished gentleman at the head of the table. There were two other men and woman at the table. Introductions were exchanged and the groups became more comfortable after a round of drinks had been served.

"Herman, I have often been amazed at the advancement of rail travel and the technologies which have come along with it. We are, after all, enjoying a meal on board a moving train. An experience that has become as popular today, as it was in the beginnings of the railroad." He raised his glass to the group and toasted.

Another man at the table added, "The combination of mouth watering food, good company, and constantly changing scenery, remains the attractiveness of long distance train travel, while the chef prepares your meal to order and the anticipation whets your appetite."

Herman replied, "I completely agree." He sipped from his glass and watched, as the chef was preparing their meal of Chicken a la Century.

Each railroad presented a variety of dining cars, "This train journey makes me feel like royalty." One of the women exclaimed, as they gazed over menu offerings that included a roast leg of lamb with mint sauce, oven-roasted chicken, or fried trout.

"I am interested in the fresh desserts and fine wines, accompanying our meal." The food was prepared, personally, by their chef and served by attentive servers. The dining car's tables were covered with spotless linen, and a vase of fresh flowers. Their server brought their meals to the table presented on real china with sparkling glassware.

After dinner, Herman excused himself, "If you would excuse me, I must return to my stateroom and prepare some of my belongings and write in my journal about this pleasant experience and dinner service."

Most passengers packed a lunch, or attempted to eat at the train depot's lunchrooms. The service was horrible and the food was served in horrendous conditions. The train had to stop about every two hundred miles to replenish the steam train's water supply. The water stations were just off the side of the train tracks. Lunchrooms were built alongside the tracks near the water tanks to feed passengers during the stops.

The average time for such stops was twenty minutes, creating urgency to feeding the passengers during the stop. Herman remained in his stateroom for the majority of the trip, only interacting with other passengers during the dinner services. His ability to gain attention from the other passengers was becoming increasingly proficient and the majority of his interactions resulted in praise and left a lasting impression.

The train arrived at the New York station and slowed to a stop. Herman's belongings were collected and loaded onto a carriage. His travel arrangements, by ship to London, had been arranged prior to his arrival. The carriage brought him to a large cruise liner and the driver began unloading his luggage as Herman boarded. Signing the ship's log, Herman used an alias to prevent any knowledge of his presence on board.

Employees of the cruise liner quickly picked up Herman's luggage and began following Herman on board. It was a grand ship containing numerous compartments and cabins. The ship was a medium sized steam cruiser and designed for the safety and comfort of the crew and passengers. Many travelers of the sea were less fortunate in their accommodations, taking weeks, if not months, to travel across the Atlantic and Pacific.

Herman's trip, across the sea, caused him much discomfort and sickness. At times, his stomach churned, as each wave launched the ship into the air and over each rough wave. The furniture in the cabin was bolted and secured to the floor. Each item on the tables was secured as well, to prevent them from sliding off and breaking.

Most of his time was spent in the cabin, to prevent extreme sea sickness from overcoming him. He wrote in his journal, drew sketches of the ocean, as the ship crossed the Atlantic. A week into the journey, Herman's sea sickness subsided and he was then able to make his way about the ship. The waves hit up against the front of the ship, as it splits through the waters of the ocean, leaving a trail of disturbed water in its wake.

Herman met with many of the passengers, introducing himself under an alias but still as a doctor, finally able to achieve the attention and respect the title of doctor would bring. In the discussions, Herman included his plans while in London and his desire to open his office, after returning to America. A number of the ship's passengers were American and the wealthier travelers continuously exchanged their contact information. His plans were to expand his practice throughout England and the United States, upon returning from London.

The passengers, although a bit taken back by the idea of supplying financing for cadavers and medical experimentation on human organs, were hesitant to show interest. However, Herman was able to use his medical knowledge and charisma to convince it was an actual business venture. One venture which could make them considerably wealthier.

The ship arrived at one of London's busiest harbors and pulled up to a large wooden dock, supported by large metal supports. The passengers slowly exited the ship and made their way along the streets leading into the heart of London. Carriages lined the street next to the docks and workers were hustling to fill the carriages with the passenger's luggage.

Herman was led to one of the carriages, where his luggage was already loaded. He instructed the driver to take him to the heart of London, one of the most widely popular districts, where he could find a more diverse and carefree population. The driver replied, "I know just the place, sir. It will not take but a few minutes to reach the district you are describing."

The heart of the city was Whitechapel High Street, extending to the east as far as Whitechapel Road, named after a small chapel which was dedicated to St Mary. Travelers to and from London on this route were accommodated in the inns, which lined Whitechapel High Street. The weather was damp and a heavy mist clung to the air, leaving limited visibility along the streets. The carriage pulled up to one of the more popular and extravagant inns and Herman was assisted inside with his luggage.

Whitechapel Road itself was not particularly as filthy and wretched compared to the smaller dark streets branching from it, containing the greatest suffering, filth and danger. Dorset Street was one such street. A private alley, described as the worst street in London, as were Thrawl Street, Berners Street, Wentworth Street and others. An endemic poverty was driving many women to prostitution.

In 1888, the Metropolitan Police estimated that there were around thirteen hundred prostitutes, of very low class, residing in Whitechapel and about sixty five brothels and opium parlors. After settling into his room and unpacking the majority of his clothing, and personal items, Herman left the inn and walked the streets dressed in a finely tailored grey suit, neatly trimmed moustache and his grey, Sebrell Fedora, hat.

He was looked upon as someone out of place, not fitting the typical citizen living in the district. Many people looked upon him with suspicion, possibly an inspector for the Metropolitan Police. This suited him fine, the less conversation he attracted the better, at least for now. He picked up a local paper from a young boy on a street corner. The paper had an intriguing headline, immediately catching his attention. "Ripper Strikes Again!"

Reading further into the article he soon found out, The Ripper, as he was being called, was an unidentified killer active in the largely impoverished areas in and around the Whitechapel district of London. The paper explained the name had originated in a letter, written by someone claiming to be the murderer, but the police stated they believed the letter to have been a hoax.

His attacks were involving female prostitutes from the slums. The first two victim's throats were cut prior to abdominal mutilations. The removal of internal organs, from the first two victims, led police to believe that the killer possessed anatomical or surgical knowledge. Thinking about the link between the killer and a man possessing surgical knowledge stirred Herman's curiosity.

Herman looked into the killer's patterns, the location of the killings, searching for anything that might be able to lead him to the killer. The first victim was robbed and sexually assaulted on Osborn Street, Whitechapel, on April 3, 1888. A blunt object was inserted into her vagina, which ruptured her peritoneum. She developed peritonitis and died, the following day, at London Hospital.

The latest and second victim was killed on August 7, 1888 and suffered thirty nine stab wounds. The savagery of the murder, the lack of obvious motive and the closeness of the location and date to those of the first murder, led police to link them as connected. Herman found the name of the inspector assigned to the case, an Inspector Frederick Abberline. Herman read past the front page cover story and discovered two stories published in the paper.

The name of the story was Sherlock Holmes, created by Scottish author and physician Sir Arthur Conan Doyle. A brilliant London based consulting detective, Holmes was famous for his astute logical reasoning, his ability to take almost any disguise and his use of forensic science skills to solve difficult cases. The first story was A Study in Scarlet and the second, The Sign of the Four.

The stories were narrated by Holmes's friend and biographer, Dr. John H. Watson. Holmes shares the majority of his professional years with his good friend, Dr. John H. Watson, who lived with Holmes for some time before his marriage in 1887, and again after his wife's death. His residence is maintained by his landlady, Mrs. Hudson.

Watson has two roles in Holmes' life. First, he gives assistance in the conduction of Holmes' cases. He is the detective's right hand man, acting as a lookout, decoy, accomplice and messenger. Secondly, he is Holmes's chronicler, his "Boswell" as Holmes refers to him. Herman read further fascinated by the knowledge and charisma Holmes possessed.

Instantly, he knew his last name would be changed to Holmes upon returning to America. For the time being, he would keep the first name of Herman. He would develop a charm and charisma similar to Holmes, which he would use to gain the complete trust and control over people. His heart raced at the notion of living such a thrilling lifestyle.

As he read on, he discovered explicit details about Sherlock Holmes' life outside of the adventures recorded by Dr. Watson is few and far between in Conan Doyle's original short stories. Nevertheless, incidental details about his early life and extended families portray a loose biographical picture of the detective's genius.

An estimate of Holmes' age in the stories placed his birth in 1854. Holmes stated that he first developed his methods of deduction while an undergraduate. His earliest cases, which he pursued as an amateur, came from fellow university students. According to Sherlock Holmes, it was an encounter with the father of one of his classmates that led him to take up detection as a profession. He spent the six years following university working as a consulting detective, before financial difficulties led him to take Watson as a roommate, at which point the narrative of the stories begins.

Herman Holmes he thought to himself or, Doctor Herman Holmes, the name did have a distinguished ring to it. In addition, it was a reputable name. Herman continued along the street, dodging the alcoholic and sick that lay along the sidewalks. Herman walked further along and came upon the Metropolitan Police building. He entered the building walking to the front desk of the station. An officer looked up from his log book, "Hello, sir, what can I assist you with?"

"I would like to speak with Inspector Abberline, to discuss some information with him."

"What would this be pertaining to?" The officer lowered his pen to the log and returned a suspicious look towards Herman.

"I am a doctor. The name is Doctor Herman Mudgett and I have information for the inspector."

The constable released a sigh and stood from his chair, "Right this way, doctor." He sarcastically emphasized, doctor. Herman followed him through the precinct and was led into a larger conference room. Upon entering the room he noticed there were photographs, evidence spread across large boards, and a few men studying the crime scene's photographs.

They arrived to a well dressed gentleman smoking a pipe. "Inspector Abberline? There is a Doctor Herman Mudgett to see you." The inspector turned and extended his hand, "Hello doctor, it would seem you are just in time. I should require a surgeon's opinion on the recent murders in the Whitechapel district."

"Inspector, it is very nice to meet you, sir."
Herman's accent caught the inspector's attention.

"A doctor from America, what brings you to London, Doctor Mudgett."

"For both business and pleasure but upon hearing about the possibility of the Ripper being a surgeon, or having some knowledge of human anatomy, I thought to speak to you of the way the women were done."

Inspector Abberline led Herman across the room and over to the pictures of the evidence. Herman studied the photographs, including the autopsy photos and carefully read the names under each victim. Some of the other photos and paperwork posted on the board had the known associates of the victims listing, Mary Ann Nichols, Annie Chapman, Elizabeth Stride, Catherine Eddowes and Mary Jane Kelly.

Herman suggested, "The killer must have been carrying a smaller surgical kit, a kit that many surgeons carry, if they should be, on call. The kits are extremely portable and perfect for doctors and physicians making house calls for their patients." Herman studied the pictures closely and realized a fascinating connection between the Ripper murders and the murder he committed on his former classmate, Billy, back in Michigan.

Much of Herman's knowledge on anatomy and dissection came into play and many of the killer's surgical knowledge and skills were discussed. Herman knew that the Ripper was somehow being connected to the five other prostitutes and determined to trail their nightly routines.

"I bid you a good day and best of luck on your investigation, inspector." He turned and left the station, setting out into the heart of the Whitechapel District.

He arranged a room, just to the west of Whitechapel Street, located near many of the bars and brothels and was soon able to locate Elizabeth Stride and Mary Kelly, after they were pointed out by the barkeep.

Herman walked over to another table, opposite the girls, attempting to listen in on their conversation. He heard that they would be meeting Mary Ann Nichols, later in the evening. They spoke about being harassed by a local street gang, which offered protection to the prostitutes after taking a large share of their profits. They noticed that Herman was attempting to listen to their conversation and stood up, leaving the bar in a rush.

Herman waited a few seconds. After the girls had left the bar, he stood up and followed closely behind. They walked down the main street of Whitechapel and cut through a back street to another darker, low lit street. There were now three of them and they continued meeting gentlemen throughout the night, performing their sexual acts and receiving their petty pay.

One of the girls set out on her own after Mary Kelly had met a gentleman and stepped into his carriage. She was all alone and walked through an alleyway. Herman followed her closely. It was Mary Nichols walking slow, showing off her body to attract men. Herman watched as she walked down Buck's Row.

Just as she passed an alley, a long steel blade reflected in the darkness. The blade thrust twice, slashing her throat wide open. A figure grabbed the body and disappeared into the night, it was at that moment he knew he had discovered the Ripper. As long as he followed the other girls, over the course of the following weeks, he would soon be able to complete his plan.

There was no need to alert Inspector Abberline. Otherwise, he would be unable to study the killer's patterns and methods. The Mary Nichols' body was discovered at about 3:40 am on Friday, August 31, 1888 in Buck's Row, Whitechapel. The throat was severed deeply by two cuts, and the lower part of the abdomen was partially ripped open by a deep, jagged wound. Several other incisions on the abdomen were caused by the same knife.

It did not take long before Herman discovered Laudanum while visiting an opium parlor. The narcotic was an alcoholic herbal preparation containing ten percent powdered opium by weight, the equivalent of one percent morphine. He found the reddish-brown narcotic extremely bitter to the taste. It contained almost all of the opium alkaloids, including morphine and codeine, making it a potent narcotic but, for Herman, he found the effects exhilarating.

Laudanum's therapeutics were generally confined to controlling diarrhoea, alleviating pain and easing withdrawal symptoms in infants born to mothers addicted to opioids. Alkaloids in opium were far more soluble in alcohol than water. In experimentations with various opium mixtures, it was discovered a specific tincture of opium that was of considerable use in reducing pain. Herman was soon using the narcotic in a mixture of absinthe.

Herman learned of four variations of Laudanum in London. The first was Best Turkey opium one oz., slice, and pour upon it boiling water one gill, and work it in a bowl or mortar until it is dissolved; then pour it into the bottle, and with alcohol of seventy percent proof half pt., rinse the dish adding the alcohol to the preparation, shaking well and in twenty four hours it will be ready for use.

Opium tincture is one of the most potent oral formulations of morphine available. Accidental or deliberate overdose was common with opium tincture given the highly concentrated nature of the solution. Herman investigated different variations of mixtures, and dosages of the drug, to ensure he was mixing it properly and only using the higher dosages when he intentionally meant to.

Herman began to dabble in using the mixture with many of the female acquaintances he made during his stay. He was careful to mix the components himself to avoid the risk of overdosing in his presence. An overdose, at this point, would compromise his medical degree and career as a doctor.

Suicide by laudanum was not uncommon, due to the current economic status of some of the residents in certain areas of London. Prudent medical judgment necessitates toward dispensing very small quantities of opium tincture in small dropper bottles, or in pre-filled syringes, to reduce the risk of intentional or accidental overdose. This was a common practice in all of the opium parlors throughout London.

The specific study of the use of the narcotic was Herman's main focus. He read about the history in one of his medical journals, "Adverse effects of laudanum were generally the same as with morphine, and included euphoria, sedation, constipation, respiratory depression, as well as psychological dependence. Long term use of laudanum in nonterminal diseases is discouraged due to the possibility of drug tolerance and addiction. Long term use can also lead to abnormal liver function tests.

Specifically, prolonged morphine use can increase ALT and AST blood serum levels."

"The French word absinthe refers either to the alcoholic beverage or, less commonly, to the actual wormwood plant. The Latin name Artemisia came from Artemis, the ancient Greek goddess of the hunt. Absinthe was derived from the Latin absinthium, "wormwood". The first clear evidence of absinthe in the modern sense of a distilled spirit containing green anise and fennel, however, dates to the 18th century." Reading out loud was one of Herman's traditional methods of retaining the knowledge.

He stopped reading aloud. Absinthe's popularity grew steadily through the 1840s, when absinthe was given to French troops as a malaria treatment. When the troops returned home, they brought their taste for absinthe with them. It became so popular in bars, bistros, cafes and cabarets by the 1860s the hour of five pm was called the green hour. Absinthe was favored by all social classes, from the wealthy to poor artists and ordinary working class people.

Herman began using preparations by The bohemian method, popular primarily due to the use of fire. A sugar cube was placed on a slotted spoon over a glass containing one shot of absinthe. The difference was that the sugar is soaked in alcohol, usually more absinthe, and then set ablaze. The flaming sugar cube then drops into the glass igniting the absinthe.

Finally, a shot glass full of water was added to douse the flames. This method tended to produce a stronger drink than the French method. A variant of the bohemian method was to allow the fire to burn itself out. This was called the flaming green fairy, removes much but not all of the alcohol. The origins of this burning ritual may come from a coffee and brandy drink, in which a sugar cube soaked in brandy was set aflame.

Many of the local parlor visitors debated over the effects on the human mind in additional to those of alcohol. One man explained, "The effects of absinthe have been described by the users as mind opening, a clear headed feeling of inebriation, a form of lucid drunkenness. Something I have experienced first hand." The indistinct chatter and conversations continued throughout the parlor, as most of the groups smoked from large hooka type devices.

Herman listened momentarily to the man and continued reading the last paragraph in his book. Many of the secondary effects of absinthe were caused by some of the herbal compounds in the drink acting as stimulants, while others act as sedatives, creating an overall lucid effect of awakening.

The long term effects of low absinthe consumption in humans remain unknown, although Herman found the herbs in absinthe to have both pain killing and antiparasitic properties. Herman was passing the point of being able to stay awake and made his way out of the parlor, down the street and back into the inn where he was staying.

'Hunt or Be Hunted'

The following day, Herman returned to the opium parlor and was sitting at one of the tables, smoking from a pipe. The mixture was a tobacco and low based opium rolled into a ball. Herman was becoming drawn into the opium parlor scene, becoming acquainted with the other patrons and more involved in conversations about the underground happenings in and about London. A man approached Herman and sat at the table with him, Herman passed his extravagant pipe to the gentleman.

"Greetings, I am Doctor Herman Mudgett."

"I am Theodor Ruess, it is very nice to meet you." The two shook hands and the man continued, "An American doctor. What brings you to London?"

"Personal business, and possibly expanding my horizons, medically speaking of course. What do you do?"

"Currently, I am a co-founder and member of the Ordo Templi Orientis."

Herman stirred in his relaxed position and inquired further, "Ordo Templi Orientis, is that a government group or a religious organization? I am unfamiliar with the name."

Theodor looked at Herman, "I have no doubts the Ordo Templi Orientis will become an international fraternal organization. Similar to many secret societies, such as the Freemasons, membership is based on an initiatory system with a series of degree ceremonies, which we use ritual themes establishing fraternal bonds, intent on spiritual and philosophical teachings."

"So what you are presenting to me, is, a type of religion? It sounds catholic? Where and when was the Ordo Templi Orientis created?" Herman remained skeptical.

"It originated in Austria, its founder is a close friend and colleague of mine, Carl Kellner, a wealthy Austrian industrialist. I collaborate with him in helping open new Ordo Templi Orientis temples and will succeed him, as head of the order, upon him leaving or his passing. Under me, charters are being passed to occult brotherhoods in London, France, Denmark, Switzerland, America and Austria.

"Sounds like an ambitious business venture. Before you ask, my financial plans are vested in the future of my medical practice. Therefore, I am unavailable to present or allow for allocating financing to your order." Herman took another toke from his pipe.

Theodor held up his hand, "No, of course Herman, I assure you this is not a pitch to obtain finances from you. The order has been successful in expanding through generous donations from its members and those who are currently becoming initiated and illuminated."

"Well, in that case, please continue."

"There are nine degrees. The first six are similar to the Masonic degrees. I purchased the right to perform the Rite of Memphis and Mizraim of Freemasonry. The order offers esoteric instruction through ritual work, guidance in a system of illumination, and fellowship among aspiring members to the great work of realizing human divinity."

Herman interrupted Theodor, "Illumination and fellowship, to realize human divinity? There seems to be more behind this order than meets the eye. Perhaps, at first glance, one might make the mistake of getting into a situation where there are secrets and unsuspectingly fall into a trap and suffer harm."

"I can assure you no harm has occurred to any member of the order. The secrets within the order, are a privilege to learn and understand, only the initiate can decide whether to take the journey into the order's degrees and rituals"

Ruess expanded, "Ordo Templi Orientis has two core areas of ritual activity, initiation into the mysteries, the celebration of Liber XV, and the Gnostic Mass. In addition, the Order organizes lectures, classes, social events, theatrical productions and artistic exhibitions, publishes books and journals, and provides instruction in Hermetic science and magick."

"Are you offering me a chance in becoming an initiate of the order and what is required of membership?" Herman replied skeptically.

"Membership is based upon a system of initiation ceremonies, which uses ritual work to establish fraternal bonds. The degrees also serve an organizational function, in that certain degrees must be completed before taking on additional levels of service within the order. There are thirteen degrees and twelve additional

numbered degrees, which are divided into three grades
or triads, the Hermit, the Lover, and the Man of Earth.
Admittance to each degree of Ordo Templi Orientis
involves an initiation and the swearing of an oath."

After listening intently to the majority of Ruess'
explanation of membership, he interrupted, "When this
illumination takes place, is it physical, mental, emotional
or all three?"

"First, advancement through the Man of Earth
triad requires sponsorship from ranking members,
which you have from me. Advancement into the degree
of the Knight of the East and West, and beyond,
requires one to be invited by ranking members. The
ultimate goal throughout the initiation process in the
Ordo Templi Orientis is to instruct the individual in the
profound mysteries of nature and therefore to assist
each to discover his or her own true identity. It is all
three."

"I am truly interested and think that I will make an
appointment with you to further my inquiries and
interests in the order." Herman shook Ruess' hand and
continued to smoke from the pipe.

They continued to discuss activities and events
taking place in London, what Herman was doing in
London, and his plans after he had returned to
America. The man sharing Herman's pipe, passed his
contact information and informed Herman, "Now, if
you will excuse me, I am late for some business that
requires my immediate attention." Herman watched as
Ruess left and closed the parlor's door behind him.

Herman spent most of the evening pursuing his
latest order of business, walking through Whitechapel
and Hanbury Street, following Annie Chapman. She
paraded the streets and alleyways, until finally stopping

and addressing a well dressed gentleman carrying a black medical satchel. A thick fog spread across the streets allowing Herman the opportunity to get in close. The man handed her some money and they walked into a smaller courtyard, surrounded by wooden fencing.

The two stood next to a wooden fence line. Herman watched, as the man reached into his bag retrieving a long slender blade, proceeding to slice her throat with two vicious cuts. Her body fell to the ground, as the Ripper was distracted, Herman slipped in closer to watch the killer work. He slashed open the stomach and worked surprisingly fast in the fog and darkness of the night.

Upon finishing, the killer returned his instruments in the case, stood up, and checked his surroundings. The surrounding area was clear. Taking one last glance at his work, he walked off into the night, Herman following closely behind. The mysterious, dark, figure walked through the streets of Whitechapel and finally reached the main stretch of road. He walked a bit further and entered a large estate, closing the door behind him.

If this was the Ripper, Herman was surprised he would allow his living quarters to be discovered, so easily. Now that Herman had found where the man lived it would be much easier to follow him, rather than the remaining girls. It was obvious to Herman, the man had some sort of obsession or fascination with the unfortunates of Whitechapel, but why not invite them home and kill them? It seemed more careful to be able to work in the confines and comforts of one's home.

The next morning Chapman's body was discovered at about six am on Saturday, September 8, 1888 near a doorway in the back yard of 29 Hanbury Street,

Spitalfields. As in the case of Mary Ann Nichols, the throat was severed by two cuts. The abdomen was slashed entirely open and it was later discovered that the uterus had been removed.

The papers were eating up the stories of the continuing murders and residents in the Whitechapel District were becoming extremely impatient with the police and began setting out on their own investigations. People were taking the law into their own hands and stopping anyone looking suspicious. Herman was stopped a few times, in the late hours of the night, but continued to follow the Ripper by parking a carriage outside his house. There was no action from the Ripper so Herman decided to call off his hunt for the afternoon.

Two days passed, Herman was now working various business contacts and making arrangements to have medical skeletons shipped from America and to London. His practices as a businessman were becoming shrewd, cunning, and most reliable. Numerous hospitals and medical universities had made agreements with Doctor Mudgett, under the name of his alias. Afterwards, he had secured large sums of financing and arranged to have the finances transferred securely to America.

That evening, Herman set out for the building that Theodor Ruess had instructed him to attend, should he choose to further his interest in the Ordo Templi Orientis. Herman arrived at the building and parked his carriage just in front of the door. Upon entering the building, he discovered various paintings and sculptures decorating the main floor and hallways.

"Doctor Herman Mudgett, I am pleased you chose to attend. Would you like to join us in our teaching hall?" He was greeted by the well dressed Theodor Ruess.

He shook Ruess' hand and replied with enthusiasm, "I would be honored to join you." The two walked down the hallway and entered a main hall. There were a few people sitting at the table, reading literature and other various books with strange symbols on the book covers.

Herman sat at the table, with the others. Ruess stood at the head of the table and began an introductory conference. "The occult refers to knowledge of the hidden or knowledge of the paranormal, as opposed to knowledge of the measurable, usually referred to as science. The term is also taken to mean knowledge meant only for certain people, or knowledge that must be kept hidden. But, for the most part, practicing the occult is simply the study of a deeper spiritual reality, which extends beyond pure reason and the physical sciences."

"We study hidden wisdom and forbidden knowledge. To us, it is the study of truth, the deeper truths that exist beneath the surface. The truth is always hidden in plain sight. It involves such subjects as magick, alchemy, extra-sensory perception, astrology, spiritualism, lithomancy, numerology, among others"

"Direct insight, or perception of the occult, does not usually consist of access to measurable facts but is reached through the mind, or spirit. The term can refer to mental, psychological, or spiritual training. Many of us have studied science to add validity to occult knowledge in a day and age where the mystical can easily be undermined as flights of fancy. These are just a few examples of the vast and numerous avenues that can be explored."

"To the occultist, occultism is conceived of as the study of the inner nature of things, as opposed to the outer characteristics that are studied by science. It focuses on the inner nature with the term, will, and suggests that science and mathematics are unable to penetrate beyond the relationship between one aspect and another. It explains the inner nature of the thing itself, aside from any external causal relationships with other things. This is often accomplished through direct perceptual awareness, known as mysticism. From the scientific perspective, occultism is regarded as unscientific, as it does not make use of the scientific method to obtain facts, or truths."

The meeting was short and Theodor Ruess invited Herman to attend one of their late night rituals and gatherings, promising his attendance was confidential and secret due to his status as a doctor. Herman agreed and was given some of the books pertaining to the knowledge of the order. That evening he read into the night and retired for the evening.

The following morning, Herman woke and attended to some of his grocery needs, returning to the inn and continued studying late into the afternoon. The knowledge and methods in the order fascinated Herman. After finishing a small meal, he set out on his carriage to see if he could find and follow the man known as the Ripper.

For weeks, the Ripper did nothing, following his own mundane routines. Until one night, Herman followed him to another yard. The man met up with a woman and walked her to another yard. Herman sat on his carriage and watched as the Ripper performed his first killing on the night, but something startled him and he quickly fled the scene of the murder.

He was clearly not satisfied with the first and continued to the next, moving into another area of the city. He waited patiently, as a drunken woman stumbled along the street and close to the entrance of an alley. The Ripper grabbed another woman and pulled her into the alleyway, slashing the woman's throat and then performing a detailed dissection for almost a half an hour. Afterwards, he calmly walked out of the alley and down the deserted street. Herman was unsure who the two women were but he had a feeling they were part of the five.

The following morning, the newspaper reporters and photographers were on the scene and quickly had the story printed on the front pages of the papers. Herman picked up a paper and read the story: Two bodies were found in the early morning of Sunday, September 30, 1888. Stride's body was discovered at about one am, in Dutfield's Yard off Berner Street, in Whitechapel.

The cause of deaths, in both cases, were one incision, severing the main artery on the left side of the victim's necks. Police are uncertain about whether this murder is connected to the Ripper, or whether he was interrupted during the attack, due to the absence of mutilations to the abdomen, as compared to the past.

An additional body was found in Mitre Square, in the City of London, three quarters of an hour after the first. The throat was severed and the abdomen was ripped open by a long, deep, jagged wound. The left kidney and the major part of the uterus had been removed. The papers were calling the murders the double event. Part of a bloodied apron was found at the entrance to a tenement in Goulston Street, Whitechapel.

There was some writing on the wall above the apron piece. The paper was unclear of the exact wording which was written. Herman was now becoming frustrated at the attention the Ripper was receiving. After all, it should be the papers writing about him. It was now time for his plan of action to be put into play.

That evening, Herman followed the streets leading to the Ordo Templi Orientis' temple. He was curious to know what the night's events would bring, but the unknown was exciting for sure. After reading some of the books about the order, Herman was ready to take the plunge and let go of everything he had been told and taught in his life. He arrived at the building and entered, greeted by Theodor Ruess, and provided a black felt robe. Ruess put a hood up over Herman's head, instructed him not to speak and for Herman to follow him into the teaching hall.

Ruess took Herman to the center of the teaching hall, knelt before Herman and quietly began to speak in a calming and gentle voice. "Herman, sex magic is a term for various types of activities used in magical, ritualistic and spiritual pursuits. One practice of sex magic is using the energy of sexual arousal, with visualization, for a desired result. An intent of sex magic is the concept that sexual energy is a potent force that can be harnessed to transcend one's normally perceived reality."

"If a man has an intelligent and loving woman, with whom he is in complete alliance, they can work out the problems of how to achieve magical results, through each other's assistance. They are a radical series of energies. The ritual is a prayer and the most powerful earthly beings can attain it. It is best for both man and woman to act together for the attainment of the mysterious intentions sought."

"Success in any case requires the assistance of a superior man and a woman. This is the law! The man and woman shall not be those who accept rewards during the process. Nor the woman a virgin; or under eighteen years of age; or another's wife; yet must be one who has known man and who has been and still is capable of intense mental, volitional and affectionate energy, combined with perfect sexive and orgasmal ability. For it requires a double crisis to succeed."

"Our order possesses the keys which open all secrets, namely the teachings of sexual magic, and this teaching explains all the secrets and all the systems." Herman was intrigued by the way Ruess spoke and his knowledge of the process of sex magic. It was deeply fascinating to him and he was curious what the evening would bring. The lighting was dim and there were many candles spread about the inside of the building.

"Instead of the sexual energy being released in a spasm, this energy undergoes sexual transmutation via willpower and the sacrifice of desire. The transmitted energies through will power is populated by billions of atoms that when rising meet, igniting it, and through many years of work causes the kundalini through the thirty three chambers or degrees of the spinal medulla."

"Because sexuality is both a creator and destroyer, one can eliminate any previously comprehended psychological defects. In other words, sexual magic is the removal of the egos, which are the animalistic or inferior vehicles of emotion, mind, and will relate to one's evolution. Thus, through the death of the ego, and the birth of the solar bodies, one can be elevated to the angelic state and beyond."

Herman and Ruess stood and walked to the door of the teaching hall, Ruess turned to Herman and spoke in a low, yet, enthusiastic tone, "Now, Herman, with the other members of the order, and some special guests, we will give you your first experience with what I have just instructed and you will have a better understanding of how it can be achieved."

Herman followed Ruess through the doors into the main hall, there were large plumes of incense rising to the ceiling and candles arranged throughout the room. The men and women were nude and there were many luxurious couches, blankets and large extravagant pillows. The men and women began pairing up and moving towards selected areas of their choice. Herman's arm was taken by a younger woman, who smiled at him and led him over to one of the larger pillows.

That evening, Herman and the members of the order performed the rituals and various positions of sex magic. At the end of the night, Herman was exhausted and returned to the inn. As soon as his head hit the pillow, he had no problems quickly falling asleep. That evening his dreams were vivid, and lucid, for the first time in his life his father no longer haunting his dreams.

A month had passed and Herman was now set on completing his plan, to follow the man known as the Ripper and kill him, surpassing his own cunning plot. To kill the Ripper would mean Herman would be better in his own hunting techniques. Herman was oblivious to the danger he was putting himself in, following a killer just a ruthless as himself. If, in fact, this was the Ripper.

Throughout the week, Herman followed the ripper to a smaller building, just off Dorset Street. The killer was watching a woman inside, stalking her every move through the evenings. Finally, one foggy night, the killer walked quietly up to the front door of Kelly's room. The Ripper broke the side window and unlocked the door, he turned and looked around to make sure the area was clear and slowly entered the room, closing the door behind him.

After an hour, he left the room and closed the door behind him. The Ripper left in a carriage and Herman entered the room Kelly lived in, lit the candles of the lanterns and slowly began inspecting the Ripper's work. It was beyond anything Herman had ever witnessed, he had clearly outdone himself. It would; however, be his last.

Kelly's gruesomely mutilated body was lying on the bed in the single room where she lived at 13 Miller's Court, off Dorset Street. The throat had been severed down to the spine, and the abdomen virtually emptied of its organs. The heart was missing, the Ripper must have taken it to his home. But for what reason, Herman wondered?

The five murders were perpetrated at night, on or close to a weekend, and either at the end of a month or a week, or so, after. The mutilations became increasingly severe, as the series of murders proceeded, except for that of Stride, whose attacker may have been interrupted. Nichols was not missing any organs. Chapman's uterus was taken.

Eddowes had her uterus and a kidney removed and her face mutilated. Kelly's body was eviscerated and her face hacked away, though only her heart was missing from the scene. There must be something more than just killing, for the Ripper, something is behind his rage and furious anger in the way he dissects them afterwards.

Herman parked his carriage close to the residence of the unknown killer, securing the reins to a post. He began shaking and wondered if he could actually follow through with it. He drank from a bottle of whiskey, followed by smoking a large dose of opium. The drug flowed through his veins and he slumped forward, blacking out for a moment. After shaking off the initial effects of the drug, he reached over and retrieved his satchel, containing his surgical kit, dismounted the carriage, carefully looking about his surroundings to ensure there were no spectators or observers.

Slowly, he stumbled across the ominous, foggy street and up to the front door. His vision was blurry and his thoughts scattered. A bell tolled in the distance. He hesitated, thinking he was not at his best and should wait for another opportunity. But there may not be another chance such as this. Turning the doorknob, he was surprised to find it unlocked. He reached into his bag and pulled out a large knife and prepared to enter the residence. He slowly opened the door and backed inside, closing the door behind him. The house was lit with small lamps and a chandelier above the main entrance.

The lights flickered, creating dancing shadow reflections on the walls. As Herman slowly walked into the front room, he heard some rustling in the hallway and footsteps approaching. He saw that it was a smaller woman, most likely a chambermaid. She walked towards Herman unsuspecting of his presence. As she stumbled into Herman, he lifted a candlestick holder and plunged it down upon her head.

Herman caught the body, before it hit the floor.
He carefully leaned it up against the wall. Pausing to
listen for any other sounds in the house and maybe
someone alerted by his presence. He waited, but heard
nothing, so he continued up the stairs. He inspected
some of the rooms, which were unoccupied and
continued down the hallway to the last room.

There was a dim light shining from under the door,
giving the wood floor a reflection for Herman to
follow. He approached the door cautiously and arrived
at the entrance to the room. The door was opened a
crack. Herman reached up and pushed the door open.
The light from the room shined upon of his face. He
looked into the room and saw a man lying in a large
bed, asleep. He pulled out his knife and walked over to
the bed. Just as he reached the bed, he saw a large paper
weight on a bedside table.

He changed his plans at the last second, putting
away the knife and picking up the paperweight. The
man in the bed stirred and turned over, opened his eyes
and rose, startled by Herman's presence in his room.
Raising the paperweight above his head and slamming it
down upon the man's head, he was knocked
unconscious. He returned the paperweight to the table
and placed the man in a chair. He took a rope tied to
the curtains and secured the man to the chair.

Reaching into his satchel, he pulled out his surgical
kit and placed the kit on the table. He removed his coat
and cut the robe from the Ripper's body, stuffing a
piece of material in his mouth, preventing him from
speaking. After a large injected of pain medication and
adrenaline, Herman took his scalpel and began to make
cuts in the Ripper's stomach, the pain caused the man
to awaken. The adrenaline would keep the man awake;

however, the pain medication would assist to relieve some of the pain during the procedure.

Herman took a syringe filled with a powerful anaesthesia, pressed the needle into the vein and the Ripper lost consciousness, again. Herman then continued his dissection work careful not to severe any main arteries, or cause too much blood loss. At this point, Herman removed the ropes and returned the man to the bed.

Securing his arms and legs to the headboard and wood, at his feet, Herman took some water and cleaned the excess blood from the body. He waited for the man to regain consciousness. The Ripper slowly came to and saw that Herman was standing over him with the knife. Herman slowly removed the material from the man's mouth. He gurgled and spit up blood, "Who are you? You are going to pay for this, boy. Do you know who I am?"

Herman smiled, "You are supposedly the infamous Ripper, the paper speaks of? I have been following your career very closely, as you might have deducted at this point."

Herman slowly walked towards the bed, as the ripper looked down at his stomach, "Oh no, this is not possible. This cannot be happening." His stomach opened slightly from Herman's earlier incisions. The Ripper became infuriated, "What is on your mind, boy, what is it you think you are doing?"

Herman didn't respond, only walked closer to the bed, reaching up towards his stomach cutting a deeper incision. The Ripper screamed out in pain and then stopped, breathing heavily, sweat pouring from his forehead. Herman began to open the stomach and remove the fatty layers from inside. He pulled out the intestines and began wrapping them around the rippers neck, tying them as one would a tie.

The Ripper was now in a state of shock, as Herman continued pulling out the remaining intestines, "You'll never be remembered, the way I will be remembered. You are an insignificant worm and you will die, dry up and wither away." He choked a few more times then managed to continue speaking in a low ominous voice, "One day. . men will look back and say. . I gave birth to the Twentieth Century." The Ripper slowly lost consciousness, and faded away, took one last breath and exhaled.

Herman reached up and checked his pulse, there was no sign of life, he had hunted and exterminated London's famous killer, The Ripper. Herman would now surpass this killer, by killing the killer himself. Cutting deep into the chest cavity, he made a few more saw and scalpel cuts then pulled the heart from the body's chest. He raised it above the dissected body and revelled in his work, placing the heart into a metal pan.

Herman placed his surgical instruments back into his case and slowly returned the case into his satchel. He reached over to the table and picked up a metal pan containing the heart, under the paperweight was a single letter signed Jack "The Ripper". He turned, just before leaving, and revelled again in the aftermath he was leaving behind. Much like The Ripper must have done, after each of his victims.

He removed the letter, walked over to the fireplace and dropped it into the fire. It slowly burned, until it was just ashes. Herman made sure to cover his tracks and remove any other information, or evidence, that might reveal the man murdered upstairs was Jack "The Ripper". Downstairs, he approached the chambermaid lying on the floor, pulling out a small metal device from his satchel and a medium sized steel hammer.

He placed the small metal device to the side of the chambermaids temple and gave two hard taps. He repeated the procedure on the other side and then towards the top of her skull. The trepanning would make it look as though the chambermaid was in a psychotic episode and slashed the man in the upstairs bed. Herman placed the Ripper's surgical blade in her hand and smeared it with blood from the heart he carried in the metal pan. Dressing the wounds on the chambermaid's head, he wrapped a cloth bandage around the freshly performed trepanning.

Completing his task, Herman returned to his carriage and placed the heart and the satchel on the carriage seat. He began to feel nauseated and leaned over the side of the carriage vomiting on the road below. He climbed from the carriage seat and into the inside of the carriage's cabin. He rolled onto his side, becoming dizzy. His head spinning, he lost consciousness and blacked out.

The morning arrived and a knock came on the side of the carriage, "Hello, is anyone in there?" A voice called out.

Herman jerked awake, looking into his medical bag. After opening the bag, there was no blood on the dissection instruments and no blood on his gloves. Did he clean up, after last night's events, or did he actually follow through with the murder of the Ripper? Was it even the Ripper, or just an innocent victim?

"Hello?" There was another tap on the side of the carriage.

Unaware of the danger outside, he opened the door to the carriage's cabin, "Yes constable?" Herman looked over the officer's uniform.

"Why are you parked here?" Herman took a deep breath, regaining his bearings, realizing the severity of the situation.

Herman rubbed his stomach, "Constable, I was feeling ill after an event this past evening."

"Overdid it, did you?" He placed his hand over his nose, "You need a shower, sir." The constable laughed, looking inside the carriage.

Herman stepped from the cabin and onto the carriage seat. There was no steel pan containing the Ripper's heart, so he untied the reins of the carriage, "I apologize for my behavior. It will not happen again, sir." As he pulled off, two additional constables walked past the carriage, their conversations echoed off the brick walls of the buildings and houses.

One of the constables looked up at Herman, sitting on the carriage and tipped his hat, "Good morning, sir." Herman tipped his hat and lifted the reins of the carriage, indicating to the horse to pull away. The carriage rode off into the thick morning fog and onto Whitechapel Street, the horse's hooves clomping on the cobblestone road and disappeared into the distance. Herman quickly returned to his hotel and fell onto the bed, asleep within seconds.

The following months, Herman continued following the Ripper's routine of murder, making it look as though the Ripper was still at large. He returned to the house he believed to be the Ripper, but it had been cleaned out and abandoned. A for sale sign hung on the fence line, just in front of the house's main entrance. Questioning his grip on reality, and the events that had never occurred with his mother and father's deaths, did he actually kill the suspected Ripper?

Holmes would continue to perform his London killings, "Ripper" style, to throw off the Metropolitan Police. Kelly was considered by the Metropolitan Police to be the Ripper's final victim and assumed that the crimes ended because of the culprit's death, imprisonment, institutionalisation, or immigration. The Whitechapel murders file did, however, detail other four murders that happened after the canonical five: those of Rose Mylett, Alice McKenzie, the Pinchin Street torso and Frances Coles.

Mylett was found strangled in Clarke's Yard, High Street, Poplar. As there was no sign of a struggle, the inspector believed that she had accidentally choked herself while in a drunken stupor, or committed suicide. Nevertheless, the inquest jury returned a verdict of murder.

Herman killed McKenzie by severance of the left carotid artery. Several minor bruises and cuts were found on the body discovered in Castle Alley, Whitechapel. One of the examining pathologists, believed this to be a Ripper murder, though another pathologist, who had examined the bodies of three previous victims, disagreed.

Later, the inspector, the Metropolitan Police, and pathologists were divided between those who thought her killer copied the Ripper's modus operandi to deflect suspicion from himself and those that believed it to be the Ripper. It seemed probable that the murder was committed elsewhere and that parts of the dismembered body were divided for disposal.

Coles was killed under a railway arch at Swallow Gardens, Whitechapel. Her throat was cut, but the body was not mutilated. A man named James Thomas Sadler was seen earlier with her, was arrested by the police, charged with her murder and was briefly thought to be the Ripper. He was, however, discharged from court for lack of evidence.

After reading the morning paper and, satisfied with his stay in London, Herman knew that he had stayed long enough. To stay any further would require him to set up his medical practice in London. Herman would be relieved to return to America and be ready to prepare his new medical practice and office. That night he packed his gear and clothing, took a sedative and climbed into bed for the evening. The following morning, Herman acquired a carriage to take him to the dock, where he first arrived in London. There were thousands of people carrying about their business, and moving throughout the city's roadways. Herman's travel arrangements had been made the prior evening by the hotel desk clerk, using the same alias as his departure from the United States. The carriage arrived at the dock and Herman's luggage was quickly unloaded and taken aboard the ship.

Herman tipped the carriage driver. Before proceeding to board the cruiser, a strange gypsy handed him a small book and amulet. Politely accepting, the man returned a strange look, as he walked towards the ship. The cruise liners for passengers were becoming more extravagant and comfortable, also faster and more streamlined. Herman signed the passenger's log book with his alias, settling into his cabin and proceeded to unpack his belongings.

He took out the small book and began to read, as he poured a small glass of whiskey. The book had a strange cover design with mysterious patterns and symbols. Upon opening the first page the word, hypnosis caught his eye. He read aloud, as he typically did. A technique he used to retain knowledge, "Hypnosis is a technique used to induce a mental state, or imaginative enactment. It is usually induced by a procedure known as a hypnotic induction, which is commonly a process of a long series of suggestions."

"Using this technique, combined with my new found confidence, would render anyone under my command." He continued reading, but this time quietly, "Hypnotic suggestions are performed by a hypnotist, in the presence of the person, or may also be self administered as well."

Hypnosis is a typical unconsciousness that resembles sleep, research suggests that hypnotic subjects are fully awake and their attention is focused, blocking out any external awareness. Amazingly, people show an increased response to suggestions. It typically involves an introduction to the procedure, during which the person is presented suggestions for imaginative experiences.

The hypnotic induction is an extended initial suggestion for using someone's imagination and may contain further elaborations. A hypnotic procedure is used to encourage and evaluate responses to suggestions. When using hypnosis, one person is guided by another to respond to suggestions for changes in subjective experience, alterations in perception, sensation, emotion, thought or behavior.

Take any bright object between the thumb and fore and middle fingers of the left hand. Herman took the amulet the gypsy had given him, before boarding the cruise liner. Hold it from about eight to twelve inches from the eyes, in a position above the forehead, as necessary to produce the greatest possible strain on the eyes, and enable the person to maintain a fixed stare at the object.

The person must be made to understand that they are to keep their eyes steadily fixed on the object, and the mind focused on the idea of that object. The hypnotist will see the eyelids close with a vibratory motion. The term suggestion refers to the act of focusing the mind of the subject upon a single idea. This strategy involves stimulating or reducing the physiological functions in different regions of the body. Place the emphasis upon the use of a variety of different verbal and nonverbal forms of suggestion, including the use of waking suggestion, and self hypnosis.

Herman closed the book and stared at the shiny amulet the gypsy had given him. As it reflected in front of his eyes the technique would have to be explored, with someone else, later in the evening. It seemed like an impossible technique, but he would try and see where it led him, perhaps it would have its advantages if it worked.

Herman took a short nap and woke, to freshen up, making his way to the ship's main dining hall. He arrived at the main dining hall and joined some older gentlemen at the bar. The men were discussing business and the recent unsolved Ripper murders. This discussion was proving to give Herman a sense of accomplishment when it came to what he, and only he, knew about the truth of the Ripper demise.

After a short while, a group of younger women entered the dining hall immediately noticing the well dressed Doctor Herman Mudgett sitting at the bar. The evening passed with much celebration among the new found friends. Herman was ordering drinks for the three young ladies and soon joined them at their table. He introduced himself, to the women with his alias, making sure to include doctor in the title.

One of the women exclaimed, "Oh, my, a doctor!"

Herman continued drinking with the women, discussing his plans, "Upon returning to America, my ambition is to start my own medical practice. Is everyone enjoying their drinks?"

The women continued drinking. One of them replied, "Doctor?" Herman felt pride upon hearing his name in that fashion, "Will you be available for house calls?" The women giggled and continuing their flirtatious advances towards Herman.

He was paying close attention to their comfort level towards him, "Would you ladies be intrigued by the suggestion of hypnosis?"

One of them responded, "I am convinced that it is impossible, but it would be interesting for you to attempt it. What about you two, are you interested?"

The others replied simultaneously, "Yes indeed!" It was agreed.

Herman escorted the three ladies back to his extravagant stateroom. The women settled in, removing their sweaters, becoming more comfortable. Herman took the amulet and sat just in front of the first young woman. His close presence caused an immediate uneasiness in the woman. She became slightly blushed, yet her friends eased her mind.

"Oh do not worry Georgiana, there is nothing to be scared about, we are right here."

Herman began to look into her eyes. The girl was taken by his gaze. Herman slowly lowered the amulet in front of her. She relaxed, as Herman continued to instruct her, "Look deep into the amulet and focus on my voice." Speaking in a low, calming, voice swinging the amulet back and forth, "Just let your eyes follow the amulet."

Soon her eyes closed, flickered and she became entranced. Herman suggested, "Stand and raise your arms." Georgiana did so. Herman then instructed her, "Bend over and touch your toes." She did so. Herman was amazed the technique actually worked.

He broke Georgiana from the hypnotic state, "I want to be next."

Herman continued hypnotizing the two others making them perform the same acts Georgiana had performed. He then instructed the two women, "Now, I want you to both, kiss each other." They followed the command. The first young woman walked behind Herman and removed his hat, sliding her hand through Herman's hair, drawing his attention to her.

In no time, Herman and Georgiana were removing their clothes and climbing onto the stateroom bed. The other two women remained in their trances. Herman used the sex magick techniques he was taught by Theodor Ruess and the woman was in disbelief at Herman's abilities.

The two other women slowly drifted out of their trances and began giggling at Georgiana and Herman and attempting to cover their eyes. After a short time, Georgiana had convinced them Herman had introduced her to new forms of intercourse. One of the other women stood and fixed drinks for everyone. Herman was lying on the bed with Georgiana and the drinks were passed around. Throughout the evening, the group switched back and forth, as Herman showed them various positions and rhythms used in sex magic.

H.H. Holmes: The Devil in Me

It did not take long before the group was now lying in the bed and asleep.

The following morning, Herman woke to discover he was alone in his room. Georgiana had left her contact information on a desk next to his bed, "Georgiana Yoke, and she lives in Denver, Colorado. Maybe a trip to Colorado will be in order?" His head was spinning from the long night of drinking and sex. The women must have left in the early morning hours. Herman prepared his luggage and clothes and freshened up in the bathroom.

After finishing, he continued reading the small book the gypsy had given him. The amulet was on a table near the stateroom's window. He picked it up and placed it in his pocket. He walked to the dining hall and proceeded to have a light breakfast. After finishing his breakfast, he cracked a smiled at the prior evening's events.

He walked back to his stateroom, removed his suit, preparing a mixture of absinthe and laudanum. He lit the cup and dropped the sugar cube in the glass. He drank the mixture and lay back on the bed. For the remainder of the cross Atlantic journey, Herman kept to his stateroom, attempting to control his desire to kill. He did this by only leaving his stateroom to eat and use of the absinthe, laudanum, mixture.

The ship arrived and docked in the main New York Harbor. Herman quickly booked a sleeper coach on the next train back to Chicago. The train left that afternoon and Herman, again, entered another chapter in his life. He wrote in his journal, drew on his sketch pad, drawing the landscapes, train passengers, and other objects in the train cars.

Practicing some of his hypnotic methods, on some of the passengers, he was improving his skills, immensely. They were quick to believe that hypnosis was a real practice and were amazed at what they were told they were doing, and how they had been acting, under the trances.

'Home Again, Home Again'

After a three day journey, the train pulled into Chicago's busy Central Train station. Herman stepped off the train and onto the station's busiest platform. He turned and walked down a busy street, on the Southside of Chicago to a nearby hotel. His luggage was to be delivered to the hotel, after making accommodations and notifying the station's director.

He walked further down the street, stopping just in front of a large abandoned building. The well dressed doctor stood on the corner of S. Wallace and W. 63rd Street. Dressed in a tailored grey suit and wearing his Sebrell Fedora hat, he looked up at the abandoned three story building proclaiming a for sale sign on the front door. The sign indicated a contact address, where any interested party could inquire about purchasing the building.

Herman reached into his pocket, pulled out a small notebook and a pen, jotting down the contact information in his notes. He stepped back checking over the entire South Wallace block, "This will be perfect!" He exclaimed, looking up another time at the building, turned and walked off in the direction of the address written in his book. He arrived at a dilapidated storefront and discovered a busy drugstore across the street.

Herman opened the door of the business office and stepped inside, "Good afternoon." The man sitting at the desk stood up.

Walking over to Herman, he extended his hand, "Hello, sir."

"I'm Dr. Herman Holmes." Herman replied.

"Dr. Holmes, it is nice to make your acquaintance. Which medical school did you attend?"

"I attended the University of Michigan, Medical School."

"That is very fine, indeed. Have you relocated to Chicago, or are you just passing through on business?"

"I want to purchase and start a practice, of sorts, at the location on S. Wallace and W. 63rd Street."

The man extended his arm towards a chair across from his desk, "Please, have a seat." The two sat and adjusted their positions in the chairs to become more comfortable. The owner took out a cigarette from a small metal case, lit it with his lighter, and held out the cigarette case towards Holmes, who shook his head declining, "I do not smoke, but thank you for the offer."

"Dr. Holmes, you are interested in purchasing my property on S. Wallace and W. 63rd Street."

"Yes, I would like to make the purchase today, assuming you have the papers and a contract prepared for the purchase?" Holmes reached into his pocket and pulled out a pen.

"My asking price for the property is $6,500. Are you prepared to pay the asking price?" The owner reached into his desk drawer, retrieving a large stack of papers.

"I am prepared to pay your asking price. I can have your money this afternoon. I will return to the hotel, and bring the money for the purchase price."

"Well then, Dr. Holmes, here is the contract for the purchase. You can sign at the bottom of each paper. I will return these papers to the bank and have the title for you this afternoon."

"Thank you, sir, it has been a pleasure to meet you and conduct business." Holmes quickly signed the contract, shook the owner's hand, stood and walked out of the office.

It was a strange transaction. Holmes never even asked to see the inside of the building. Making such a quick purchase was surely unorthodox to the owner, but he shook his head and walked to the door of his office. Reaching in his pocket, he pulled out a set of keys, opened the door and closed it behind him, locking it with his keys.

"I forgot." Holmes was standing just behind the man.

The sudden interruption startling him, "Oh my, Dr. Holmes, you startled me."

"Please excuse me; I was wondering if you knew of any establishments in the area that are hiring?"

"As a matter of fact, I know the owner's of the drugstore next door. Mrs. Holton runs it, the majority of the time. Doctor Holton is unable to work, as much as he did in the past, due to an illness."

"Oh that is terrible to hear, what is the diagnosis?"

"Cancer, I'm afraid, the incurable type."

"After I return from the hotel with the money, I will speak the Holton's, further, about the possibility of helping in the drugstore." Holmes bowed his head, turned and walked off in the direction of the hotel. Afterwards, he smiled knowing that his plans were now in motion.

He returned to his hotel room and collected a large leather satchel, opened the flap, reached into the satchel and pulled out neatly wrapped bundles of money. He counted out exactly $6,500 dollars, placed the money into the satchel and hid the rest in the closet. The murderous desire began flowing through his mind, surging inside him.

Walking over to the desk drawer he pulled it open, retrieving a loaded pistol, opening the pistol's cylinder checking to ensure it was loaded. He was never impressed with men who resorted to using weapons, in a fight, but still believed in protecting himself from an unwanted attack. He put the pistol in a holster hanging from his belt, turned, picked up his leather satchel and left his hotel room. He walked down the hotel's hallway and was greeted by an older man smoking a cigar in the hallway.

"Good afternoon, young man!"

"Good afternoon, to you." Holmes tipped his hat at the man and continued walking past him, down the hall and descended the large stairway to the hotel lobby.

The hotel lobby was decorated with extravagant statues, large paintings of local Chicago politicians and businessmen that had donated to the hotel's admirable environment. Holmes approached the desk clerk and waited behind an older gentleman checking into the hotel. The man completed his check in transaction and reached down, picking up his large suitcase.

"Pardon me," the man exclaimed, as he walked towards the staircase. Holmes looked over the man's clothing, determining he was well off and might be worth a chance encounter, later, in the dining hall.

"Hello sir." The desk clerk exclaimed, attempting to get Dr. Holmes' attention. "How may I assist you?"

"Yes. Excuse me, can I ask you to place an advertisement in the paper, for immediate release?"

"Absolutely, sir, do you have the advertisement with you?"

Holmes reached inside his suit pocket and unfolded a large piece of paper. "Here it is. I need all the advertisements to run in the next paper. Could you kindly send it over to the paper and have the price of the advertisement charged to my room?"

"Yes, sir, I will have the total price for you when you return and confirm the advertisement will run in the next paper. Will there be anything else, sir?"

"Yes, could you put together a list of contractors in the area? I prefer general construction, electricians and plumbing contractors."

"Yes sir. I will have those contacts, along with the results of the advertisements."

"Thank you." Holmes reached into his pocket, withdrew a bill from his pocketbook and slid it across the desk to the hotel clerk.

"Thank you very much, sir." The clerk took the bill and placed it in his pocket. Holmes turned and left the hotel, walking off in the direction of the building owner's office.

Walking down the avenue he watched the people passing him, paying close attention to their dress and their actions. He was seeking out sophisticated individuals and the sharp dressed, indicating they were well-to-do. He was following them throughout the city, watching their shopping and dining habits. Later, he would return to the hotel and determine his next move.

Holmes arrived at the building owner's office and knocked on the door, rattled the doorknob and discovered it was locked. He walked in the direction of the drugstore and stopped short in the doorway, looking around at the individuals passing by. He looked through the window of the drugstore, surveying the occupants and the general layout of the drugstore.

Mrs. Holton was standing behind the counter speaking to a couple. She was short and wore heavy, thick glasses which magnified her eyes, making them appear larger than they really were. She turned, reached for a package from a shelf and handed it to a well dressed man. He handed her some money and she placed it inside a drawer, under the counter.

This would be the perfect place for him to work, but he needed to convince Mr. and Mrs. Holton that he was the right fit for the job, even if it meant working in a simple drugstore. It would give him the connections and networking opportunities he needed to carry out his elaborate schemes. The couple left the drug store. Holmes tipped his hat and watched as they walked into the distance and down the sidewalk of the crowded street.

Horse drawn carriages passed on the street behind him and thousands of people walked up and down the neighborhoods. As he stood, looking in the doorway of the drugstore, he gathered himself opened the door and walked into the drugstore, "Hello, Mrs. Holton." He greeted her, removing his Fedora and arranging his hair.

"Hello, sir, can I help you?" She replied.

"I spoke with the owner of the building across the street, earlier about the building for sale on S. Wallace and W. 63rd Street."

"Oh, yes, he was an excellent businessman?"

"That is correct. It is very nice to make your acquaintance. I also understand that you might be requiring some assistance in the drugstore? I am looking for something just like this, to gain networking opportunities. I am also planning on opening my new practice and medical operation in the building I am purchasing."

"Do you have a family, Dr. Holmes?"

"I'm afraid I do not but I was married for a short time, back in New Hampshire."

"Oh dear, I'm sorry to hear that. Well, we do need someone to help me in the drugstore and if you would have dinner with us, we could speak more about it." She arranged some medicine bottle on one of the shelves behind the counter.

Holmes was thinking of his plans for the evening, scouring the social clubs and the hotel dining hall, later that evening. He also had to make sure that his advertisements would be running and contacts for the contractors would be available to him, later in the evening.

"I'm afraid the next few days may be a little busy for me. How would this Saturday be for the two of you? I would enjoy having dinner at a time I could completely focus all my attention on the occasion."

"Then it sounds like the doctor and I will see you this Saturday evening." Mrs. Holton replied with a smile on her face.

Just as the dinner arrangement was made, Dr. Holton walked into the drugstore with some papers and a briefcase. He was in a rush and seemed a little frantic. "Hello, sir."

The owner of the building entered the drug store, "Hello, Doctor Holmes and Mr. and Mrs. Holton. I have confirmed the bill of sale and received the final title, which transfers the ownership of the building over to you. I assume you have the funds for the purchase with you?"

"Yes, the $6,500 is in this satchel." Holmes handed the satchel to the owner who, in turn, handed over the building's title and the final paperwork to Holmes.

"Shall we go to my office and finish the transaction. I have the keys to the building inside, as well." The owner extended his arm towards the door, motioning for Holmes to exit first.

"After you." He motioned to the door, "I have also arranged for dinner Saturday evening with the Holton's."

Doctor Holton exclaimed, "Oh, that's splendid, we rarely have company at the house. All of our children have left the state and are now living in Philadelphia." The two men left the drug store and walked across the street, entering the office, closing the door behind them. The satchel, full of money, was placed on his desk. He opened it and pulled the money from the satchel, counting it as he hummed an upbeat tune to himself.

"All of the money is here. These are the keys to the building. I assume you will want to inspect your purchase. If you should find anything disagreeable, or not to your liking, I will still allow you to take back the transaction. I will keep the money in the office and give you a little time to think over the purchase."

"I'm sure the property will be to my liking, but should I decide otherwise I will let you know." He was eager to look at the property and quickly stood up, "I will be leaving to attend to some final construction matters for the property." They shook hands and Holmes walked towards the office door, placing his Fedora on his head. He left, closing the door behind him.

Walking down the streets of Chicago, he continued surveying the population observing their habits, where the majority would go during certain hours of the day, and where would they go during the hours of the night. He would need to spend the next few days networking and spreading the word of his, up and coming grand opening of the hotel.

He made his way back to the property on S. Wallace and W. 63rd Street, placing the key in the lock and opening the rickety door. The door was the first thing that would need to be replaced. A rickety door, that did not keep his affairs private, would most certainly expose his plans and operations.

He looked over the building, quickly making mental notes on the construction needed in order to carry out and efficiently execute his elaborate fantasy. The building was perfect but would require major renovations to meet his standards. The third, second, and main levels were separated and the sound was restricted from above. He would use the third floor as the main section of hotel rooms and the lower levels to focus on the majority of his business.

Once his plan was in motion, there would be little interference from the authorities. He knew medical services, and the production of medical products, were becoming a big business. The city had become lenient

on construction permits and inspections, since the
unprecedented Chicago fires of 1871, in order to
rebuild and restore the city's beautiful landscapes and
monuments. A medical operation would also keep the
authorities unsuspecting and unaware of his operations.
He made his way to the basement by climbing down
the sturdy, metal staircase which was secured into the
bricks of the wall by large steel bolts.

His delight came to fruition, as he lit the lanterns
on the wall and discovered the basement room was
wide and high enough to install another cremation
furnace and two to three more large tanks, which would
be required to hold the chemicals needed to produce
his medical products. He mentally noted the floor plans
in his head and was ready to draw out the plans for the
contractors, major electrical installations would be
necessary to renovate and provide power to the hotel.
A luxury many guests would find appealing amongst the
other amenities.

He climbed up the staircase and made his way to
the front of the building. Pulling the keys from his
pocket, turned one last time and decided the following
day he would have the contractors in the building
regardless of the price involved. He opened the door
and closed it, locking the wiggling door handle behind
him. Holmes stepped back slowly, looking back up at
the complete picture of his purchase.

He brushed his hand through his mustache,
straightening it with his fingers. There was a twisted
smile on his face and a glimmer in his eyes, as he let his
fantasies play out in his mind. He returned to the hotel
and approached the hotel desk clerk.

"Hello, sir, how was your afternoon?"

"Wonderful thank you. Were you able to get the advertisements placed in the paper?"

"Yes, Dr. Holmes, here is what the advertisement will read, as your paper instructed." The clerk handed the confirmation to Holmes. He looked at the paper to confirm the details were read in the newspaper as instructed. It read: Wanted; Female Help, only bookkeepers and clerks. Address: S. Wallace and W. 63rd Street.

Wanted; A young lady who is a thorough and expert bookkeeper and accountant. No attention paid to answers that do not give full particulars and salary expected. Address: S. Wallace and W. 63rd Street, also; Wanted - A bright and intelligent young lady who writes well and rapidly. The work is mostly copying: state age and salary expected. Address: S. Wallace and W. 63rd Street.

He looked back up at the desk clerk and replied, "That is exact and precise. Thank you for taking the time to place the ad for me."

"You are welcome, sir, and here are the contacts for the contractors you asked for. I also added multiple contacts, in order for you to have the option of receiving multiple bids for anything you may have planned."

"Very good, sir, could you also provide me with city officials, commissioners and zoning departments, anything that I will get me in touch with Chicago officials?"

"Absolutely, sir, I will have them for you later this evening. Would you like me to bring them to your room?"

"That will be fine, thank you." He handed the clerk a bill. "How much do I owe for the advertisements placed in the paper?"

"No charge, Dr. Holmes." He quickly turned and walked towards the staircase leading back up to his room. He spent the next few hours drawing out plans for his newly acquired building. The building plans would be required to have prepared before the morning, if the contractors were to start on the construction. He had called and received competitive bids, which also included starting work the next day.

He smiled as he completed the precise and rough drawings of each floor of the building. After finishing the plans, he walked over to his closet, opened the door and reached in to retrieve some spending cash for the evening. He straightened up his room, looking around to make sure everything was in order and nothing was left out to be disturbed, or possibly stolen while he was gone.

He walked down the staircase of the hotel and casually into the dining hall. Seated near the windows, he was able to get a good view of the people passing in front of the hotel, carefully watching, as men and woman moved rapidly down the sidewalks. The waiter approached his table, "Have you had a chance to look at the menu?"

"Excuse me?" He replied.

"Have you had a chance to look at the menu, sir, and have you decided what you would like to order?"

"No, I have not. Could you allow me a few more minutes?" Herman sharply replied to the waiter with an aggressive tone in his voice.

"Of course, would you like to order a drink?"

"No, thank you, I should be ready to order in a few moments."

The waiter turned, walked towards the next table and approached a well dressed businessman. Holmes watched intently, as he recognized the man from earlier. Just as he had guessed, it was the man from the lobby checking in from earlier and he was now in the hotel dining room. The man had yet to order his meal, as well. Holmes closed the menu as the waiter was walking pass his table.

"Are you ready to order now, sir?"

"I am and I will take the steak platter. Steak, rare, also I would like to buy that man a drink, the gentleman sitting at the table near the wall." He motioned towards the businessman, sitting in the corner.

"Why of course, sir, I will let him know."

The waiter walked over to the man's table and informed the man that Dr. Holmes had offered to buy him a drink. The man spoke to the waiter and the waiter returned to the kitchen. The man stood from his table and approached Holmes' table.

"Thank you for the offer." The man said as he held out his hand.

Holmes shook the man's hand. "I'm Dr. H.W. Holmes, it is a pleasure to meet you sir."

"I am Henry Howard," the man replied, "May I join you?"

"Yes, of course, please sit down." Henry pulled the chair out and sat in front of Holmes.

The two proceeded to order their meals and multiple drinks throughout the evening, the two were becoming well acquainted. Holmes spoke about his education in Michigan and Henry was explaining his business affairs across the United States and his affiliation with the Freemasons. The two were experts in their fields and knew the ropes when it came to securing financing.

Henry began explaining his involvement with Freemasonry and its history. More intent on discussing the organization, rather than tedious business transactions, "Freemasonry is a fraternal organization that arose from unknown origins in the late sixteenth to early seventeenth century. Freemasonry exists all over the world, with a membership estimated to be at or around one million."

"Henry, I was involved with a similar organization, in London, but my plans do not include distractions and require my full attention." Holmes took a sip from his glass.

The man was persistent in continuing, "Herman, the fraternity is administratively organized into independent Grand Lodges, each of which governs its own jurisdiction, which consists of subordinate Lodges. The various Grand Lodges recognize each other, or not, based upon adherence to landmarks. There are also other bodies, which are organizations related to the main branch of Freemasonry, but with their own independent members and operations. You would decide your overall involvement within the lodge you choose, there is really not much to it."

"Explain more." Herman politely replied thinking of the possible doors it would open, for business transactions, should he decide to join the organization.

"According to Masonic tradition, medieval European stonemasons would meet, eat and shelter outside working hours in a Lodge on the southern side of a building site, where the sun warms the stones during the day. Freemasonry uses the metaphors of operative stonemasons' tools, and implements, against the allegorical backdrop of the building, to express what has been described by both Masons and critics as a system of morality veiled in allegory and illustrated by symbols."

"The fascinating part about the history is how far it dates back. A poem known as the Regius Manuscript has been dated to approximately 1390 and is the oldest known Masonic text. There is evidence to suggest there were Masonic lodges in existence in Scotland as early as the late sixteenth century. There are clear references to the existence of lodges in England by the mid-17th century."

"So, are you saying that membership is a possibility for me, is that your intention?" Herman's skepticism kicked in and reminded him to be cautious.

"Well before the membership, let me expand on some of the other aspects and meetings that take place within the lodge. A Lodge is the basic organizational unit of Freemasonry. Every new Lodge must have a Warrant or Charter issued by a Grand Lodge, authorizing it to meet and work. Except for the very few 'time immemorial' Lodges pre-dating the formation of a Grand Lodge, masons who meet as a Lodge without displaying this document are deemed 'Clandestine' and irregular."

Without skipping a beat, the man continued expressing his excitement and knowledge of history, "A Lodge must hold regular meetings at a fixed place and published dates. It will elect, initiate and promote its members and officers. It will build up and manage its property and assets, including its minutes and records. It may own, occupy or share its premises."

Henry looked up at Herman with a serious look in his eyes and said, "A man can only be initiated, or made a Mason, in a Lodge, of which he may often remain a subscribing member for life. A Master Mason can generally visit any Lodge meeting, under any jurisdiction, in amity with his own and as well as the formal meeting, a Lodge may well offer hospitality."

Herman interrupted Henry, "So this is where you ask for my payment?"

"No, it is not what you think. Most Lodges consist of Freemasons living or working within a given town or neighborhood. Other Lodges are composed of Masons with a particular shared interest, profession or background. I am not from Chicago, so it would be necessary, should you become interested, to join a local lodge."

"So it is exclusive to prohibit certain people from membership and keep its secrets from being told to others, who might not be able to keep secrets?"

Henry slightly dismissed Herman's remarks and continued, "While Freemasonry has often been called a secret society, Freemasons argue that it is more correct to say that it is an esoteric society, in that certain aspects remain secret. The most common phrasing is that Freemasonry has, become less a secret society and more of a society with secrets."

"God, Henry? I have little belief in a supreme being that created and controls the very essence of all life, in fact, how can a God exist in such a seemingly forsaken time?"

"All Masonic ritual makes use of the architectural symbolism of the tools of the medieval operative stonemason. Freemasons, as speculative masons, use this symbolism to teach moral and ethical lessons of the principles of brotherly love, relief and truth. Or as related in France, 'Liberty, Equality, Fraternity'."

"Sir, I am not within the boundaries of moral and ethical principles. Someone such as myself and the secrets I possess also, striving to be a successful businessman, sometimes has to disregard the moral and ethical practices. How can one expect to be successful?"

"Herman, candidates for regular Freemasonry are required to declare a belief in a higher power. However, the candidate is not asked to expand on, or explain his interpretation of a higher power. The discussion of politics and religion is forbidden within a Masonic Lodge, so a Mason will not be placed in the situation of having to justify his personal interpretations."

Herman was becoming tired of the conversation, he was obviously starting to become uninterested in the man's involvement and commitment to Freemasonry. He was not getting the feeling that Henry was going to be a pushover for one of his schemes. Henry was just as a much the shrewd businessman as Herman and he knew, it would not be easy to pull one over on him. So his thoughts changed to the next step in his plan, which would be to excuse himself and return to his room.

Henry was beginning to remind Herman of his father the, violent, raging alcoholic. Herman was suddenly reminded of his father taking him to his room and tying him to the bed, while he went out on the streets of New Hampshire on extended binges and the other abuse. The binges would last for days and he would be left at home tied to the bed.

Herman suddenly broke free of the flashback and was now becoming more and more enraged towards the businessman and could no longer sit with him for an extended period of time. If he were to learn that he could pull one of his financial schemes on him, he would have waited longer. However, now that the man would be able to spot a scam, Herman had decided to take his plan one step further.

"You will have to excuse me, Henry; I need to return to my room."

"Are you feeling ill?" Henry replied.

Herman did not respond and walked out of the hotel dining room, leaving Henry sitting at the table, alone. Walking up to his room, he was now enraged at the businessman in the dining room. Sweating heavily, his breathing was deeper and his pulse, racing. He put his hands on the desk and closed his eyes, trying to remain focused on the construction plans the following day.

He was still not satisfied, pulling out a long piece of tubing from the closet and stepping over to the door. Quietly walking down the hallway, he slipped into Henry's room closing the door behind him. He walked across the room and slipped into the closet keeping the tube tightly gripped in his hand. In his right hand, he held a syringe containing a heavy sedative.

Holmes was now well educated on the medications used in the medical field. As an expert on human anatomy, and what medical examiners looked for in an autopsy indicating foul play, he could easily mislead the trained eye. His breathing slowed, as he waited silently in the closet of Henry's hotel room. He stood, with the closet door slightly opened, staring out at the door. Within moments, the door handle turned. The door opened and Henry walked through the door.

He placed some items on the desk and lit the small lantern. He walked over, near the closet and turned to place his jacket on the bed. As he turned his back, the closet door opened revealing Herman standing just behind him. Henry stood at the end of the bed, straightening the wrinkles out of his jacket. Holmes approached Henry from behind and stuck the syringe into the side of Henry's neck, draining the entire contents of the syringe.

Henry let out a loud scream, as the pain from the syringe needle struck the nerves. Herman quickly took the tube and wrapped it around the neck of the weakened man. It prevented any screams and Henry was quickly overcome by the effects of the drug. He fell to the bed, Herman standing over him turned and walked over to the desk and put out the lantern and the room went dark.

Walking out of the room, he locked the door behind him and returned to his room. Preparations were made for the next day. Afterwards, he left the hotel and continued walking the streets of Chicago, looking for signs of nightlife and crowded social clubs. He was beginning to get a feel for the streets of his new playground and a comforting feeling overtook him, "Hello, son."

The familiar voice which had been absent for years, had returned, "You have been doing well for yourself. I am proud of your accomplishments. I will return, in time. For now, you have much to accomplish. I'll let you get to it, son." The mysterious voice faded. He never questioned who the voice was or where it was coming from, or the fact that he may have a mental condition. He just let the voice comfort him, which it did.

Anticipation for the preparations for the building construction, and moving into the next phase of his plans, overtook him. That night, Herman lay in his hotel room bed tossing and turning. Beads of sweat rolled from his forehead, as he mumbled incoherently in his sleep. Dark images raced through his mind, vivid and descriptive.

He was walking over cadavers which had been disemboweled, his bare feet slipping into the inside of their stomachs. Pulling his feet from the insides of the stomachs, they would become tangled in the intestines and cause him to trip and fall to his knees. After regaining his balance and walking further through the bodies, they suddenly began to snap and crunch beneath his feet. The bodies were now decayed skeletons and their flesh was burned from their bones.

He reached down, picked up some of the bones and watched, as they turned to ash in his hands. He rubbed the ash over his face, and chest, painting his skin a black and greyish tint. Holmes screamed, as he woke clutching the sheets draping his sweaty body. Sitting up on the bed, he wiped his forehead with the sheets. His thoughts remained on the beginning of the construction work on the building. He stood up, walked over to the closet, opened the door and pulled out a long rope from a suitcase.

A noose was tied at the end of the rope. Herman threw the rope over his right shoulder and walked to the door of his hotel room, opening it a crack and peering down the hallway, to ensure there were no other guests present. His deceptive eyes reflected in the dim lighting. The hallway was empty and dark. He knew that now was his opportunity to make his way back to Henry's room and finish setting up a misleading suicide scene.

H.H. Holmes: The Devil in Me

He walked into the room. Henry's motionless body was still lying on the bed. Taking the rope and quickly sliding the noose around the corpse's neck, he then tied the other end to the small chandelier on the ceiling. Pulling the rope tightly, Henry's body was hoisted upright and he finished tying off the rope under the bed. The body swung slowly from side to side, making it look as though the traveling business man had simply hung himself.

Herman turned and walked to the door, looking back to make sure he did not overlook any minor details in his charade. He opened the door and stepped through it, pulling the door closed quietly behind him. His plan went exactly according to the time frame allowed. He returned to his room in hopes of attempting to get a few hours of sleep.

'IN MOTION'

The following morning, Herman walked down to the hotel desk and informed the desk clerk, "I am checking out, today."

"Will you require a carriage Dr. Holmes?"

"Yes, thank you." An employee gathered his bags and waited near the hotel's front doors.

The bill was settled and he walked out of the hotel doors, where the carriage awaited to transport him, to his newly acquired property.

The employee loaded his bags onto the rear of the carriage, "Thank you sir." Holmes tipped the employee.

The carriage rode a few blocks, along side other carriages and turned onto W. 63rd Street, slowly rolling to a stop, where the driver of the carriage informed him, "We have arrived at your stop Dr. Holmes." Holmes exited the carriage, standing in front of his newly acquired three story building with a satchel and large suitcases in both hands.

There were already contractors and construction workers arranging materials in front of the building.

Holmes walked over to the door and unlocked it, turning to the contractor and workers, "Here are the plans for the required woodwork and framing. Here are the plans for the piping to be installed in each of the smaller rooms on the second and third floors, and the basement will only require the installation of another heater." Groups of passersby were stopping and looking at the cities newest undertaking.

He distributed the plans to the contractor and entered the building. He went upstairs to a room, in the back corner of the third floor and looked out the window. The unobstructed view revealed the rooftops of the surrounding warehouses and buildings. Smoke was coming from some of the chimneys of the buildings, their roofs coated with a thick black tar. Holmes walked down the stairs on the third floor and made his way to the front office.

A contractor stood near the door, instructing the workers to bring in the building materials and where to place the tools, "Place the tools, over against that wall and the materials against this wall, over here." The contractor spoke with a thick accent.

"Sir, do you have everything you need here?" He asked the contractor.

"Yes, Dr. Holmes, there is nothing elaborate on the plans which would keep us from finishing on time."

"Very good, everything will go according to plan and I will be able to start bringing in supplies for my business. I shall return, this afternoon, and follow up with the progress." Holmes turned and walked out of the building leaving the contractors and workers to begin their work on the building.

Walking down to the city's main offices, he arrived and discovered the building's directory of departments

183

listed on the placard. He looked up the zoning department and the other various departments of building planning. He walked into the building carrying his leather satchel filled with contracts, papers, money and his revolver. Inside the building he changed the names on his title, contracts and zoning permits to reflect H.H. Holmes.

The initials would be a sick and twisted tribute to his first murder victim in Chicago, Henry Howard. He added Henry's initials as his first name and then Holmes for his last name, as a tribute to the charismatic detective, Sherlock Holmes. After a light meal, he returned to his building. The third level was almost completed, wired and the piping installed in the plumbing and ventilation systems.

There were no questions asked about the elaborate use of the piping creating the peculiar ventilation system, or the mysterious compartments and additional passage ways hidden from view. Holmes had taken extra precautions to pay off the contractors to remain silent about the construction plans. The second level was near completion, only requiring some additional designing and woodworking.

Construction was halfway completed near the end of the first week. Holmes approached the contractor, "I am afraid your progress is falling below my expectations. I will have to let you go and hire a new contractor and construction crew."

"I do not see how some of these plans can be finished within the time frame you expected. It's just not feasible."

"The progress is unsatisfactory."

"Very well." The contractor turned, "Listen up everyone. Load up all the tools!" The workers cleaned up and placed their tools near the entrance of the building.

Holmes immediately contacted a new contractor, who assured him the construction would continue the following day and they would work longer hours than the last crew. The overall construction took the better part of the month.

Near the end of the construction phase, the contractor announced, "Dr. Holmes, we will be returning tomorrow morning to finish the cabinets and stair work to some of the rear hallways. The wood floors were in surprisingly good condition. The furnace in the basement has been installed, along with the tanks and plumbing systems you requested."

"Thank you, sir." Holmes replied.

"I almost forgot to inform you. The beds, drawers and chests for the third floor have arrived and have been placed in each of the rooms."

"Excellent, that will be all for today. Now, if you will excuse me I am going to take advantage of one of those beds. Please close the door on your way out, sir."

"Certainly, we should only be a few more minutes, see you in the morning." The contractor replied. Holmes climbed the freshly painted staircase and made his way to the third floor. Bright sunlight shined through the newly installed windows, as he walked down the hallway. Towards the end of the hallway, and into one of the back rooms, he opened and closed the door behind him.

He slept well into the evening, woke, put on a hand tailored grey suit and his favorite Sebrell Fedora. He set out for an evening of networking, in order to establish business connections with the well-to-do and connected businessmen of Chicago. He walked to a

popular dinner and social club and entered through the
front doors.

A well dresses host greeted him, "Good evening,
sir, can I get you a table in the dining room?"

"Yes, thank you that would be fine." He
responded.

He was led to the center table in the crowded
establishment. A waiter approached his table, filling his
glass with water, "For tonight's special, we are serving
lamb in a light gravy sauce and a special blend of
seasoned vegetables." He ordered a drink and decided
on the light meal of lamb and vegetables.

Throughout the evening, he walked from one table
to another, using his charm and newly established
outgoing personality, introducing his new business and
hotel to the highest class and elite business members of
Chicago. They were impressed with his energy and
unique idea of supplying medical supplies,
pharmaceuticals, and learning tools for medical
universities.

However disturbing his idea was, providing human
skeletons to universities for learning instruments; it was
still a unique and an unchallenged business model. He
had quickly lined up investors, and distributors, in order
to assist him in delivering his finished products. He
convinced them all; his materials were from cadavers
and additional plaster casts made in his factory.

At the end of the evening, he had become an
established businessman by using his title as a doctor
and charming wits. He embellished in his abilities to use
his con, without the slightest suspicions from his
financers. With a long list of names in his black-book,
he was now ready to return to his building and finish
construction on his building, the following day.

His progress on the building was swift and quickly completed. The contractors and workers had finished cleaning up and were in the process of removing the last of their tools. He shook hands with each of them, as they left the building and closed the door behind them. Holmes stood in the main lobby of his newly renovated business and hotel lavishing in his accomplishments.

Within a month, he had purchased a building, finished the construction and remodel. In one night, he established strong connections with the business community at the social club, secured investors and for the distribution of his products. He returned to the back room on the third floor, removed his hat and suit and lay down on the bed. The beds were one of the hotels more extravagant features, providing an unprecedented comfort other hotels and inns lacked.

He looked up at the ceiling thinking of additional ideas for his elaborately constructed building and the many methods involved in the ventilation for all three floors. If he were to be using gas in the rooms, he would need to ensure there are no issues with ventilating the rooms. He closed his eyes and drifted off to sleep. His dreams flashed through his mind and the recurring voice he had begun speaking, "How are you feeling with all your success?"

Herman thought about the success he had achieved over the past month and a sense of pride filled his mind, "Very good, son. That is the feeling you will achieve if you continue to follow what you have been instructed to accomplish. Keep your wits about you, for this is the most crucial and important step along your path."

Colby Van Wagoner

Herman stirred in his bed and under the sheets. His mind was racing. Holmes woke in his third floor room, staring up at the ceiling. It was Saturday. He needed to prepare to meet with the Holton's for dinner that evening. He walked around the building, inspecting the construction and was beginning to think that he did not need to pay the contractors anything, at this point. They accepted the work on credit vouchers. Therefore, he could make the new investors direct their funding to the contractors.

Being free of paying for the construction, would leave him ample finances to create other opportunities and purchase additional properties on the block. He collected his materials for the additional construction and returned to work on the doors and rooms on the upper floor. Some of the rooms were left untouched to make them look like normal, inviting hotel rooms. In the other rooms, he began studding sheet metal over the windows, replacing the walls and floors with soundproofing material. The door handles were replaced with one way handles leaving the rooms accessible only from the outside.

He rigged some of the windows and doors with intricate magnetic alarms, which would sound off, should someone attempt to escape the room. After finishing up with the third floor, he prepared for his evening dinner with the Holton's. He washed up and prepared his suit and hat, brushing them with a lint brush. After dressing, he walked through the hallways of the building and an idea struck him.

Sunday, he would spend the day preparing the hallways, with trap doors, hidden staircases, secret passages, rooms without windows, chutes that led into the basement and a staircase that would open over a steep drop to the alley behind the house. He would then begin executing his plan.

He walked through the cobblestone streets of South Chicago tipping his hat at people, as they passed him. The air was hot and humid. He made his way to the Holton's house and knocked on the door, Dr. Holton answered. "Just in time, Mrs. Holton has finished the salad and the lamb chops. I know that she mentioned you were particularly fond of lamb."

"Wonderful, Dr. Holton, I have developed quite an appetite from the construction work the past few days."

"Wonderful, you will have to tell us all about it and show us, after dinner that is." Dr. Holton replied with a hint of curiosity, little did he know about Holmes' overall scheme.

The three ate dinner and finished. After an hour of conversation, about working in the drugstore, his charismatic personality and charm won over Dr. and Mrs. Holton. The couple agreed and Mrs. Holton replied, "You should begin working in the pharmacy on Monday."

"I look forward to it." After helping the couple clean up, and finish the dishes, Holmes suggested the three take a walk over to his building. "I think it is time to take a walk over to the building. You can both see the renovations I have made."

"Oh wonderful, I think it is just fantastic how ambitious you are! You should have your business up and running in no time. I hope that working at the drugstore will not interfere with your other business affairs?" Mrs. Holton added.

"Not at all, in fact, I have arranged advertisements in the paper to hire some help, so, I should have enough employees to help me run my business, allowing me to help you in the drugstore." The three prepared to leave and put on their coats for the walk over to his building. They walked through the streets chatting about the plans for the coming week and even for Holmes to use Dr. Holton's office to conduct the interviews for his business. It was agreed and his plan was now moving along smoothly.

"Here we are." Holmes indicated, as he opened the door to his building.

He flipped on a light. Dr. and Mrs. Holton gasped in delight at the renovations he had made. He showed them the first level and explained the offices and other rooms on the first floor. They climbed the exquisite staircase to the third floor. Holmes led the unsuspecting couple to the first room, on the right. He showed them one of the actual hotel rooms and then one of the next rooms.

"I must say, this room is a bit peculiar. What is the purpose of having the sheet metal over the window?" Dr. Holton inquired.

"This room will be for the storage of the materials for guests of the hotel. As a matter of fact, let me show you the security features I have installed." Holmes pulled Mrs. Holton from the room and closed the door behind him, leaving Dr. Holton alone in the locked room.

"Now, Mrs. Holton, I want to show you to the next room and you can see the amazing security feature of the rooms. As a matter of fact, if you listen carefully you will not even hear your husband through the walls."

"No noise at all? That is a great idea, the other guests will not be complaining about the noise from the other rooms. It will be peaceful and quiet. I do hope that you will have us for the grand opening?"

"You are my special guests?" He replied, with a sinister tone, leading Mrs. Holton to the door of the next room. She walked into the room and looked around. "There are not any lights in these rooms?"

"No." He replied, "There is no way to open the doors from the inside." He pushed the door closed and waited for Mrs. Holton to respond. There was no noise, so he walked to the room Dr. Holton was locked in and waited. From inside the room he could make out low grumbling and thumping on the walls. He smiled, realizing Dr. Holton was now panicking and had realized he was locked in the room without escape.

He walked back to the room where Mrs. Holton was held, hearing muffled screaming coming from the cracks in the door. He put his head to the door and listened to her scratching at the door. He smiled, turned from the door and strolled down the hallway to his room. Before he walked into his room, he had turned off the hallway light, moved through the entrance to his room and closed the door behind him.

The following day, Holmes walked from his room wearing a dark apron and gloves. He descended the stairway, down to the lobby of the building. He walked down the hallway, passing pictures of flowers and landscapes. Upon reaching the end of the hallway, he gripped a large sliding steel door with both hands and pulled it to the right. The door opened with ease and Holmes walked through the entrance, down to the basement.

The furnaces were lit and there were large bags piled in the corner. He pulled large steel grates from the wall and slid them into position. There were two steel plates, which were held in place and covered by a brick enclosure. He slid long piping under the grates and connected tubes to the end of the pipes. He walked over to the two large metal tanks, turned the handles at their bottoms and they began to fill with corrosive acid. Above the tanks were two openings, connected to trap doors, leading up to the third floor.

He walked to a steel door in the floor, towards the back of the steel tanks. He reached over to the wall and pulled a large metal handle, which opened the steel lids. Looking down into the hole he smiled, turned, and walked over to the bags piled in the corner. He lifted the first bag, ripped it open and poured the quicklime into the pit. Upon finishing, Holmes walked up to the first steel tank, shut off the acid and then did the same to the second tank.

After he prepared the basement, he took off his apron, hung it on the wall and walked back up to the first floor. He looked through the windows of the front door and saw that the streets were relatively empty, with the exception of a few passing horse drawn carriages. Holmes was now in the beginnings of fulfilling his desires and the familiar voice, inside him, spoke, "Take whatever you want, no matter what you may fear, no matter what complications arise. No matter what obstacle you have to overcome. You will kill, without consequence." The voice faded.

He walked back up the main staircase, down to the second door on the left, where Dr. Holton was locked. He pounded on the door, "Dr. Holton, how are you doing in there? Are you enjoying my new hotel?"

He pressed his head up against the door and could hear Dr. Holton yelling out, indistinctly. Herman was unable to make out the words. He reached to the top of the door frame, turned a small handle and listened, as the gas sprayed from the pipes. He used the same gas medical buildings used to heat the furnaces of the crematories. The same gas supplied to his basement crematory to fumigate the room. It was a toxic dose.

Inside the room, Dr. Holton recognized the smell of the gas and covered his mouth with his shirt, but he knew that it would not be enough. After a few minutes, he began to feel light headed and fell to his knees losing consciousness, soon after. Holmes returned to the room Mrs. Holton was in and knocked on the door. This time he opened the door revealing Mrs. Holton lying on her side. Holmes let out a horrendous scream which caused her to jump and wake from her sleep, screaming.

"Why are you doing this?" She insisted, sobbing hysterically.

"Why? Because, Mrs. Holton, I can!" Screaming angrily back at her and slamming the door closed. She crawled slowly across the floor, lifted her body up to the door, attempting to push the door open.

"Please, let me out of here! I will not tell anyone, I promise."

Pressing his ear up against the door, Holmes lifted his hand placing it softly on the steel frame, using his other hand to slowly rub up and down the front of his pants. He walked back to his room and shut the door behind him determined, now more than ever, to begin the interviewing process bringing more and more young ladies into the hotel.

After sleeping for over three hours, he woke up and walked back to the room where Dr. Holton was gassed. He slowly opened the door, smelling the air inside, discovering the ventilation system he designed was working properly. He stepped inside the room and stood over Holton's body. Holmes reached down and felt for a pulse, there was no sign he was alive. He dragged the body to the wall, opened up a small door in the wall and pushed the body into the opening. The body dropped down the chute, banging against the sides of the metal as it fell echoing up and out of the opening.

Holmes turned, walked out of the room and down to the basement. He put on his apron and walked over to the first metal tank. Pulling down a long handle, the tank's lid opened up on top. With the lid of the tank opened, he walked over to the wall and pulled another lever. The body of Dr. Holton dropped from the ceiling of the basement and into the tank of corrosive acid.

He walked back over to the side of the tank, pulled the lever back down, closing the metal lid to the tank. Holmes was convinced of his flawless design. It was perfect and now, it was time to take care of Mrs. Holton. He walked upstairs and repeated the same process with her, finishing up the process. Afterwards, he prepared to spend a quiet evening at the social club, just down the street. Inside the social club, he proceeded to make the usual business arrangements, procuring additional finances, with ease. He also announced his plans of a glorious opening for his hotel.

Monday morning arrived. Holmes was standing in front of the drugstore, unlocking the door, as the first customer arrived. "Well hello, sir, I do not think I know you. It is very nice to meet you."

"It is very nice to meet you, as well." Holmes shook the ladies hand, opened the door and ushered her through the door.

"Where is Mrs. Holton, is she feeling well?"

Holmes walked behind the counter and replied, "I guess it was sudden, but Dr. Holton passed, Saturday evening, and Mrs. Holton made arrangements to return to the west coast to be with her family."

"I am so sorry to hear that. Did she leave a forwarding address?" The woman inquired. Holmes paused in his work and quickly replied, "No, I am afraid she did not. She was shaken up and hardly able to make all the arrangements for travel and transport of her husband, for herself. She was going to have me start work today, but after the shock of her husband's death, she decided to sell the drugstore and avoid the memories she had of her husband, should she continue to work here."

"Oh, well, that is a tragedy. I need to get this script filled, I will be back to pick it up this afternoon." She handed the paper to Holmes.

"I'll have it ready for you within the hour." He smiled and finished with a calm and charismatic response, "It was very nice to meet you." The lady smiled and allowed him to take her hand and lightly kiss it. She giggled, turned, and walked to the door. "I'll be sure to tell everyone about the death of Mrs. Holton's husband and there is a handsome new doctor taking over the drug store." The lady opened the door, closing it behind her and turned to get one last look of Holmes, who stood, just behind the counter.

Through the day, he worked at the drugstore filling orders and explaining the mysterious and sudden death of Mrs. Holton's husband. He also explained to all the regulars that Mrs. Holton had left town and moved out west. He was very convincing in his explanation about how she left, in such a hurry, and had also transferred ownership of the drugstore to him.

At the end of the afternoon, he had closed and was now in the office next to the drug store. He finished two interviews with two older women, for the bookkeeping position, but was unimpressed with their attitudes. A few minutes after the last interview, a young lady walked into the office. She was quiet and shy. Holmes immediately stopped filing his papers after having a look at her.

"Hello, have you come for an interview?"

"Yes, I have, I am looking to write and thought it would be good for me to take up a position that involved writing." She looked down at her dress, adjusting it by pulling at the bottom and stretching it down to her knees. She seemed very modest, walked over to the chair at the desk and sat down.

"My name is Julia. I have moved here with my husband, Ned, and my daughter, Pearl.

"Where have you moved from?" Holmes replied, sitting back in his chair.

"Iowa. My husband is a watchmaker and a jeweler, who recently lost his job, so we decided to move to Chicago and make a new start."

"About the job, you must be able to type and read well. You also must be proficient in grammar and punctuation as the ad indicated."

"I can type around sixty words a minute and my understanding of the English language, grammar and punctuation, is very efficient." Julia replied with more confidence. So taken by the young woman, at this point Holmes was not interested in her abilities, only hiring her to work in his office. When there were not enough typing and writing needs, she could fill in at the drugstore and assist him with additional responsibilities.

"You are hired. And another thing, are you looking for a place to stay?"

"Yes, for now, we are staying at the hotel just around the corner."

"The apartment, above the drug store is available and at night, it is a quiet place. There would not be much rent involved. You will have to pay for the water and electricity you use."

"Oh that will be perfect. I will let my husband know. He will be happy when he hears we can move out of the hotel and into a real place." Holmes was also thinking about her husband and what he could offer, should he put a jeweler and watchmaker in the empty space in the rear of the drug store.

"So, you can have your husband come in and see me tomorrow, as well? I believe I may be willing to set him up in the additional space of the drugstore, where he can operate his watch making and jewelry talents." Julia stood up quickly and shook his hand, walked to the door and turned. "Thank you, Dr. Holmes." She opened the door and closed it behind her.

Holmes walked out of the office and back to his building to begin planning the grand opening the following Monday. In the meantime, he was going to focus on a weekend of social clubs and dinner halls. He was filled with confusion and rage, unable to understand where these feelings of jealousy were coming from, most likely the fact Julia spoke so highly of her husband.

Holmes had met with Julia's husband the following day, Ned Connor, and was impressed with his knowledge of jewelry and watch making, "I think this will be a beneficial arrangement for both of us, Ned." The two had agreed on business terms and after moving into the apartment above the drug store, when Ned would begin work in the drugstore.

Julia would be starting work in the main level of the building on S. Wallace and W. 63rd Street, the following week, arranging files and writing up business contracts. Holmes spent the majority of the weekend meeting with couples and businessmen, offering them tours of his new office and hotel. He drew them in with his charm, wit and charisma and they quickly accepted his invitations to tour the hotel.

At the end of Saturday night, Holmes had drawn in twelve people, quickly had them separated and locked inside the hotel rooms on the third floor. Low, muffled screams and banging emanated from the rooms. He knew he would have to complete their gassing through the night and have the room's sound proofing improved. That night he walked from room to room, listening to the occupants scream, begging to be freed. Some of the rooms had already gone silent.

Inside one of the rooms, a young woman he had met at one of the social clubs was being held. She was at the club with her fiancé. The two were interested in seeing the new hotel and working in the offices on the first floor. Opening the door and stepping inside the room, the girl rushed towards the door. Holmes easily knocked her back to the floor with his right arm.

"Please let me go. Why are you doing this? We have done nothing to you. Where is Jesse?"

"He is gone now." Holmes whispered, as he walked closer to her. "He is gone. Would you like to see him one last time?"

"What have you done to him?" She sobbed.

"He is asleep, asleep, forever." He walked over to her and pulled some rope from his side, tying her arms and legs with the rope, then took some tape, wrapping it around her mouth. He took his tongue and slowly ran it up her cheek, licked his lips and whispered, "You taste so sweet."

"You are sick!" She was sobbing hysterically and squirmed in the ropes. Holmes took out a syringe from a bag, near his side, removed the lid and held the girl's arm. Slowly inserting the needle into her vein and draining the contents of the syringe into her arm, she relaxed and drifted away. He pulled the needle from her arm and the girl continued her feeble attempts struggling to move away from him.

He stood up and pulled out a knife from his pocket, opened the blade and reached down to her shirt. He cut the shirt and removed the fabric, revealing the young girl's chest. He cut her skirt, and threw it onto the floor near her, removed his shirt and unbuttoned his trousers. He lowered himself just above the girl, took the knife placed it at her throat and whispered, "You are mine, now." Holmes forced himself on the girl and after he was finished, took his knife and ran it across the girl's cheek.

Afterwards, he lifted the drugged girl over his shoulder and walked her down into the basement. He took her over to the dark corner of the room and chained her to the wall, reached up and pulled a lever on the wall. Lights lit up the room, revealing the body of her fiancé. Holmes began to peel back the man's face with a scalpel, carefully removing the skin and completely pulling the remaining skin away from the muscle.

After a few hours, the medication began to wear off and the girl looked up to see the mangled body of her fiancé and continued struggling with the ropes.

Holmes walked over to the dissection table and picked up a scalpel from the instruments carefully arranged on a metal table. Taking the scalpel and cutting an incision in the man's arm, he reached over and drained the blood into a cup, carefully placing the cup back on a table.

After finishing, he took the cup and walked over to the girl tied to the wall. Standing above her, Holmes slowly walked into the light, revealing her husband's skin over his face. He poured the cup of blood over her head. She began screaming though the tape covering her mouth and pulled at the ropes restraining her arms and legs.

Holmes walked back over to another table, reached under a blanket covering the body. He removed the blanket revealing the body's severed limbs. Picking up one of the legs he carried the severed limb towards the girl. He took the legs and began to hit her in the face repeatedly. The girl became so overwhelmed, she lost consciousness. Holmes walked over to the pit, filled with quicklime, and threw the leg below.

He walked back over to the girl and untied her, carried her back up to the third floor and locked her back in a room. He walked from room to room turning off the gas. Other rooms, he turned on the gas, filling the room with the deadly fumes. He spent the rest of the evening raping and molesting the girl, tied in the room, and before going to sleep had turned off the rest of the gas allowing the remaining rooms to ventilate.

He woke the following morning and went from room to room, sliding the bodies into the chutes, which fell into the trap doors located just above the tanks filled with corrosive acid. After letting the bodies soak in the tanks for hours, he climbed the ladder to the top of the first tank. Wearing thick, rubber, gloves he retrieved the skeletons hanging them in metal frames spread across the basement. The skeletons were allowed to air dry, and become ready for preparations.

After finishing the dressings over the skeletons, he used a brush to coat the bones with a preservative. Allowing them to dry for most of the day, he prepared a lunch in the dinning room, finished the meal and walked the plates into the kitchen, placing them in the washbasin. Tired from the preparation of the first group of skeletons, he walked up to the third floor of the building, into the last room, and went to sleep on the bed.

He woke and walked down the hall on the third floor. Arriving at the room containing the drugged girl, he slowly turned the handle on the gas pipe. Gas began hissing and seeping into the room. The girl choked and squirmed on the floor, within ten minutes her body became motionless. She was dead. Holmes had finished off his twelfth victim in his weekend killing spree.

He spent the remainder of the evening arranging for the distribution of the skeletons from the basement to local, Chicago area, medical universities. To cover up his murderous scheme from the authorities, Holmes would say the skeletons were from cadavers obtained from local hospitals and Chicago coroner's offices. If the authorities investigated any missing person reports, he would be able to confirm his trail through various hospital employees and city employees he had easily bribed.

The grand opening of Holmes' hotel was in full swing. Local officials and successful businessmen had come to see how their investments had come to fruition, "Glorious building Dr. Holmes." One of his highest financiers was admiring the main dining hall, and the fine details of the decorations, to the artwork carefully placed on various walls throughout.

"The sculptures and statues will be arriving shortly, and there will be some additional improvements on the roofing. However, I am quite pleased with the final results." Holmes continued, "If you will please excuse me, I must spread my praise and thanks to the other donors."

"Yes, of course, Dr. Holmes."

Dr. Holmes continued giving his thanks and praise to all his guests, then announced, "Can I have your attention?" He called out, "Ladies and gentlemen, thank you for attending my grand opening. I thank each and every one of you for your involvement, and a special thank you to my very special guests attending this evening." He raised his glass, as the others followed suit, taking a drink from their glasses. The grand opening continued into the afternoon. Holmes had hired special security detail to keep the guests from entering the more private areas of his hotel.

That evening, after the grand opening celebration, he attended a dinner with Ned, Julia, and their daughter Pearl. They discussed the progress of their move into the drug store's apartment. "Ned, have you finished getting settled into the apartment?" Holmes inquired.

"Yes, we have, and I have to make a few more arrangements with some suppliers in the area. I will have a shipment of watch making materials, and some additional jewels, coming within the next week."

"If you need any additional business contacts, I can provide you some numbers from my office." Holmes offered.

"Thank you that would be very helpful. I can start working towards the end of the week, which should give me enough time to set up the extra space in the drugstore."

Holmes was watching Julia for most of the night, careful to make sure that Ned was unaware of his interest towards his wife. The group finished up with dinner and parted ways for the evening. Holmes returned to his building, added some additional sound proofing to the rooms, worked on some more secret passages in the walls and made adjustments to the gas flow running into the rooms. Once finished, he retired for the evening.

Colby Van Wagoner

'The Lesser of Two Evils'

The following day, the newspaper announced
Chicago was hosting the first world's fair May 1st, 1893.
It would attract millions of businessmen, tourists and
travelers, from all across the country, to the area. Upon
reading the news Holmes rushed to the store and
quickly drew up advertisements for his hotel. The
cunningly drafted advertisements would attract
attention and customers, unaware of the dangers they
would be facing. The success of his hotel and elaborate
schemes hung in the balance.

Submitting the advertisements to the newspaper,
for print, would have to be accomplished as quickly as
possible. He would let the advertisement run for the
majority of 1893. He ran the drugstore for most of the
day and had Julia typing up the advertisements, "Julia,
the drafts must be delivered to the papers, today. After
delivering the advertisements can you return to the drug
store?"

"Yes; afterwards, I can return." As she spoke, she
remained vigilant with her typing, paying close attention
to every detail and aspect of the grammar, and spelling.

Holmes replied, "When you return, I will train you in the drug store's accounting and bookkeeping."

She quickly proved her efficiency and attention to detail, "I have the rough drafts completed. You should proofread these to make sure they meet your requirements." She went to hand Holmes the papers.

He made an advance towards her, "Please, Dr. Holmes, I am a married woman." Julia was hesitant, but his charismatic personality and charm began winning her over.

Ned was in and out of the store, making arrangements with distributors and moving equipment into the drug store's extra space. He was unaware of the consequences of his marriage, as his wife was spending much of her time with the charismatic and charming, Dr. Holmes. The gap of space, in the rear of the drug store, was soon filled with metal polishers and tables filled with watch making tools, which would allow Ned to begin offering his services in the drug store.

As the weeks passed, Ned was working in the drugstore, full time, and becoming well known for his precision as a jeweler and watchmaker. He attracted multiple customers who were returning for his skills and technical knowledge. Yet, he was beginning to have his suspicions about his wife's involvement and flirtatious interactions with Holmes.

Holmes and Julia worked late into the evenings at the building across from the drug store, "This is your introduction to my latest business of distributing skeletons to medical universities, schools and hospitals. It may be horrifying and a bit disgusting to think about; however, using cadavers from hospitals for the materials is a no cost supply, and the universities pay top dollar for skeletal models."

"How do you prepare the skeletons?" She replied and was intrigued at the business model Holmes was explaining.

"I will show you more. However, for your own safety, I cannot allow you to explore, or stay in the third floor hotel rooms." Slight, suggestive hypnotism was another technique he was taking advantage of in order to further his advances towards Julia.

"Will you show me the rest of the hotel, Dr. Holmes?" Julia inquired.

Holmes quickly insisted, "This is not something that you want to be involved with, trust me." He was using reverse psychology and a suggestive technique to further spark her interest and see how far she was willing to become involved.

"I do not mind, really." She replied, moving closer to Holmes placing her hand on his knee. Her touch caused him to shutter and laugh, as he reached for her, placing his hand on her shoulder and sliding it up to the back of her neck. Julia moved in closer and kissed him. Holmes pulled her in closer and wrapped his arms around her, returning her kiss. He reached around and began unbuttoning the back of her dress. The two began passionately rushing to remove their clothing.

Within moments, the two were on the floor. He reached down and pushed himself inside Julia. She moaned with pleasure and began to move her hips further up into him. They remained in the office of the hotel for a few hours, until Julia stood up and dressed.

"I need to get back to the apartment. Ned will start wondering if there is something wrong."

"Ned is not going to notice any differences, or anything out of the ordinary. He will just think that you are working hard on handling the books and keeping my finances in order."

"Well you are sure keeping me in order." She replied, blushing, "I think that you underestimate Ned. He is very inquisitive when it comes to certain social situations."

"You mean situations when it comes to intimacy with his wife? If he understood intimacy you would not be with me, here, tonight." Julia was not expecting Holmes to have said it, but he was right.

"You are right, you know? Ned would never understand my needs and has become too caught up in his jewelry and watch making. He started neglecting my needs, years ago." She retrieved her bag, walked to the office door, and smiled back at Holmes who was still lying on the floor. Julia left, closing the door behind her.

The following day, Holmes was working in the drugstore watching Ned, as he was fixing watches. His mind raced, as he thought about ridding Ned from the picture. Eliminating Ned would allow him and Julia to be together, but what about her daughter, Pearl? How would he handle living with Julia's daughter? Children were curious and nosey. Pearl would most likely interfere with the business he was running from the basement of his building.

Ned looked up from his work and saw that Holmes was watching him, "Dr. Holmes, is there anything the matter?"

Holmes shrugged, "No, Ned, why do you say that?"

"Well, for starters, you seem to have had your eye on me today. Is my work interfering?"

"Ned, I was just lost in thought. That is all."

"Dr. Holmes, I am not a naive person. It seems that you are having thoughts about Julia and me. We are happy here. It seems that you are trying to interfere with that?"

Julia walked in, just as Ned had finished his sentence. She stopped at the front door of the store, "What is going on?" Julia exclaimed, as she sensed Holmes and Ned's awkward expressions.

"Well, we were just discussing your relationship with Dr. Holmes, Julia!" Her husband replied walking from behind his worktable.

"I do not know what you are talking about. Why are you saying this?"

"Just shut up, Julia, I know! I am not the naive schoolboy you knew back in college! I know!" He slammed his fist down on the table. Holmes reached to his belt and gripped the handle of his revolver, waiting to see what Ned's next reaction would be. Julia knew that she could no longer hide the charade from her husband.

"I'm so sorry, Ned. I didn't want it to happen like this. You have just been so distant and shut off from me." Ned didn't respond, picked up a satchel from beside his work bench and slid the valuable watches and jewels into the bag. He walked from behind the desk and towards the storefront. Julia stepped towards him.

"Get away from me, you whore!" Ned pushed Julia to the floor, "I am taking my belongings, Pearl, and I am leaving you. Do not bother trying to track me down, because I will not ignore it and the next time we meet, I will kill you both!" Ned knew Holmes carried a revolver and was in no hurry to test him to see if he would actually use it or not.

Holmes did not react to the confrontation and simply stood behind the pharmacy's counter. Julia was on the floor in tears, as Ned opened the door of the drugstore, turned and glared at Holmes giving him one last scowl; afterwards, slamming the door and walking off into the distance.

Holmes walked over to Julia, lifting her from the floor, "Come Julia, our decision last night led us to this moment. Let us close up the store, for today, and get away."

"Where will we go?" Julian stood, wiping the tears from her cheeks.

"How does the lake sound? I'll pack a lunch and we can take the carriage for an afternoon ride." She sniffled. Holmes handed her a white handkerchief from his pocket and she used it to finish wiping the tears from her eyes. She walked with him to the door. He led her through the door and turned, locking the door behind him.

That afternoon, Holmes and Julia spent the day walking around the lake, after eating a picnic lunch, and returned to the hotel. Holmes walked over to a cabinet in his office, pulled out a vial and a needle from inside, walking back over to Julia and rolling up her sleeve, "This will calm you down and help you sleep." Holmes had pressed the needle into the vial, extracted the liquid and injected the mild sedative into Julia's vein.

"What is it?" Julia inquired.

"This is a mild sedative; there is no cause for alarm." Julia rolled down her sleeve, leaned over and kissed him, as she walked into the room, in the rear of the first floor and laid down into a small bed.

"Now get some rest. I'll go check on a few things, over at the drugstore."

Walking over the door, Holmes turned to look at Julia and shut off the light, closing the door behind him. Julia slept for the better part of the evening. Holmes remained in the office next to the drug store. There was a knock at the door and he stood up from behind the desk. After opening the door, two police officers walked into the office and stood next to the door. It was an obvious precaution preventing him from leaving the office.

"How can I help you officers?" Holmes arranged some paperwork and stood.

"Dr. Holmes?" One of the officers inquired.

"Yes, I am Dr. Holmes."

"Doctor, we are investigating the disappearance of some citizens and wonder if you have seen anything unusual, or any suspicious, in the area?"

"No, I can not say that I have. Are there any leads?" Placing his hand and leaning on the desk, the officers began looking around his office.

"We have a few, which are from the social club you have been known to frequent just around the corner. Some of the employees mention you were speaking to a couple there. Just about a week later, they were reported missing."

"Well officers, did you also ask them if I was speaking, or sitting, with anyone else at the restaurant?" One of the officers looked at the other and shifted his stance, realizing that Holmes made a good point. They would not be able to pin the disappearance of a couple on an upstanding citizen, who was simply speaking with the couple at the social club.

"Officers, I have answered your questions and should it be necessary, I can personally see the commissioner about your investigation. I am sure a personal friend would be very interested in your line of questioning?" The tone in Holmes' voice became defensive and aggressive.

While the officers recognized the tone, it did raise some suspicions about Holmes' involvement in the couple's disappearance. They knew that an upstanding citizen such as Holmes would not be brought up on charges with just circumstantial evidence.

One of the officers coughed and replied, "Dr. Holmes, if you do see anything suspicious, or something that might raise concern, you will be responsible enough to report it, correct?"

"Right away officers, now if you will excuse me, I have some paperwork to finish up here. That is unless you would care to join me?"

"That is quite all right, good evening, Dr. Holmes."

"Good evening, gentlemen." Holmes responded with a sinister tone. The two officers showed themselves out, closing the office door behind them. Holmes stared at the door with thoughts of being caught racing through his mind. Being accused of kidnapping and murder would certainly send him to the hangman's noose. He reached into his desk drawer, pulling out his revolver and placing it in its holster.

Holmes walked across the street to his hotel and was now focused on making arrangements for his grand opening. He had to delay the grand opening, due to some final construction on the security features of the doors on the third floor. He spent the better part of two days upgrading the security features and was becoming agitated the work had distracted him from his other business affairs.

Now that the final adjustments to the security of the building were completed, he was ready to open and

invite guests into his hotel. He opened the front door
of the building to find Julia standing in the front lobby,
near the clerk's desk. She looked concerned and was
fiddling with some papers.

"Hello, Julia, did you rest well?"

"Yes, I did darling, but there are a few concerns I
have. I know that you do not want me looking around
on the third floor, but you know a woman's intuition
and curiosities?"

"What is it that you think you saw on the third
floor? There is nothing but rooms, desks, chairs and
beds, for my guests." Holmes walked over to the desk,
pulled out his revolver and laid it on the table. Julia
looked down at the revolver and smiled at him. She
walked over to him, reached down to his slacks and ran
her hand between his legs.

"Now, what is it that you plan on doing with that
revolver, Dr. Holmes?"

"What do I plan on doing with it?" He replied and
continued, "First, that all depends on what it is you
think you saw on the third floor. What do you plan on
doing about what is on the third floor."

"Doctor Holmes, I saw the desks, chairs and beds
in the rooms on the third floor. But what I also saw are
the handles connected to the gas lines running into the
rooms. I also saw the trap doors in the corners of the
rooms, which seem to lead to the basement. And in the
basement, there are two tanks underneath the chutes,
which open, indicating whatever comes through the
chutes falls into the tanks."

Holmes reached behind Julia with his left arm, as
she continued to rub between his legs, pulling her into
his body. With his right hand, he reached for the
revolver on the desk, raising it in front of Julia and then

to her chin. Cocking the hammer, he slowly rubbed it up her cheeks and brought it down in front of her nose, leaving the barrel directly in front of her lips.

With his left hand, he reached up to her jaw, grabbing it with significant force, pushing her head back to open her mouth, placing the barrel of the revolver into her mouth and looked deep into her eyes, "Now what is it that you saw on the third floor?"

She pulled her arm free, reached up to the barrel of the revolver and pulled it from her mouth. At the end of the barrel, she closed her lips, lightly sucking the end and kissing it, as it came out of her mouth, "There is something I should let you know, because like my soon to be ex-husband, I am not as naive as I look. Unlike my ex-husband, there is something that you do not know about me and I think you might be surprised, if you just trust me." She unzipped his trousers and reached inside.

She dropped to her knees and began performing fellatio. Holmes dropped his head back and began to inhale deeply. He lowered the revolver, placed his hand on the back of her head and pulled it in closer, pushing himself deep into her throat. Julia let out a deep moan and continued to press her mouth against Holmes' groin.

After a few moments, she stood up in front of Holmes and pulled his ear to her mouth continuing to fondle him. "When I was a young girl, my father came into my room while my mother would be in the kitchen downstairs, or in their bedroom sleeping. He forced himself on his own daughter, Dr. Holmes. I was only a child and he took advantage of the trust between a father and daughter."

She stopped talking and licked his ear, sliding her tongue up the side of his neck, and continued, "When I was finished with him, I took a large hunting knife from underneath my pillow and plunged it into his back. I forgot how many times I stabbed him. Repeatedly, I know that for sure. When I was finished, I could see his insides, behind the spine, after that I tore into his body and broke every bone of ribs. I pulled out his intestines, liver and heart, took them into their room where my mother slept and spread them all over her sleeping body."

Holmes began to moan, his breathing accelerated, along with his heart rate. Julia continued whispering in his ear, "I ran the knife across my mother's cheek, until she woke up. She was in a state of confusion, but I remember the look on her face when she saw what was covering her body. She was terrified. I took the knife and pushed it into her neck. Then, with a quick jerk, I slit it from left to right."

"You cut your mother's throat?" Holmes said excitedly.

"Yes, I did. Next, I took the blood from the knife and licked it till it was clean. I continued slipping the knife into the blood; afterwards, licking it each time. The taste was bitter and salty." She dropped back down to her knees and continued, closing her mouth tightly, until Holmes finally let out a loud groan, pulling Julia's head tightly against his crotch.

Holmes stood frozen, as Julia stood up and whispered again in his ear, "Tastes something like that, but has a different sweetness to it." Julia walked over to the staircase leading up to the third floor, lifted her finger and motioned it towards Holmes. He zipped up his pants, walked over to the staircase and followed her up the stairs, down the hallway and into the last room on the left. Holmes had unknowingly stumbled upon another human being that finally understood the rage and emotion stirring inside him.

The following morning, Holmes and Julia woke in the bed, draped only in a sheet. They stood up and walked down the hallway, naked, down the elaborate staircase and into the kitchen. They prepared their breakfast, in the nude, and discussed the nature of last nights somewhat confrontational act in the lobby, "I take the guests to their rooms, the doors only open from the outside, leaving them locked in the rooms, without escape. After I have kept them locked in for an hour, or even days, I get bored of them and turn on the gas for a while. Sometimes I stop the gas and listen to them choke, scratching at the door, and the pleas to release them."

"Nobody knows that they are missing, after you do it?"

"Nobody, as long as I make sure to put them in the corrosive acid tanks, or cut them up and put the remains in the quicklime pits, or dress their skeletons and sell them to medical universities."

"Selling their remains to a medical university, and the corrosive acid tanks, is brilliant. You are going to have to be careful with the quicklime pit, which leaves some evidence of the bodies."

Holmes looked up at her, as he ate some of his eggs and replied. "Not if there is no one left to find any evidence."

"I have nothing to worry about Holmes, my life is already over. I accepted that a very long time ago, after my first husband and now Ned. Do you really think I am concerned with my life, at this point? You could kill me right now and I would not feel the slightest sense of fear, terror, or regret about it. In fact, Dr. Holmes, I would welcome it."

Holmes was now in disbelief at the, before, shy and quiet little young woman that walked into his office for the interview. He was now deeply impressed with her disregard for life, including her own. He did not understand the last part. In fact, it made him feel pity for her. Similar to the way he felt towards cats and dogs when he was younger. He would punish them, to see their pity, to make them, make him, feel he was in control of their lives, like he was God.

After the two had finished breakfast, Holmes led Julia back upstairs to the third floor. He reached into the desk drawer, pulled out a syringe and acted like he injected something into his arm. After he placed the syringe back on the table, Julia looked over with curiosity. "What is that you injected yourself with?"

"It was a sedative. Every now and then I need something to keep me calm among the living. Otherwise, I would run the streets like an enraged beast."

"Can you give me another one?" Julia slid next to him.

Holmes did not think twice and reached over to the table. This time, he reached into the drawer and pulled out a different sedative, a much stronger one. He was now going to test Julia's disregard for her own life and see what her threshold was. He reached towards her arm and took it in his hands, injecting the sedative into her arm and removed the needle. This time the sedative worked much faster and within minutes, she was unconscious.

Holmes walked to the closet and dressed. Afterwards, walked down to the lobby of the hotel and saw a couple standing, just outside. It was a man and a woman, holding suitcases and peering in through the glass. Holmes walked over to the front door, opened it and greeted them. "Good morning, can I interest you in a room?"

"Yes, sir, my name is Gerald and this is my wife Cynthia. We are both from Michigan."

"I am also from Michigan." A ploy Holmes would often present to make his guests feel more comfortable, even though he was originally from New Hampshire, "Come this way, let's get you signed into the books and registered." He led the couple to the hotel's front desk and opened the registry. He started to write their names, "So, it is Gerald and Cynthia?"

"Thompson." Gerald enthusiastically exclaimed.

"Very well, then, Cynthia and Gerald Thompson." He finished writing what looked like their names on the paper. However, the names that he wrote in the books were different from their actual names. Holmes led them up to the third floor and into the first room on the right. "You can leave your suitcases here, for now. I would like to show you the washrooms. They are down the hall, to the left."

"Certainly, I could freshen up a little. Gerald could as well."

"It is this way." He replied, instructing them to follow him into the hallway.

He led Gerald into the first room on the left, opened the door and informed him, "The light is near the window and there are towels next to it." He closed the door and led the woman to the next room on the left. She unknowingly walked inside, assuming the light is in the same place, as the last room. After Holmes closed the door to the room, he turned and closed his eyes, "How can it be so simple? These unassuming people are so trusting and convinced they are going to be safe from harm, they just walk right in."

He walked back to the first door, reached up to the valve and turned it on. He listened, as the gas hissed into the room, walked back down the staircase and out of the hotel. He walked down the street and over to the drugstore, where a man was waiting just outside. Holmes walked over to greet the man.

"Hello sir, how can I help you this morning?" Holmes tipped his fedora.

"Just need to have a prescription filled, can you have it for me this afternoon."

"That should not be a problem." He took the script and walked into the store, opened his books and wrote in the description of the medication and the man's name.

"It will be ready for you this afternoon." The receipt was provided to the customer.

The man turned and left the drugstore, leaving Holmes to tend to some paperwork and close the store just as soon as he had opened it. He walked back out of the store and left a message: Store temporarily closed for the remainder of the morning.

He walked back across the street to his hotel, opened the door, closing it behind him and rushed upstairs to the third floor. He reached up and closed the gas valve by turning the handle. He left the door closed and walked back over to the next door. There was a light whimpering coming from the crack in the door, Holmes banged on the door and screamed, "Don't worry Cynthia. It will not be much longer." He changed the tone of his voice to a scared voice of a woman, "Don't be scared." He pounded on the door.

He walked down the hallway and into the last room, where Julia was drugged. He reached into the drawer and pulled the needle back out. He gave her another injection of the sedative to ensure she would remain asleep. He finished and lifted her from the bed, carrying her into the basement.

He tied her to the chain bolted into the brick of the wall and left her, returning to the third floor. He walked into the first room and smelled through the crack of the door ensuring the gas had been cleared out through the ventilation system. He opened the door and discovered the man had covered his face with the cloth from his shirt, somehow surviving the gas. He was slowly moving across the floor, extremely disoriented from the fumes.

Holmes walked over to him. "Gerald, Gerald?" He repeated his name and smacked his face. "Are you there, Gerald?"

The gas had apparently seeped into his lungs and circulation, enough to cause him to become slightly paralyzed and discombobulated. Holmes walked over to the trapdoor, opened it and walked back to Gerald. He pulled him over to the chute and slid him inside. Gerald's body crashed and banged against the steel of the chute. Holmes then walked over to the door, closed it behind him and approached the room Cynthia was in.

He opened the door and rushed over to Cynthia, punching her as hard as he could, until her jaw was broken. She fell to her side and was knocked unconscious from Holmes' blow. Holmes slowly shook his hand, walked to the trap door, opened it and stopped. He reached down to his trousers, walked over to her and began urinating on her face. After finishing, Holmes slid her over to the door and pushed her inside. She fell down the chute the same way as her husband, crashing and banging against the metal of the chute.

Holmes then walked out of the room and back down to the basement, to surprise Julia when the sedative wore off. As the hours passed, Julia was lying on the floor and regaining consciousness. She opened her eyes to see that Holmes was standing near the large, steel dissection table busy at work with instruments in hand. Using the smaller instruments, he cut deep into the man's tissue, the man was still moving but unaware of what Holmes was doing to him, because of the effects of the gas.

Julia did not speak when she woke. She watched, as Holmes continued his work. He turned to see that she had awoken and pulled down his mask. "Oh you have woken my darling. Would you like to see what I have done?"

"Yes." She replied with excitement.

Holmes cranked the wheel at the base of the table and turned Gerald's body to an upright position. He adjusted a light on the wall and shined it directly on the body. Holmes then took out a syringe and injected adrenaline into the man, causing him to wake on the table. His eyes came into focus, "Why do you have me tied to the table?" He looked over, "What are you doing to my wife? You sick bastard!" He screamed, discovering his wife had been secured by large railroad spikes, which were hammered through her wrists and ankles securing her to the wall.

"Now, Julia, do you know how much pain the body can endure? This man has been gassed, dropped down a thirty foot steel chute, broken the bones in his legs. And, now, has had his stomach exposed by my surgical scalpel."

She looked on impressed and excited for his next move, almost like she was watching a horse race. The butterflies in her stomach fluttered.

"No, what are you doing?" The man panicked, "Why would you do this?" Gerald's pleading continued, "I have money in my suitcase. Please take the money and just let me and my wife go, I beg you!"

"Please, please, let me and my wife go, I beg you." Holmes imitated Gerald's shaky voice. "Gerald, I thank you for telling me where your money is; although, I would have found it, eventually. Now, you can relax and watch, as I introduce you to your new and improved wife!"

Holmes walked over to a table that had been turned upright and was against the wall, hiding what was on the other side of the table. Slowly, Holmes walked over to another light and turned it on, revealing an additional dissection table.

"Now, Gerald, are you ready? Is the anticipation killing you?" Holmes let out a sick and twisted laugh, turning the table to reveal Cynthia's body. Gerald screamed, as he discovered what Holmes had done to his wife. Her body had been completely cut and sawed open. Holmes had taken her face and peeled the skin off it, revealing the muscular facial features underneath. He had also retracted the chest and rib cage revealing Cynthia's insides.

Gerald began to sob, hysterically. Holmes quickly rushed back to him, "Now, Gerald, first we shall see what your legs and arms look like underneath. Julia is that where you would like me to begin?" Julia shook her head and clapped her hands together.

Holmes took a scalpel and began to slice up Gerald's legs with quick incisions. He then took a large metal scraper and peeled the skin from his leg, pulling in a downward motion. Gerald was now screaming in pain, as Holmes moved to the next position. He made an incision and cut into Gerald's arms, peeling the skin away in the same fashion. Afterwards, he walked over to Julia, placing the skin of Gerald's wife's face over hers and untied her bonds.

She stood up and kissed Holmes, then walked over to the metal table where all the remaining surgical instruments lay, "Show me what is used to open the chest. I want to see his heart beating inside him, while he is still alive."

Holmes reached for a saw and quickly cut into Gerald's chest, the saw cutting through the arteries sprayed blood across Holmes' white apron and Julia's face, covering her cheeks in blood. Holmes finished cutting open the chest and pulled a retractor from the floor and inserted it deep into Gerald's chest, spreading the rib cage, "He is almost dead!"

"Take this saw and open that section right there," pointing at an area of cartilage and fat covering the heart. As she peeled open the cartilage, Gerald screamed and finally lost consciousness from the pain. Julia peeled open the chest to reveal the still beating heart.

After a short time the heart slowed and stopped its pumping motion, "Gerald has finally endured all that the human body could suffer. I am always fascinated with how much the body can endure. How much pain it can be put through and still allow someone to survive for so long."

"I have never seen a live, beating heart before."

Holmes looked over at Julia, realizing she was truly his partner in business and in crime. He smiled and she turned to catch sight of it. She walked over to him removed her blouse and dress and took off Holmes' apron, next his shirt, and then his trousers. Holmes was surprised she was still wearing the woman's facial skin over her face. Standing nude in the spotlights, lighting up the basement, the two began to run their hands up and down their bodies, rubbing in the blood from the floor as they knelt down.

Holmes reached over to Julia's hips and pulled her in front of him. Julia was on her knees facing Cynthia's lifeless dissected body, as Holmes knelt behind her. He began to pull Julia's buttocks into his body from behind. The muscles of her ass pressing firmly up against Holmes' thighs. Pumping faster and harder, Julia began to moan and scream in a passionate rhythm to Holmes' motions. The two made love under the lights and in the presence of the freshly murdered bodies of Gerald and Cynthia, "This is my special gift to you. I wanted to give her something that no other person on Earth could provide."

She moaned in satisfaction, "I love it my dear!" She screamed, as she reached climax.

The coming year brought the World's fair to the Chicago area. Holmes had purchased a majority of advertisements for the hotel's grand opening from the money he found in Gerald's suitcase. Over the next few months, Holmes had prepared to manufacture multiple orders for medical universities and now hospitals.

With Julia's help, he was now moving into the medical market and not only providing entire human skeletons, but also various bone fragments used in instructing students and patients of the hospitals.

Holmes would be seen escorting a number of females into the hotel. Two women in a store watched as Holmes escorted the two women into his hotel, "That man is some sort of a playboy!" The woman poked at the other.

"Wouldn't it be nice?"

"Oh stop it, now!" The two women giggled and went about their work in the store.

As the World's Fair opened, hundreds of thousands of tourists began arriving in the Chicago area. Holmes and Julia were now operating the hotel with a few other unsuspecting employees, who had some ideas about what went on in the hotel in the late hours of the night. As Holmes continued his interviews, in the office next to the drug store, he decided to hire a woman named Minnie Williams. She was very confident and presented her work experience to be extremely efficient in accounting and bookkeeping. Holmes was also taken by her good looks and fashion sense.

He quickly made the decision to hire her and allow her to work in the drugstore, freeing up his time to focus more on the operations of the hotel. Holmes returned to the hotel, across from the drugstore, to inform Julia of his new hire. Julia was in the rear office on the first floor of the hotel.

Holmes walked into the office, "Julia, I have just hired a woman named Minnie Williams. She moved here with her sister, Nannie, and has been working as a school teacher. She understands bookkeeping and accounting, well. This will free up more time for me to be here, in the hotel, and with you."

Julia suddenly looked frustrated and dropped the pen she was writing with, "How can you hire another woman? Do you really think I do not know what is going on in that mind of yours? You plan on seducing her, just like you did to me."

"Darling, there is nothing to be worried about, besides what if I did? Would you object to me being with another woman?"

She shoved Holmes back from the desk and stormed out of the room, slamming the door behind her. Holmes stood at the desk and knew that she was going to become a distraction. He walked out of the office and into the lobby. Julia was nowhere to be seen. He walked up to the third floor and looked in the back room. Julia was not there, so he walked back into the lobby.

Minnie and her sister Nannie were standing near the front doors of the hotel's entrance. She was holding a suitcase and a small purse, "Minnie, this is a surprise, what are you doing here? You do not start till tomorrow." Minnie walked over to Holmes and stopped just in front of him. "I know what you want. I saw it in your eyes, as you interviewed me. You do not hide your intentions well, Dr. Holmes, and we need a place to stay."

Holmes, taken back by Minnie's directness, replied, "Well, this is a pleasant surprise."

"You said that before. Now, do you have a room for us, here?" Holmes, not ready to throw her directly into the mix, replied, "I have an apartment, above the drug store. You are welcome to stay there. Of course, you will have to pay for the water and electricity you use. But we can take that out of your pay for working at the drugstore."

"Fine, show us the way and we can get settled in." Holmes walked to the front doors, opened them and instructed them to follow him across the street to the drugstore.

"This is the apartment, there is the bedroom, in there is the washroom and in here, is a small kitchen."

"This will be just fine," Standing next to her sister, Nannie, who was just as beautiful as Minnie. Minnie saw that Holmes was looking at Nannie, the same way he looked at her in the interview and stepped between them, "Dr. Holmes, allow us to settle in. Afterwards, maybe we could interest you in an invitation for dinner and drinks?"

Holmes looked intrigued at the invitation and replied, "I look forward to it. Should we say around eight?"

"Eight o'clock it is, Dr. Holmes."

He walked over to the door of the apartment, turned and lowered his hat at the two ladies. "Good day ladies." Holmes returned to the hotel and walked into the basement. He was upset at Julia's reaction from before and paused at the bottom of the staircase, picked up a shovel and threw it across the room it smashed against one of the large metal acid tanks.

He made his way to the dissection table and stood over the body of a man who had been tied with leather bindings to his wrists and ankles. Holmes walked to the top of the table and began turning a large wheel stretching the man's body, the man screamed in pain. He took a long piece of rope and wrapped it around the man's head, tying the rope as tight as he could, to restrict the man from screaming.

Holmes continued to stretch the ropes, contorting the man's body. The bones in the man's arms and legs cracked, as the tension increased. Finally, the man lost consciousness and went still. Holmes checked the man's pulse and realized that he had been put through too much. His heart must have given out. Holmes proceeded to cut the man's limbs into pieces and throw them into the quicklime pits.

After finishing with the body parts, he cleaned up at the washbasin in the basement, placed his apron on a hook near the door of the basement and walked back up to the hotel lobby. Julia was standing near the desk at the front of the lobby. He walked over to her and stopped just in front of her.

"So are you still upset Julia?"

She did not respond at first. Holmes moved in closer and used his charm and charisma to make her smile, "I'm sorry. One thing I do know is that you are your own person and how can I expect to keep some twisted control on someone that needs to maintain his freedoms."

Holmes hugged her, "Would you care to join me upstairs?"

She smiled and Holmes led her to the third floor bedroom, at the end of the hallway, closing the door behind him. A few moments later, Holmes emerged from the room holding a syringe. He closed the door behind him and made his way to the first chamber of the third floor. He opened the door and walked back to the room where Julia was, walked over the bed and pulled her motionless body from the bed.

Dragging her into the first chamber and closing the door, Holmes reached up to the handle above the door. He slowly turned the nozzle, releasing gas into the chamber. He began to cry, as the gas continued to flow into the room. His emotions clashed, he was torn between letting the gas continue to run or to shut it off.

He walked away from the door, down the stairs and out of the hotel, leaving the gas running into the chamber.

He stood out in front of the hotel and waited. After thirty minutes passed, he walked back into the hotel and up to the room where Julia was. He turned off the gas and walked back down to the lobby of the hotel. Many of the workers had left for the day and there was one clerk behind the lobby's check in desk

"Is there a problem, doctor? You look a little disturbed."

"No, there is not a problem. Take the rest of the evening off, I can take things from here." The man behind the desk quickly wrote down his hours worked for the day and walked to the front doors.

He stopped and turned to Holmes, "Sir, I hope you try and have a good evening." Holmes did not respond, as the employee walked out of the hotel. Holmes walked back up the stairs to the third floor and opened the door to the first chamber. Julia's body lay motionless on the floor near the window. He walked over to her body, picked her up and carried her to the basement.

The remainder of the evening, Holmes prepared her body for preservation. Holmes walked over to the door leading up from the basement and hung his apron on the hook. He looked back, one last time at Julia's body and walked out the door, closing it and securing the lock.

'More is Always Better'

Holmes arrived at the apartment, above the drug store, at precisely eight o'clock. Nannie was just outside smoking a long cigarette and greeted Holmes with a seductive voice, "Hello Doctor!"

"Hello Nannie, how are you doing this evening?"

"Better, now that you're here." Holmes reached for her hand, raised it to his lips, kissing it softly. She smiled at him and dropped her cigarette to the ground. Holmes extinguished it with the sole of his shoe, "What a gentleman you are, Dr. Holmes." Nannie exclaimed, as they both walked to the upstairs apartment's door, Holmes followed closely behind.

As they entered the apartment, Minnie turned from the stove to greet them, "Well, it is the good doctor himself. Would you like to start the evening with a drink?" Holmes took off his hat and jacket, hanging them on the hook near the door, "I would kill for a drink right now."

"Be careful doctor, you do not want to use such harsh words around the ladies." Nannie replied.

"Pardon me, Nannie." Holmes gave Nannie an evil grin, causing Nannie to become unsettled by the look. Minnie walked over with a small glass and handed it to Holmes. He raised his glass to Minnie and Nannie, "Here's to new friendships." Nannie and Minnie raised their glasses, tapping them with Holmes' glass.

The three walked into the main room and sat on the couches, surrounding a long wooden table. Holmes looked at the two and wondered what their intentions were for the evening. Was this going to be an uneventful dinner, filled with cliché conversations, or would the two present some surprise to Holmes' fantastical macabre?

"So, how is business at the drugstore?" Minnie inquired.

Holmes took a sip of his liquor, "Business is excellent. There are a number of clients, who is spreading the word for me."

"Well, that's good for saving on advertising costs, correct?" Nannie added.

"Yes it is, Nannie. And with the hotel just across the street, travelers are also aware of the drug store. That opens up another opportunity, for me, at least."

Holmes informed the two, "My intention is to make my hotel the most attractive hotel in Chicago during the World's Fair. There is a lot of money to be made in Chicago, right now."

"That is very impressive, doctor." Minnie replied, pouring another round of drinks.

He spoke about his additional business ventures, "I am also operating a business from the basement of the hotel." He waited to see if the two would inquire further, wondering what their reactions would be upon hearing his other operation.

Nannie placed her glass on the table, "What type of additional business?"

"I am processing cadavers into skeletons, for sale to the nation's medical universities, schools, and hospitals for educational purposes."

"Well, Dr. Holmes, a business of making skeletons for medical universities and facilities, sounds dreadful." Nannie stated.

"Well, I have been a medical doctor for years and the market needs to have someone supplying the necessary educational materials. Once you get past the skeleton's preparations, it is really not all that difficult."

"Where do you get the bodies?" Minnie inquired.

"I get the bodies from the morgue and hospitals in the area." Holmes replied, with a less than convincing response for Minnie to accept. She gave Holmes a strange look, which caught his eye. Holmes raised his eyebrow at her, tipped his glass, raising it to his lips and took a drink.

After the three finished their dinner, salad, lamb chops and potatoes, they walked from the apartment and over to the hotel. Holmes took them up to the third floor, only showing them some of the completed rooms, keeping them from seeing the gas chambers. He walked them through the kitchen and out the back, into a long hallway leading down to a larger dining room.

There was a billiards table and a bar stocked with all the finest top shelf liquor money could buy, "Wow, Dr. Holmes, I must say this is quite the establishment." Minnie exclaimed. "My father was a wealthy realtor and left me his entire estate. He would be quite taken by a room such as this!" Minnie walked behind the bar and pulled three glasses from under it, "Can I fix you two a drink?"

"Yes thank you that would be great." Holmes replied. Nannie walked over to a bar stool and sat just beside Holmes.

"Here you are." Minnie handed Nannie the first glass and Holmes the second.

The three continued drinking late into the evening. Holmes was becoming extremely forward in his advances towards both women, sitting in between both of them, on an extravagant couch. They had a bottle of whiskey placed on the table in front of them and were now drinking right from the bottle, passing it between the three of them.

Minnie, holding the bottle, reached over to Holmes' chin, took a drink and kissed Holmes, exchanging the liquor from her mouth to his. Holmes swallowed and continued to kiss Minnie. She stopped and put the bottle on the table in front of them. Minnie reached down to Holmes' zipper, laughing while she opened it, reaching inside his trousers.

She lowered her head down to Holmes' lap, as Nannie moved in closer to Holmes. She kissed him and reached for the bottle, sitting on the table in front of them, giving Holmes a drink and then taking one for herself, placing the bottle back on the table and returning to kissing Holmes. She stopped after a moment and looked into Holmes' eyes, "Would you like us both, at the same time, Doctor? Or, better yet, how would you like to give me an examination?"

Holmes smiled and continued to kiss Nannie. Minnie stood up and removed her dress, returning to sit on Holmes' lap. She reached down and began sliding up and down on his lap. Holmes felt himself slide inside Minnie, as she released a moan. Nannie continued to kiss Holmes and rub her fingers across his chest.

Minnie moved up and down on Holmes' lap, moving faster and faster. She let out a loud scream that echoed throughout the room and into the hallway leading from the dining room. After her climax, she stood up and reached for the bottle on the table, watching, as Nannie climbed on Holmes' lap, continuing where Minnie had left off. Minnie took the bottle and walked around the room, turning off individual lights throughout, lighting candles in their place. The room was now dimly lit by candlelight, as Holmes and Nannie continued on the couch.

Nannie was riding Holmes on the couch, continuing to move faster and faster, as Holmes reached around placing his hands on her back. He pulled her down harder and harder into his lap. Nannie rose up, above Holmes, and arched her back in satisfaction. Minnie walked behind the bar, reached into a drawer and pulled a knife from it. Nannie was lying on top of Holmes with her back turned to her, as Minnie walked slowly over to the pair. She was now extremely jealous of Holmes' interest in her sister, little did Holmes know about the jealousy Nannie's sister carried for her.

She stopped at the table just in front of the couch and raised the liquor bottle above her head. Holmes looked up and was startled to see Minnie, standing over them with a bottle raised in the air. Minnie waited till Holmes looked up and then smashed the bottle over her sister's head. Shards of glass smashed off Nannie's head and scattered over their bodies.

In a furious rage, Minnie screamed and jumped onto her sister's back. Holmes, at the last minute, moved from underneath Nannie's body, as her sister plunged the blade repeatedly into her sister's body.

Minnie screamed, as she stood up breathing heavily, covered in her sister's blood. She looked at Holmes and then back down at her sister's bloody body, slicing at it, blood gushing from the wounds spraying onto her and Holmes.

The blood spatters covered the couch and the wall behind it. Holmes unprepared for the event looked on with confusion, but also a curiosity, "Where did that come from?" Holmes inquired.

Minnie dropped the knife to the floor, walked over to the bar and pulled another bottle from the shelf, "Well, you are the doctor, figure it out." She opened the bottle and took a long drink from it.

"We are going to have to get rid of the body. What was the reasoning behind that?"

"I have hated my sister, ever since she was born. My parents began paying her all the attention. They gave her better gifts, better toys, took her on the vacations and left me with our grandparents, because they thought I enjoyed spending more time with them, rather than my own parents!" Minnie walked from behind the bar and over to her sister's body. "She always got daddy's attention. Daddy was always going into her room at night, instead of mine. I mean look at me, Dr. Holmes. I am much more woman than she will ever be!" Minnie spit on her sister's motionless body.

Minnie was surprised at Holmes' calm reaction to the whole situation, "Well, we need to get rid of her body, Dr. Holmes."

"What do you suggest Minnie? She was your sister and your kill."

Minnie looked at her sister's body and replied, "Let's take her to the lake, weigh her body and throw her in. I want to see her sink in the water, below."

"We will need to hurry, if we are going to get back and clean up this mess, before tomorrow." The blood from the gruesome killing was spattered on the wall and collecting in a puddle, on the floor, beneath the couch.

"Minnie, I have an establishment to think about, not to mention the consequences of being caught in an act such as this." Holmes took Nannie's legs, pulled her from the couch and slid her near the table. Walking over to a closet in the dining hall, he opened it and pulled out a large piece of canvas tarp and proceeded to wrap the body in the canvas tarp. He covered the remaining parts of the body in the canvas and pulled it over to the rear entrance of the hotel.

Minnie looked at Holmes and was now beginning to see where his plan was going. Holmes walked to the bar and poured a drink, raised the glass towards Minnie and threw back his head, drinking the entire contents of the glass. "I'll pull the carriage around to the rear of the hotel. We can load the body in the back and take it to the lake." Minnie and Holmes spent the remainder of the night cleaning up the blood in the dining room.

The blood was easy to clean from the wall and the floor, underneath the couch, but cleaning the couch was a different story. Holmes was exhausted and wanted to take the body to the basement, but Minnie was not having it, "Let's just go take care of the body. We can return to the hotel and get some rest, afterwards."

Holmes and Minnie rode out to the lake in the middle of the night, taking back streets and dirt roads leading out to the lake, in order to avoid suspicions. When they arrived at the lake, Holmes pulled the horse's reins, bringing the carriage to a stop, pulling the brake and locking it into position.

They carried the body to the dock, which extended far from the shoreline, drug the body the remainder of the dock and reached its end. Holmes weighed the body down with some rope and cement blocks, tying them to her ankles. What Minnie was unaware of, was the additional rope Holmes had secured to the dock and Minnie's leg. This would allow him to return and recover the body to be cremated at a later time.

He slid the body to the edge of the dock and pushed it into the water. The body splashed, as Minnie watched her sister's body bob up and down and then sank deep into the darkness of the water. Holmes and Minnie returned to the hotel, where they finished some additional cleaning in the dining room.

Holmes took the bloody rags to the basement and threw them into the furnace. He quickly returned to the dining room and poured another drink. Afterwards, he walked from the dining hall, into the lobby of the hotel and wrote a note to the hotel staff instructing them of the tasks that needed to be completed the next day.

The following day, Holmes woke to find Minnie had already left the room, walked over to the washbasin, washed his face and dried it with a clean towel. He threw the towel onto the bed, walked to the closet and dressed for the afternoon. He had slept for the better part of the morning. Holmes walked into the lobby, to see if any guests had checked in.

The first part of the morning was slow, so he dismissed the staff and the desk clerk for the remainder of the day. He called the staff to the lobby and announced, "The remainder of the month will be slow and I will not require many of you to be here."

One of the staff members stepped forward, "But what of the World's Fair? It should bring in a steady flow of guests?"

"It may and if it does I will call you in, as required." They walked from the hotel, "I bid you each a good day." Each of the employees left the hotel. He retreated to the third floor and joined Minnie in the last room on the left. He walked slowly into the room, remembering the time he spent with Julia. Minnie was lying on the bed. Holmes reached into the desk drawer and pulled out a syringe.

Raising the sedative bottle, he inserted the needle into the bottle and drew out a large amount from the bottle, and reached down to Minnie's arm. Holding it gently, he inserted the needle into her vein. She hardly noticed the needle prick, turned, looked up at Holmes and smiled. She was soon sedated and Holmes stood, looking at her, as she slept on the bed. He walked from the room, down the hallway, on the third floor and into the hotel lobby. As he stood by the front desk, two couples walked through the door of the hotel.

"Welcome, guests. Are you looking for accommodations?" Holmes stood upright in his finely tailored suit.

"Yes we are. Your hotel comes highly recommended at the social club, just around the corner."

"Well, you are in luck. We have plenty of rooms available. Would you like two rooms, or will it be more than that?"

A man stepped forward and replied, "Two rooms will be fine."

Holmes walked behind the desk and opened the registry book. "Can I have your names, please?"

"I am Ben Pietzel, and this is Jeptha Howe. This is Emmeline Cigrand, and Emily Van Tassel." Ben Pitezel shook Holmes' hand. Emily immediately caught Holmes' eye, being young and dressed very innocent.

"Where are you from?" Holmes asked.

"We come from Dwight, Illinois. I was a businessman and worked with insurance policies, for a brief time."

Holmes was interested in Ben's experience with insurance. He avoided showing them the third floor and directed them to the rooms, in the rear of the first floor. "Here are the rooms, there are washrooms across from the rooms should you need to freshen up. I can have a lunch ready for you, within the hour. Would you all care to join me, in the dining hall, later?"

"That would be great." Ben replied.

"Now, if you will excuse me, I have some work to attend to." Holmes excused himself. "Oh and please stay off the third floor, it is currently under reconstruction and very unsafe to occupy. I would hate for anyone to come under harm in my hotel."

He returned to the lake to recover Minnie's body. Pulling the rope and recovering the body, a man watched from a distance. Holmes untied the ropes and placed the corpse into his carriage. A few couples passed by; however, the majority of people were unaware of his cargo. The man who had been watching from a distance, climbed onto his carriage. Holmes left the lake and after a short ride, pulled the carriage to the rear of his hotel, unloading Minnie's corpse and taking it in through a rear doorway.

The man, following Holmes parked his carriage a safe distance and followed. Holmes laid the body on the basement floor, returning to the rear entrance, watching as the man approached. He slid behind the door, waiting, in silence. The man looked up and down the alley way, rushing for the door. Peering around the entrance, he placed his first foot on the step. Moving in through the door, Holmes grabbed the man's over coat and threw him down the stairs. The man crashed against the cement floor, his face crushed by the force of the fall.

Holmes walked from the hall and down into the basement. He closed the sliding, steel door and locked it behind him. Holmes walked into the center of the basement and began to prepare a row of skeletons for shipment. After sealing the crate of skeletons, he turned and walked over to a chair sitting against the wall. Sitting in the chair was Julia's preserved body. He sat next to her and leaned his head on her shoulder, reached his arm over and ran it up her leg, sitting up close to her face, he leaned in and kissed her cheek.

Holmes lay next to her for a moment, stood and walked over to the shelves he had recently constructed. There were large glass jars on the shelves, containing various human organs; hearts, livers, lungs, kidneys and other organs, which Holmes, in addition to the skeletons, intended to begin selling to medical universities and hospitals. He slowly ran his hand along the bottles of organs, turned and looked back at Julia's body.

Minnie's corpse and the man were slid into the crematorium and burnt to ashes after Holmes had fired up the flames in the furnace. His eyes glowed as the orange glow from the fire reflected in his eyes. He smiled at the scene, knowing that there was no evidence left behind, yet again.

He returned to the first floor, and into the kitchen, to prepare a lunch for his new guests. Holmes opened the fridge, reached past some of the various trays and plates inside, pulling out a long tray of strangely colored meats. Holmes had prepared the sandwich meats himself, from various parts of muscles from his last victim. Bending over the tray, he took a deep breath smelling the contents of the tray.

After removing some of the slices of the meat, he prepared some bread and carefully arranged the meats on the breads. He placed some salad in some smaller dishes and walked the plates and sandwiches into the dining hall. A few minutes passed. Ben, Jeptha, Emmeline and Emily entered the dining hall, pulled the chairs from under the table and sat down, ready to enjoy the meal Holmes had prepared for them. The group was unaware of the meat content in the sandwiches. The group immediately picked up their food and began eating.

"Hmm this is delicious, Dr. Holmes." Howe replied, after swallowing the first bite. "What kind of meat is this? It goes great with the mustard."

Holmes looked up from the table and replied, "The mustard gives the roast beef an additional kick." Holmes continued to watch the group eat their meal and smiled, sitting at the end of the table. After the guests finished, Holmes began discussing his business plans with local hospitals, and rest homes, to expand the option of life insurance for patients. Ben Pitezel was suddenly interested, since he was recently in the life insurance business.

"Dr. Holmes, with your connections in the medical industry and my experience with life insurance, I think that it would greatly benefit the both of us to work together on this venture."

"Well, certainly Mr. Pitezel." Holmes replied.

"Dr. Holmes my wife's children, Alice, Nellie, and Howard will be joining us. I hope that will not be an issue?"

"That will not be an issue, because the more the merrier." Holmes replied, thinking about the life insurance schemes he had thought up and carried out back in Michigan. He made a great deal of money by convincing and manipulating people into taking out life insurance policies. He would then manipulate the documents, leaving him the beneficiary in the policies.

By killing the people he had the life insurance policies on, he would get rid of the bodies and replace the bodies with cadavers, making it look like an accident. The cadavers would be disfigured, and burned. Some would have died from natural causes, throwing off any signs of foul play. Holmes decided to speak to Ben Pietzel, later in the evening, to bring him up to speed on the real intentions of his insurance scheme.

Ben and Holmes sat in the dining hall, at the bar, sharing a bottle of aged whiskey, "Dr. Holmes, I am in agreement. Your plan is actually quite a brilliant idea. You obtain the bodies from the morgues and local hospitals. I will then arrange the insurance policies and manipulate them to make you and me the beneficiaries, and we will collect the payouts from the life insurance companies." Ben raised his glass towards Holmes and they both took a drink, sealing the deal with a handshake.

'Murder Castle'

Pitezel's family had arrived to join him at the hotel for the World's fair, which was now in full swing. Minnie was running the drugstore full time and becoming frustrated with Holmes' new interest in the young woman Emily, who was now working in the hotel. Holmes was admitting a large amount of guests to his hotel. People in the neighborhood were now calling it the castle.

Some of the hotel employees were noticing the guests checking in, but not checking out. They whispered their quiet rumors of the suspicious activities taking place. Other employees were well aware of the events taking place in the hotel's basement, but were paid large salaries, happy to be receiving the additional money and remaining quiet about the operations.

An outspoken and ambitious employee approached Holmes on the first floor, "Excuse me, Dr. Holmes."

"Yes, Dan, what can I do for you?" Holmes' response was quick and harsh.

The young employee was intimidated by Holmes, "I notice a large number of guests checking into the hotel, but I never see anyone checking out. Some of the other employees have their concerns, as well."

"Dan, I understand the concern. The hotel guests are usually in a hurry to get home, or to their next destination, and end up checking out late at night or early in the morning. This is before you or the other employees have arrived for the morning shift, or have left from the evening shift."

"Oh, well, that makes sense, I guess. Why would anyone want to check out so early in the morning though? It would seem they want to sleep in and get some good rest for their travels?"

Holmes thought Dan would be more naive or, at least remembers the warnings he was provided when he decided to hire him, "Dan, do you remember when I hired you, the main thing that I informed you, in order for you to work here?"

"Yes, sir, you told me that you wanted your guests to have their privacy and that there were many other competitors, in the hotel industry, that would be looking to get to you and obtain information about how you run your businesses so successfully."

"That is correct, Dan." Holmes walked over and placed his hand around Dan's shoulder, walked him towards the front of the hotel and then suddenly turned to the basement door. "Now, Dan, you have been doing a great job working in the hotel. I want to show you some additional business ventures that I work on, down in the basement."

Holmes unlocked the door to the basement and slid it to the right, "I am thinking of offering you a promotion. Would you be interested?"

Colby Van Wagoner

"Yes, Dr. Holmes, I would be very interested indeed."

"Excellent, now would you care to join me below?"

Dan walked through the door and entered the basement, Holmes following behind him, closing the door and walking into the dimly lit basement. Holmes led Dan over to the rows of metal hangers where he had hung the skeletons. The steel hangers were empty and Dan slowly investigated them, "What are these used for, Dr. Holmes?"

Holmes walked slowly past the dissection table, picking up a scalpel from the metal tray beside it, "Those, my dear innocent, boy are for hanging skeletons and preparing them for distribution to medical universities and hospitals."

Dan turned and replied, "Where do you get the bodies for the skeletons?" He stepped back, beginning to get a bad feeling about entering the basement. He turned and saw the large tanks to his right and looked to the left and discovering the dissection table.

The familiar voice entered Holmes' head, speaking calmly and instructed, "You know what needs to be done." For the first time, Holmes answered the voice while in the company of another, "I know what must be done. That is why the boy is here."

"Who are you speaking to, Dr. Holmes?"

Holmes shook his head, realizing that for the first time, he spoke out loud to the voice and answered the questions aloud, and in front of another person. He coughed, "No one, Dan. Well, actually . . ." He was now comfortable admitting his confusion, "I hear a voice from time to time, a comforting voice. I can assure you, no one will hear this. This is between you and me."

"Of course, Dr. Holmes, you have treated me very well and I appreciate you hiring me to work in your hotel."

Holmes scoffed, "I get the bodies from the guests, who check into the hotel and then never check out. Where do you think I would get them?"

Dan turned to see Dr. Holmes directly behind him, lifting his right hand up to Dan's throat and pressing the scalpel against it.

"So, Dan, are you still interested in your promotion?"

Dan replied in a shaky tone, "Yes, Dr. Holmes, I am." His voice cracked and his muscles were trembling, uncontrollably.

Holmes reached up with his left hand and grabbed Dan behind the back of the neck. Dan was shaking and trembling, Holmes took the scalpel slowly pressing it into Dan's neck. Dan shrieked out, Holmes quickly dug the scalpel into his neck and thrust it to the right, cutting Dan's throat open and spraying blood across his face. Holmes let the body fall to the basement floor, as it twitched and slowly became motionless.

Holmes took the body, lifted it to the dissection table and proceeded to dissect the main organs, placing each organ into jars and arranging them carefully on the shelves. After he finished, he lit the cremation chamber in the center of the basement, the flames lighting up the room with a bright orange glow. Holmes pulled the table over to the oven and slid the body into the flames, "I won't need you for the promotion, Dan, and I have no open orders for skeletons, at the moment. So, your fate is the furnace."

The voice returned to remind Holmes, "You and I have come along way, together."

"If we have, then why have you not revealed who it is you are?" He yelled out.

"Yes, I do believe it is time." The voice paused, as Holmes waited impatiently for the mysterious voice to respond, "I am Lucifer, the devil and I have been with you since you were born. Your father must have somehow known this, which is why you received the ill punishments from him." Holmes was slightly shocked. The voice continued, "You must need some time to comprehend this newly acquired knowledge of discovering who I am. I will give you some time to reflect." The voice faded.

Holmes continued receiving more orders and worked tirelessly preparing skeletons, covering up their disappearances, and swindling insurance claims with Ben Pitezel. As the Chicago Worlds Fair was nearing its end, Ben and Holmes had swindled over twenty couples and other lonely women into taking out life insurance policies. After the couples and the women would take out the policies and sign them over to Holmes, he would create fatal accidents, explosions, fires and then collect on the life insurance policies.

With his growing wealth, Holmes was now traveling the country. He stayed in Fort Worth Texas for a period of time, contending with Minnie and Nannie's property; however, the authorities were questioning his intentions of constructing a new hotel on the property and the documents he possessed, claiming that the railroad heiresses had signed over the property to him. The documentation and signatures were not matching up. Before the authorities could question him further, he fled Texas.

Holmes was still collecting large sums of money from his business selling skeletons and organs to the universities and hospitals for research and other uses. Holmes used the finances to travel to St. Louis, and complete another swindle. He was arrested and after being released, decided to return to Chicago and work on the Ben Pitezel situation.

Holmes and Ben were in his office counting out the cash they collected from the last payout, "Now, here is your cut and this is mine."

"That's only $2000! Why should you keep the other $5000 and I only get two?"

"Ben, my good man, you need to understand the amount of work that is involved on my end. I am going into people's houses, setting up these accidents, killing the victims and replacing them with cadavers. That, Ben, is more work for one man and that, Ben, is why my cut will be more."

"I guess, Holmes. What am I supposed to say about it?"

"Well, I have an idea that would get you more of the money."

"How is that?" Ben inquired.

"Take out a life insurance policy on you, your wife, and your three kids. I can take cadavers over to the Holton residence and set it up to look like an accidental fire. I will collect on the life insurance and you can get a major split from it."

"How much would that be, Dr. Holmes?"

"I think about ten thousand dollars!" Holmes counted out the remaining split of the cash and slid it across the table to Ben.

Ben placed his hand on his chin thinking for a moment, looking down at the money before him and then replied, "I am in. I'll file the life insurance policies tomorrow and we can finish up with this, next week."

"That sounds good, Ben."

After they finished up the arrangement, Jeptha Howe walked into the office,

"Holmes, there is a gentleman here to see you." A man came through the door and stepped into the light. It was Ned Conner, Julia's ex-husband. He walked into the room and removed his hat.

"Hello, Dr. Holmes, I need to know where Julia is."

Holmes lay back in his chair and stretched his hands behind his head, "Ned, let me see, Julia went back to Michigan. Things did not work out between us."

Ned looked up at Holmes with a perplexed look, "Is that so? Just where did she have to go?"

"She went back to her family's house."

"Is that so Holmes? Because her family is dead, she killed them!" Ned raised his voice, "Now tell me, Holmes, where she went? Where is she?"

"I do not like your tone, Ned."

Holmes stood up from his chair and walked from behind the desk. He reached into his jacket, pulling his revolver from its holster, cocked it and lifted it in Ned's direction. Ned stood without a reaction to Holmes.

"What are you going to do, Holmes, shoot me with all the guests in the hotel? What will you do with my body if you shoot me?"

"Holmes, please stop it!" Ben exclaimed as he stood up and lifted Holmes arm. Ned ran from the room, down the hallway, and out of the hotel. Holmes was furious, pushing Ben away and rushing out of the office. He ran through the hotel and up to the third floor of the hotel, walked into the back room slamming the door behind him.

On the bed, Minnie lay motionless. Holmes paced back and forth in the room, wondering if Ned would go to the police. What would he do if Ned did? He needed an alibi, someone to place him out of town for a while. He looked over at Minnie, walked to the bed and shook her, she did not move so Holmes shook her again. He reached up and felt her pulse but there was nothing there.

The sedative must have been too strong but he was too distracted to care about it. He would have to get rid of her and her remains due to the recent events in Texas. Minnie also suspected him of being responsible for the disappearance of Emmeline. If she ever found out he was seeking to take over her property she may report him to the authorities, "Do not worry, my son." The voice returned to his head.

Holmes screamed out, "Do not worry? That is easy for you to say, you're just a voice in my head. I have to contend with being discovered and captured."

Holmes went downstairs and found Ben in the office, "You need to take out those life insurance policies and have them ready tomorrow morning. Sign me as the beneficiary and we will have Jeptha help me with the cadavers at the Holton house. After that I'll burn the house and collect the insurance. After that, we split ways, I'm going to Boston."

"Sounds good, but are you not worried about this Ned character?"

"Not at all, because by the time the police or investigators figure this out, I'll be long gone."

The following day, Holmes and Howe put two adult cadavers and three children in the Holton home.

The home was still abandoned and under Holmes name, so there was no curiosity raised when Holmes was seen going into and leaving the house. Holmes walked over to the drugstore and placed a note on the door, after collecting most of the medication and money. The note read: drugstore closed due to renovations, open soon.

He then returned to the hotel, and dismissed all the employees, except for one of the caretakers and a janitor. He would keep the janitor on staff, because he was still an immigrant working on getting his papers and becoming a citizen. The employee understood saying anything about the operations of the hotel would mean his job and deportation. He also knew more than the other employees when it came to the hotel's operations.

Holmes rushed to the bank, withdrew his savings and returned to the hotel vault. He placed his gun into his desk and walked out of the office. He went up to the third floor, slid Minnie's body from the bed, down the hall and into one of the gas chambers. He opened the door to one of the chutes leading to the basement, pushing her body into the chute and closed the chute's door.

Holmes needed to think of the way he was going to get out of this mess. It was now becoming a major distraction and the possibility of becoming exposed and captured was near. He decided to concoct a backup plan. He would take Ben's wife and kids to the third floor when Ben was in hiding. Ben needed to stay out of sight, after the fire and leave town after the whole thing went down.

The following morning, Ben returned with the life insurance policies. Holmes took the papers and locked them in his safe, along with the rest of his money. Ben agreed to cross town and stay in a hotel on the north side of Chicago. His wife and kids would stay in Holmes' hotel. Holmes went to the Holton's residence and torched the building with the cadavers inside. The house quickly went up in flames and Holmes returned to the third floor of the hotel, watching the house burn in the distance.

That evening, Holmes was in the dining hall when Mrs. Pitezel and her three children walked in, "Dr. Holmes, I am worried about Ben. He has been gone all day. Do you know where he has gone?"

Holmes knew where Ben was staying and put his plan into action, "Carrie, Ben came to me with a plan to take out life insurance policies on you and the children. He then wanted me to kill you all, leaving him to collect on the life insurance policies."

She looked at Holmes, seeing the sincerity in his eyes and broke down into tears. The children rushed to their mother, hugged her, attempting to console her. Holmes hugged her and put his arm on her back, rubbing up and down slowly.

"I know this is hard and I know where he is staying. If you want me to confront him, I will do that and convince him to turn himself into the police."

She wiped her tears and looked up at Holmes. "No, Dr. Holmes, I want you to kill him! Take your revolver and kill him for me. He can threaten me, but not my children."

Holmes told Mrs. Pitezel, "Stay at the hotel with the children, go up to the third floor and hide in the back room. Ben may return, to check on them and see if I had killed them."

She agreed and walked up the staircase to the third floor. Holmes quickly retreated to his office, retrieved his revolver and medical bag. He walked out of the hotel room, stepped into his carriage and rode off to the north side of Chicago. Holmes arrived at the hotel, where Ben was staying, and unassumingly entered the hotel. He approached the desk clerk and inquired where Ben was staying.

"Excuse me, sir; can I get the room number for Ben Pitezel?"

"Yes sir, room twenty-two, on the second floor."

Holmes walked to the staircase, up the stairs and down the hall to Pitezel's room. He arrived at the door and knocked. The door opened and Pitezel stood at the door.

"Can I come in? I need to talk to you."

"Come in, Dr. Holmes." Ben motioned for him to come in.

Holmes walked over to the desk and placed his medical bag on the table. Pitezel walked over to the window and opened the drapes, staring out at the horizon and the city beneath it. Holmes reached into his bag pulling out a rag and a bottle of chloroform, walked over behind Ben, poured some liquid into the rag and wrapped his arm around his neck, covering his mouth with the rag.

Ben fell to the floor. Holmes kept his hands over Pitezel's nose and mouth, keeping his airways restricted. After a few minutes, Pitezel stopped breathing. Holmes stood up put the rag and the bottle of chloroform back into his medical bag. He pulled out a small bottle of fluid spraying it over Pitezel's face. The smell of sulfuric acid filled the room. Holmes walked to the window and opened it, attempting to remove the chemical smell. He left the hotel room, walked down to the back staircase and left the hotel through the rear entrance.

Holmes returned to the hotel, walked up to the third floor and opened the door to the back room, "Quick Carrie, it is Ben, he is here and he has a pistol, come hide the children in the room down the hall. She rushed the kids down the hallway and into one of the chambers on the left. Holmes shut the door and led her to the next room.

"Now you hide in here, I will stop him." Holmes reached for his holster, pulled out his revolver and pushed her into the chamber, closing the door behind her. He put the revolver back into his holster and walked down the hallway, descending the staircase to the lobby on the first floor.

The police and fire brigades had responded to the fire at the Holton residence. Most of the squad, and fire brigades had been called to the fire. Word spread through the precinct that it was the old Holton residence which was recently taken over by Holmes. After the fire was extinguished, some of the officers returned to the station to inform the detectives there were bodies at the residence and they were all killed in the fire. They were now charged with investigating the fire and questioning Holmes about his whereabouts during the event.

In Philadelphia, Detective Frank P. Geyer sat at his desk. Frank stared ahead, at his case load with a vacant gaze in his eyes. He wondered what their stories were. Everyone's victim tells a story, along with the crime scenes he investigates. How was he going to put the pieces of the investigations together to find those stories?

Colby Van Wagoner

He worked Philadelphia precinct three's homicide department, and was very close friends with the majority of the officers and detectives of the surrounding state law enforcement agencies. He was also involved with the notorious Pinkertons. It was a grim and tedious process to have multiple victims without any leads or evidence to suggest a suspect. He had multiple unsolved cases which he kept in a pile on the desk to his left, unsolved and taunting his mind repetitively. The majority of cases was missing persons and deaths caused by mysterious circumstances.

One of the lead detectives from one of the Chicago precincts was on the telephone consulting with the infamous detective Geyer, regarding the rash of missing person's cases accumulating in the areas. After consulting with Detective Geyer, a lead detective who was part of a large team of detectives charged with investigating the numerous missing persons turned. He addressed the team, "We have all this, so far."

He pointed to boards and desks surrounded by scattered piles of files and photos. The photos were grainy black and white pictures of brutally murdered women and men, "Let's get to work!"

Meanwhile, upstairs in Holmes' hotel he had already had the gas running for over an hour in the room. The children lay on the floor, motionless but still alive, as Holmes walked towards the room where Mrs. Pitezel was. He went to reach up and turn on the gas, when a voice called out from the hotel lobby.

"Hello, is anyone here?"

Holmes rushed and shut off the gas in the first room, straightened his suit and went down the stairs into the lobby. Holmes discovered a single detective, standing near the front desk, looking through the hotel's registry.

"Detective, I am Dr. H.H. Holmes, how can I help you?"

The detective was watching Holmes very carefully, as he moved across the lobby, "Dr. Holmes. I'm afraid the residence around the corner has caught fire and burned, nothing was saved."

"Oh my, is everyone all right?"

"Why would you ask if everyone was all right?" Holmes felt he was on the verge of being found out and was now cornered.

"Well, I was renting the house to Ben Pitezel and his family."

"What are the names of the other family members?" Holmes appeared a bit nervous, as the detective wrote down the information on a note pad.

"There is Mrs. Pitezel and her children, Alice, Nellie and Howard."

The detective walked from the front desk and started to look up the stairs and down the hallways leading to the dining hall and the kitchen.

"Do you have any other guests staying in the hotel, at the moment?"

Holmes reached for his side, walking towards the detective, "No, right now there is no one staying here."

"That's a bit odd. What about your employees, where are they?"

"I dismissed them for the day."

The detective walked over to the front door, turned and looked back at Holmes, "One other thing, Dr. Holmes," He paused, observing Holmes' facial expression and body language. "What about the registry? It shows that Ben Pitezel signed the registry on his own, why would he do that if he were renting the home around the corner?"

Holmes knew there was no name on the registry for Ben Pitezel and walked over to the desk. He looked down at the registry and saw that Ben Pitezel had written his name in the registry. He must have overlooked it, but why would he sign his own name in the registry? The detective saw that the question flustered Holmes, his actions were nervous and the Detective could see his body language had become shifty.

"Dr. Holmes, do you mind if I take a look upstairs?" He reached to his belt and pulled out his revolver, knowing that Holmes often carried one of his own.

He walked over reached into Holmes' holster, pulling out his revolver placing it on the desk. Covering Holmes with his gun, he reached for his handcuffs, cuffed Holmes to the steel bar which extended from the wood of the desk, "You stay here, doctor. Is there anything I need to know before I go upstairs?"

The detective looked at Holmes, who said nothing to the detective and looked down at the signature on the registry. It was not Ben Pitezel's handwriting, whose was it? Holmes suddenly thought of Jeptha Howe, he must have had some suspicion about him over the deal he had made with Ben and wanted to cover his tracks with a back up plan of his own.

The detective walked up to the first door on the right and opened the door. The room appeared to be a regular hotel room. The bed was made and the room was clean, well organized. The detective stepped back, closed the door and moved to the first door on the left. Down in the lobby, Holmes stood locked to the desk.

Jeptha walked through the front door and saw that Holmes had been detained with handcuffs.

Holmes immediately asked for his help, "Jeptha, quick, I need you to reach behind the desk, on the floor and pick up the gun behind the counter. There is a detective upstairs and I need to take care of him." Howe walked to the desk, looked down at Holmes' gun on the floor behind the desk. Holmes had managed to free one of his hands from the cuffs and was staying still in order to get Robert to pick up the gun.

Upstairs, the Detective opened the first door on the left and discovered Mrs. Pitezel. She was lying on the floor, crying and hysterical. She looked up at the detective holding the gun informing him, "Please do not kill me, I am Carrie Pitezel, I did not do anything wrong, Ben was going to kill me. Dr. Holmes is protecting me."

The detective was now confused about Holmes' role in this whole scenario, still unaware of what was going on. Why was Carrie, Ben's wife, locked in a room in the hotel and supposedly dead at the house around the corner with her family?

"I am going to get to the bottom of this, but I need you to stay here for now." He shut the door behind him and slowly walked to the staircase, looked down and discovered another man in the lobby. The detective raised his revolver towards the two men. Howe heard the detective coming down the staircase and moved towards the gun on the floor. He reached down, hid behind the counter and picked up the gun. The detective slowly moved down the staircase.

Holmes looked over at Jeptha Howe and demanded, "Give me the gun Jeptha. I can kill him. I have killed before. What are you going to do kill a cop?" Holmes knew that Carrie Pitezel thought that Ben was going to come and kill her. Holmes believed Jeptha Howe was unaware about Ben's death and if he could get the gun, he could finish off both the detective and Jeptha.

"Give me the gun Howe, I will kill the detective and we can flee the hotel. I am planning on fleeing to Boston!"

"Just like you killed Pitezel, Holmes?"

Holmes looked at Jeptha, realizing that he must have somehow found out about Pitezel's death at the hotel. The detective was listening to the conversation from the top of the staircase.

"Put down the gun!" The detective ordered.

Jeptha Howe stood up from behind the desk and fired at the detective, but his shot missed. The detective fell to the staircase, injuring his arm, and held his shoulder with his left arm. He stood up and returned fire at Howe, but missed. Jeptha fell forward to the ground, hunched over and crawled to the front door, escaping. The gun fell to Holmes' feet. Holmes stood still, pretending that he was still cuffed, as the detective descended the staircase. Holmes slid the gun behind his feet out of view from the detective.

"Holmes, do not move." The detective ordered, as he walked down the remaining stairs. He kept his gun pointed towards Holmes, slowly making his way closer to the desk.

Holmes slowly released the cuffs from his hands, as the detective walked closer to him. When the detective reached the desk, Holmes swung his arm at the detective, striking the detective on the side of the jaw. The detective fell to the floor dropping his gun and falling to the ground.

"Stop, Holmes, according to Mrs. Pitezel you were protecting her."

Holmes turned from the desk revealing he had escaped from the handcuffs restraining him. The detective gasped and grabbed for his gun, as Holmes reached down and picked up his revolver. He pointed it at the detective and fired off one round, "This is your chance to survive." The first shot hit the floor next to the detective.

Holmes stepped forward and pulled the trigger again, but the gun misfired, pointed the gun, pulled the trigger and again, it misfired. The detective reached back and grabbed his gun which was right behind his head, lifted it towards Holmes and fired. The gunshot echoed through the lobby, striking the lobby reception desk. Holmes fell backwards, to the ground.

The detective rolled over to his knees. Holmes jumped towards the detective and kicked the gun from his hands. Reaching down to his ankle, slid up his pant leg revealing a knife tucked underneath. He pulled the knife and pressed it against his throat. The detective cried out, "It's still not too late, Dr. Holmes." Holmes beat the detective, repeatedly, across the face. After knocking the detective unconscious, he rushed up the stairs and opened the door where the children were.

The gas had overtaken them and they were not moving. One by one he carried them down the stairs and loaded them into a trunk inside his carriage. The detective was still lying on the floor. Holmes took a medical bag and rushed up to Mrs. Pitezel, "We need to leave, now. Ned is coming. I am going to give you this injection to calm your nerves during the carriage ride."

"Where are we going?" She inquired.

Holmes finished administering the injection, "I am not sure, yet." She became groggy, and Holmes lifted her from the bed and carried her to the carriage. After placing her inside the carriage, he whipped the reins and the horse and carriage rode off into the busy Chicago roadways.

'The Jig is Up'

After fleeing from the back of his hotel in his carriage and down the busy streets of Chicago, Holmes was on the road towards Philadelphia. As time passed, the detective struggled on the floor of the hotel, unable to regain his bearings from the severe beating Holmes had put on him. Moments later, two officers opened the hotel's doors and slowly entered, revolvers in hand, quickly spotting the struggling detective.

"Detective, are you all right?" One of the officers raised the detective's head. As he slowly came to, the detective jerked back screaming in pain. The officers tended to the wounds on his face. The detective screamed out, again, "We are going to need as many officers down here as soon as possible."

One of the officers handed his pair of cuffs to the other officer and ran out the hotel door to make the call. The remaining officer rushed over to the detective. The detective looked up at the officer and gasped,

"Holmes is going to Philadelphia or Boston. He has a woman named Carrie Pitezel and children."

The detective managed to muster enough energy to call out to the officer, "There is another man who was involved with Holmes, but he fled the hotel. We will get some carriages and pursue Holmes." The officer rushed up the stairs to check the rest of the second and third floors. The detective had rushed off in his carriage with two other carriages in pursuit of Holmes. The carriages pulled in front of the police precinct.

"We need to notify Detective Geyer in Philadelphia. We may be in luck if Holmes is headed to Philadelphia or Boston. Detective Geyer is one of the nation's top detectives with the Pinkerton Services."

After leaving a message for Detective Geyer, of the possibility Holmes may be on his way to Philadelphia, the team of detectives and officers set out on carriages in an attempt to catch up and detain the suspect. There were a few main roads leading to Philadelphia and if they rode through the night would eventually catch Holmes. They would have to tend to the wounds on the detective's face and check for a possible concussion.

Holmes, Mrs. Pitezel, and the three Pitezel children traveled across the Northern United States and into Canada, "Ned will still be looking for you and the children."

"Do you believe he has any ideas where we will be traveling?" She replied.

Holmes directed the carriage across Toronto and to their first stop, "I have a feeling we have covered our tracks well enough to keep him off the trail. There was even word that Ben has fled to London, with Jeptha Howe."

He escorted Carrie Pitezel and the children into a small hotel along the route, "I will need to keep you and the children calm and relaxed. Therefore, these sedatives will allow me to do just that." Holmes administered the drugs and they were soon in a sedated state. That night he carried out the murders of the two Pitezel girls, suffocating them and leaving their bodies in a trunk.

The following morning, Carrie Pitezel woke, "Where are the children?"

"They are staying with a caretaker, on their way to England. I have to make a stop, before we return to Detroit. Then we can join the kids in England." Carrie was unaware the girls had been murdered and the remaining boy was drugged and placed inside the carriage's storage compartment.

Holmes used various aliases, as they interacted with the people along their route. Detective Geyer arrived in Toronto and had Holmes' last known whereabouts quickly narrowed down to a small town, where Holmes was thought to have been seen by a local resident. Geyer had discovered the bodies of the two Pitezel girls in the cellar and had learned Holmes was heading east.

He was following Holmes through Indianapolis, where Holmes had rented a cottage. Holmes was reported to have visited a local pharmacy to purchase drugs, and a repair shop to sharpen the knives; he planned on using for his final act.

That night Holmes worked throughout the evening, dismembering the body of the remaining Pitezel boy, Howard, "Goodbye." He calmly whispered, as the extremities and other bones were buried underneath the house. He attempted to disfigure the face by removing some of the teeth and bones. After finishing his dinner, Holmes spent the remainder of the night collecting and placing wood into the fireplace to incinerate the evidence.

The following morning, Carrie Pitezel had fled the cottage and was hiding in a local hotel. Holmes had already fled the Indianapolis cottage, when Detective Geyer arrived on the scene. He approached a field, near the cottage, where a man was tending to his crops, "Excuse me, sir."

The farmer approached the detective with caution, "What can I help you with?"

Detective Geyer produced a photograph, "Have you recently seen this man?"

"I believe this is the man who rented out this cottage, a few days back." The farmer studied the photograph, further, "Yes, I am positive. That is the man."

"Thank you very much. Would you know who owns the cottage?"

"Well, that would be me." The farmer answered, leaning on his shovel, "Is there a problem?"

"I am Detective Geyer, from Philadelphia. Would you grant me access to the cottage, so I can have a look around?"

"Follow me." The farmer led the detective to the front and unlocked the door, allowing the detective inside.

When he was given access to the cottage, by the owner, the detective smelled the scent of freshly burnt flesh. He immediately investigated the fireplace ashes. The boy's teeth and other bits of bone were discovered in the cottage's fireplace, "Would you be willing to write your testimony, regarding seeing this man and renting this cottage to him?"

"I certainly would, anything to help you with your investigation." The farmer seemed a bit rattled by having someone in his cottage that would perform such horrifying acts. The detective discovered freshly disturbed ground under the home. Upon retrieving a small shovel, he removed some of the remains of the Pitezel boy.

"Who is this man, detective?"

"Doctor Henry Howard Holmes. He is suspected of being involved in the disappearance of many people." Detective Geyers placed the evidence and remains of the boy with the other children.

After the farmer had finished writing his statement and the detective had gathered the necessary evidence, he turned to the farmer, "Thank you for your cooperation. If I should need anything further, I will contact you."

"I am happy to help, detective." The two shook hands and the detective departed in his carriage. As he was pulling away, two more carriages joined him.

"Glad to have some fellow members from the Pinkerton Service join me." Detective Geyer and the Pinkerton's exchanged handshakes.

"Sir, we found Carrie Pitezel in one of the local hotels."

"Return her to Philadelphia and lock her in a cell, along with these trucks, containing evidence against Dr. Holmes and Carrie Pitezel."

Carrie Pitezel called out from the rear of the carriage, "We did nothing wrong!"

"What about the murder of your husband, and your children?" Detective Geyers accusations seemed outrageous to Mrs. Pitezel.

"You can give your testimony back in Philadelphia. Take her away! The rest of you follow me." The rest of the group headed east, hoping to keep hot on the trail of Holmes.

Back at Holmes' hotel, the hotel's janitor informed police, "I was never allowed to clean the third floor. I had strict instructions that I would lose my job and I was paid very well."

Police and detectives began their investigation over the course of the month, "We are uncovering Holmes' efficient methods of committing murders and then disposing of the corpses." The captain was informed by one of the detectives, as he entered the hotel.

"Show me more, detective." Throughout the day, officers and detectives scoured the hotel.

The detective walked into the hotel with the captain, "These are the gas chambers, on the third floor and here are secret chambers where we believe people were held and over here is one of the hotel's hidden passageways."

The captain looked over the rooms, "How could this go on for so long, unreported by any of the guests, or hotel employees? I believe there are more people involved with Holmes in this operation and we need to find out."

"Sir, I believe the employees were paid, handsomely, to remain quiet and we were told as much during the interview with the hotel's custodian, Patrick B. Quinlan. In the hotel safe, they found more bodies, which had been asphyxiated. There were suspicious life insurance policies next to Holmes' savings withdrawals."

The captain left the room, followed by the detective, "Strange, Holmes would leave behind his savings withdrawals."

"As far as we know, he assaulted a detective and was forced to leave the hotel, very quickly."

"In the basement, we discovered numerous organs; Holmes had removed from his victims." They descended the staircase, from the third and second floors, "Sir, before you enter the basement, you should know this is a highly indescribable scene. We found tanks of acid filled with half dissolved bones floating inside."

"Good God almighty! Show me the way." The scent from the basement rose from below, leaving the captain and detective covering their mouths and noses with handkerchiefs. They walked through various tunnels.

The detective continued, "Pieces of dismembered body parts were discovered, here, in the quicklime pits." Officers and detectives were gathering evidence, placing each piece into their individual evidence bags.

The captain looked over to a table, "This is the body of a half dissected man, strapped to a steel table. What kind of monster are we dealing with? This is unbelievable."

"Sir, no one in their right mind would carry out something like this."

"The man will be dealt with according to the law. Continue gathering the evidence and photographing the scene. I want all of this documented, with precision and with the utmost attention to detail!" The captain was obviously more shake by witnessing what had taken place in the hotel's basement.

"Before you leave, sir, take a look over here." The detective showed the captain the where they discovered half burned bones and pieces of jewelry in the makeshift crematories and hair and skin lying all around the floor of the basement. Some of the officers fled from the basement and out of the hotel, to get into the fresh air.

The captain turned, "Any of the officers that cannot handle this crime scene return to headquarters for further orders." Rumors quickly spread throughout the precinct and the word on the street was that the Chicago police had discovered a "House of Horrors." The papers quickly picked up the story and announced the case would be quickly brought to trial, once Holmes was apprehended. The hotel was also being dubbed, the "Murder Castle".

Holmes rode along the bumpy dirt road, towards Boston. He rode for the better part of the day and evening. He allowed the carriage to be led by the two horses, as he attempted to stitch a wound he had received from one of his knives. However; was unsuccessful in fully stitching the wound. He rode; half awake, allowing the horses to do most of the work traveling along the dirt road.

Early the next morning, Holmes reached a clearing just outside the Boston city limits. He lowered himself from the carriage and struggled to reach for his medical kit. After pulling out the old stitching from the wound, he repaired the wound, carefully cleaning the wound with disinfectant. After an excruciating amount of pain, and unaware of the amount of blood loss, Holmes lost consciousness.

The afternoon passed. In the distance, a carriage approached Holmes who was lying on the ground, just near his own carriage. A man and a woman pulled up to the side of Holmes' carriage. The man jumped from the carriage and approached the scene with caution, "Stay there, dear. We don't know what has happened here."

Holmes was still unconscious, as the man walked up and opened the door of the carriage. The rotten smell struck him and he placed his hand over his nose at the overwhelming stench. He placed a handkerchief over his nose and mouth and inspected the truck inside. Upon opening it, he discovered the blood and pieces of clothing.

The man ran from the carriage and recovered a rope from his carriage, instructing his wife, "Ride into Boston and inform the police there is a man here with a compartment filled with blood, inside his carriage." The man's wife quickly slid over to the middle of the carriage seat and whipped the reins, leaving her husband at the scene.

The man rushed to Holmes and tied the ropes around his wrists and legs, restraining him from fleeing or escaping. Holmes slowly stirred and was regaining consciousness, as he moved he realized he was restrained. Just as he opened his eyes, Detective Geyer and two other carriages arrived at the scene. The Pinkerton crew quickly took Holmes into custody, "This is Holmes, Detective Geyer."

Detective Geyer limped over to Holmes' body, along with the rest of the Pinkerton crew, and looked down at him as Holmes recognized the detective, "So, you got me? I guess you have a few questions to ask?" Holmes laughed. The detective reached back and struck Holmes across the jaw, knocking him unconscious. The woman, who rode into Boston, had also arrived back at the scene along with two other police carriages.

Holmes' murder spree finally ended when he was arrested, on November 17, 1894, after being tracked across the country, from Philadelphia, by the Pinkerton crew and Detective Geyer. He was held on an outstanding warrant, "It appears he was prepared to flee the country." The detective found a suitcase and an additional bag of money.

It was agreed by some of the members of the Pinkerton service and the detective, "Holmes should be taken into custody and placed in Moyamensing Prison, to be held over for trial." Holmes was taken to the prison, restrained and placed in a cell.

One of the prison guards instructed the others, "Attention guards, Holmes has a deceptive and devious way about him. You are not to look into the murder's eyes. Looking into the eyes of this man could lead to a hypnotic state and then, ultimately, you will be under the killer's control."

Outside the prison, guards patrolled the perimeter and there were guard towers strategically positioned around the prison walls. The Moyamensing Prison dominated 1400 South 10th Street, at the southwest intersection with Passyunk Avenue and Reed Streets in South Philadelphia. It was built to house four hundred inmates, with a separate attached wing that would serve as a debtor's prison.

While Holmes sat in the Philadelphia prison, not only did the Chicago police investigate his operations, but the Philadelphia police began to try to unravel the Pitezel situation in particular, the fate of the children. Detective Geyer was given the task of finding out. His quest, like the search of Holmes' Castle, received wide publicity. He never discovered all the remains of the small boy; however, the discovery of the two girls in the cottage essentially sealed Holmes' fate, at least in the public's mind.

Holmes sat in his cell, in between the numerous confessions and false statements, drawing sketches and writing in his journal. The confessions and interrogations by the prosecutor, led nowhere, " If you are not going to cooperate, the judge is not going to be lenient with your final sentence."

"I will tell you this, I will not be aiding the police to discover the exact body count I left behind. You already have evidence to use, as you will."

"I believe you must have disposed of the bodies by selling them and distributing them to medical university, schools, colleges, and hospitals across the country. Is that what your paperwork will reveal?"

Holmes leaned forward, "Do you have the paperwork?" He smirked and leaned back against the wall.

The interrogation was abandoned, "We possess all the evidence we need, but it is hard to believe you would not want to give the families of the deceased some peace of mind."

Holmes scoffed, "There is no peace of mind in this world."

"Well, Doctor Holmes, the trial will be underway, as soon as I have gathered and examined the remaining evidence for your trial."

Once the trial date arrived, the prosecuting attorney and his team gathered in the courtroom. The jury filed in from a back room and took their seats. The judge addressed the jury, "You are instructed not to look Holmes' eyes and to avoid any eye contact, at all costs. Holmes is manipulative and it is rumored he can use his hypnotic stares to put the power of suggestion into your head. These powers of suggestion could make someone do whatever it is he desires, including taking their own lives and the lives of others."

Doctor Holmes was escorted into the courtroom, "Please be seated. Prosecutor, you have the floor." The judge began reviewing paperwork.

The prosecuting attorney stood and began presenting the evidence, "We learned from a man who informed the police about his most recent scam. It involved insuring a man named Benjamin Pitezel, his wife and children, for $10,000, with the Fidelity Mutual Life Association in Chicago and then faking his death in a home explosion by substituting cadavers."

"All participants were then to split the insurance payment, but Holmes had reneged and planned on running off with the money. We soon learned that Herman Webster Mudgett was actually Doctor Howard Henry Holmes, clearly a con and fraud. A company representative of the Fidelity Mutual Life Association, who had already expressed suspicions about the scene at the Holton residence, re-opened the investigation and circumstances surrounding the discovery of a body at 1316 Callowhill Street in Chicago. It had been found in a state of rigor mortis and so badly burned from chemicals, and sun exposure, that identity of the person could not be judged. Holmes had indeed identified this body from certain characteristics as the remains. After he collected the money, he disappeared."

The judge continued taking notes and the jury was listening intently to the prosecutor's presentation, "Given these details, company officers tried unsuccessfully to track him, so they hired additional agents from the Pinkerton National Detective Agency to search for and detain Holmes."

The prosecutor began presenting more evidence as he continued his case, "As these more experienced men followed his trail, across the country, they gathered information about his numerous frauds, thefts and schemes, including other insurance scams years earlier in Chicago that had provided him with funds to build his three story hotel. They finally caught up to Holmes just outside of Boston. He was taken into custody and transferred over to police."

"The best sources for the Holmes case are the documents and evidence from the investigation itself: Detective Frank P. Geyer's testimony and evidence from his experiences and the autobiographical pieces that Holmes has penned. At first, Holmes tells one story, including mundane details about his life and numerous lies to cover up his crimes and then he offers sensational confessions."

The Holmes case was an immediate sensation. Editions of the major Philadelphia and Chicago newspapers carried the story from the moment Holmes was arrested. The judge spoke, "Doctor Holmes, please stand. Holmes remained seated, as the judge looked up from his paperwork, "I am moving forward with the prosecution request for a trial. You will be held over throughout the case, with bail denied. Do you wish to have representation, or have you sought counsel with an attorney?

"I will be representing myself." Holmes answered.

Holmes requested he represent himself and the judge replied, "You will be allowed your constitutional right to do just that. I will continue the case, for the following morning, allowing Doctor Holmes time to prepare his case." The judge tapped his gavel and Holmes was escorted from the courtroom and returned to his prison cell.

The following morning, the prosecuting attorney continued presenting more of the evidence from a Chicago detective, "Going back to Chicago, a detective looked up real estate agents to find out if a man had rented a house and hotel room for only a few days. It took considerable time to impress each agent with the importance of making a careful search for us. He found a house that Holmes had rented, which was surrounded by a six-foot fence. The family residing there knew about some loose dirt under the house. They dug it up, firmly believing they would find one or more bodies. However, there were no bodies found at the location."

"Geyer discovered Holmes with a large trunk containing blood, inside the carriage. A woman identified Holmes from a photograph as the man who her and her husband came across while Holmes was unconscious from a wound. In short order, Detective Geyer discovered the corpses of two unclothed girls, Nellie and Alice Pitezel, back in Toronto."

"Alice was found lying on her side with her hand over Nellie, Geyer wrote. Nellie was found lying face down, her plaited hair hanging neatly down her back. A crew of officers lifted them from the cellar and transferred them to coffins. Gruesomely, as Nellie was lifted, her heavy braid pulled the scalp away from her skull. The bodies were doused with corrosive acid, leaving little of their remains identifiable."

"Searchers found a toy in Holmes' Chicago hotel, which was listed in Mrs. Pitezel's inventory of things that her children had owned. Geyer still knew there were more victims to find. His trek was not yet done, although it now appears to be fully pessimistic."

The prosecutor described the inside of Holmes' hotel and the evidence from the investigation, "Holmes' "Castle" included soundproof sleeping chambers with peepholes, sheet metal walls, gas pipes, sliding walls and vents that were controlled from another room. Many of the rooms had low ceilings and trapdoors in the floors, with ladders leading to smaller rooms below. The building has secret passages, false floors, rooms with torture equipment and a specially equipped surgery table."

"There were also greased chutes that emptied into a two level cellar, in which Holmes had installed two large furnaces. It is believed that Holmes placed his chosen victims into the special chambers into which he then pumped lethal gas, controlled from the hallways and then listened to them react. Apparently, he gained some fiendish pleasure from this activity."

"It is believed that he would sometimes ignite the gas to incinerate them. When finished, he might have slid the corpses down the chutes into his cellar, where vats of acid and other chemicals awaited them. Perhaps even place them on a table, an elongated bed with straps, just to see how far the human body could be stretched during torture."

"Investigators discovered several complete skeletons and numerous incinerated bone fragments in the hotel's basement, including the pelvis of a fourteen year old. There was also a bloodstained noose and a vault filled with quicklime. Yet, Holmes insists he had nothing to do with any murders. Those people had either taken their own lives, he claimed, or was killed by someone else."

The judged ordered, "We will break for the day and return tomorrow morning where, you, Doctor Holmes can present your case." Holmes did not speak a word, but had been writing for hours in his cell, writing up his defense. He was determined not to speak a word or cross examine any of the witnesses, hoping to prevent any further, damaging testimony against him.

The following day, Holmes then took to his defense, "To exonerate myself, I present the journal I penned and allow for my defense, allege the evidence against me as being a multi-murderer and arch conspirator, telling of the twenty-two tragic deaths and disappearances in which I am said to be implicated. Furthermore, the evidence presented against me is all speculation and there is no incriminating evidence against me, as no witnesses have come forward that I was the one who in fact committed these crimes."

The judge replied, "Unfortunately, for you Dr. Holmes, the prosecutor and Detective Geyers have presented witness accounts and even testimony from Carrie Pitezel that you were in fact involved with the crimes you are being charged with. The court will be dismissed for the weekend and coming holiday. Doctor Holmes, the evidence against you is overwhelming. I suggest you present truthful statements and cooperate with this court room and the prosecuting attorney."

Holmes knew his time had run out, the voice he heard throughout his life was gone and had not spoken to him in months. It was now a matter of time and he knew it. It was time to pen another story. He hired a journalist the work with him over the weekend and was paid a large sum of money for the publishing of his confession. The weekend had passed and Holmes was back in the court room, to continue his defense.

H.H. Holmes: The Devil in Me

"Are you prepared, Doctor Holmes?" The judge inquired.

Holmes answered and stood, "I am and I present, to the court, my memoirs. In my original confession I described the Gilmanton Academy, N.H., the town in which I grew up as Herman Webster Mudgett."

The judge received the memoirs and read them aloud, "I was born in Gilmanton, New Hampshire in 1861 and claim to have experienced an ordinary life, with an ordinary set of parents and a normal schoolboy routine. However, this is not true. In this new memoir, which I had a journalist assist me in writing over the break, tells of the real life I lived. Please feel free to share this with the court." Holmes was now attempting to gain sympathy from court proceedings.

The memoirs were read aloud. They describe a turning point in his life as the day some older boys bullied him in school, his mother, and him being molested by his father's estranged mistress. It was a wicked and dangerous thing to do to a child of tender years and health. Holmes claimed, though he admits that the experiences cured him of his fears. He attributes his desire to go into medicine to this memorable incident.

"Had my early life and associations been such as to predispose me towards such criminal proceedings, still the want of motive remains. I can show that no motive exists."

Holmes memoirs continued to tell that he was a mother's boy and an avid reader, spending nights with the works of Edgar Allan Poe and Jules Verne. His father, Levi, was a farmer and strict disciplinarian who used his belt to punish him, or banished him to the attic without food for bad behavior. His mother was devoutly religious and constantly insisted her husband and Holmes to pray with her, he wrote.

Apart from my strict upbringing, little foreshadows my transformation into H.H. Holmes. However, in this book, I offer up one incident that had a lasting effect on me as a child and into adulthood. He describes how he often would walk by the office of a town doctor. The door to the office was typically open, and recalling the scent. Partly, from it being associated, in my mind as the source of all the nauseous mixtures of that had been my childish terror and partly because of vague rumors I had heard regarding its contents. This place was one of peculiar abhorrence to me.

At seventeen years old I left Gilmanton, with Clara Lovering to Alton and we were married. From there, I served some time as a doctor's assistant in an asylum. We had a son, but I soon left without notice. My marriage to Clara proved to be a rare exception for me and the women who I kept company with, because she survived. I knew that if I stayed with her, I would eventually be overcome with the desire to murder her as well.

It was in college, where I did my first truly dishonest act. I began robbing and stealing from the citizens of Michigan. I received a medical school diploma, from the University of Michigan's Medical School. I continued to commit insurance fraud, faking deaths with stolen cadavers. I was extremely profitable in these endeavors.

I made it a point to stretch the Christian character of Minnie Williams, however, retract the statements I had made about her, regarding her state of mind and the alleged murder of her sister, Nannie. I persuaded her to give me several sizable sums of money and forged documentation to secure her Texas land.

I had offered a number of rooms for many young women, and individuals, arriving to attend the Chicago World Fair, but many of those women associated with me had left my hotel, alive. In addition, I had employed a number of young women, who also had left without notice. From what can be reconstructed, it seems that the prosecutor and police would lead the public and the jury to believe I tortured and murdered these women, then processing their corpses in the basement crematories.

Even with the most absurd of accusations by removing their flesh and selling the skeletons to medical universities, and hospitals, which in some cases I had but strictly from cadavers collected from local hospitals and city morgues. I was paid $7,500 by the Hearst Newspapers in exchange for this confession. I gave various contradictory accounts of my life, claiming innocence and even I am possessed by Satan.

Minnie was killed so that no one in or about the hotel should know of her having been there. Investigators claim she did leave something behind, her footprint on the door of the room where she was killed, which she produced during an unsuccessful struggle to survive. This is how Chicago authorities seek to prove I was her murderer.

I told Minnie that her sister had given up her journey north and had decided to stay with me. I then secured Minnie's property in my own name. I drugged her with a heavy sedative and left her in the upstairs room of my hotel. I was going to attempt to implicate her as the murderer of her sister and the Pitezel children, which I am now repudiating. This is the saddest and most heinous of any of the crimes, I committed."

Next, I turn my statement to Pitezel. From the first hour we met, I knew that I was going to kill the man. Everything I did for Pitezel, which seemed to be a partnership in committing insurance fraud, was merely a way to gain his confidence. Pitezel met his death and I informed Mrs. Pitezel he was going to kill her and have me assist in collecting on a life insurance policy he had me take out on her and the children.

I packed my bags preparing to flee and then went to where Pitezel was in the hotel room, saturated his clothing and face with corrosive sulfuric acid. I literally melted the face of my former accomplice. Pitezel cried out and prayed for mercy, begging me to end his suffering with a speedy death, all of which had no effect on me.

When Pitezel finally expired, I poured chloroform into his stomach, to make the death appear to be accidental brought about by an explosion. That way, the insurance company would quickly pay the full amount of the claim. I left his body in a position that exposed it to the sun, for however long it would be before someone would discover him, presumably to further deform it for difficulty in identification. I left the hotel, without the slightest feeling of remorse for my actions.

Included is my prison diary is an appendix. The diary was read as a boring rendition of his routine and was his intention to make him appear to be ordinary, with an interest in books and was presented as a means to cast favor on him during the trial. He viewed the memoir as a literary work, as befitted his narcissistic temperament, claiming that "It was written with mature deliberation and against the protest of the charges and that said the charges be dismissed."

I claim that the murders I have been accused of being a blatant attempt to ensure that my trial would not be fair and impartial. I claim to formally and publicly deny all these accusations. Thus, I offer this narrative of my entire life, including a full disclosure of my dealings with the Pitezel family.

In ending the story and final protest, Holmes wrote; my sole object in this publication is to vindicate my name from the horrible aspersions cast upon it and to appeal to the American public for a suspension of judgment. Doctor Holmes never questioned any of the witnesses and it was an apparent failure to successfully defend against the evidence presented by the detective and prosecutor.

After hearing all the evidence and testimony presented in the courtroom, the judge and jury quickly came to his decision in the case, "Dr. Henry Howard Holmes, as it stands in this courtroom and in the case against you, you are found guilty as charged for the murder of five people and to the kidnapping of Carrie Pitezel."

Holmes only confessed to the murders of the five people in one confession and in others twenty six, he did not bring to light the murders of the hundreds that he made into skeletons, only that he sold processed cadavers to the medical universities and hospitals around the United States.

The judge looked over at H.H. Holmes, who looked back at him winked and smiled, "Dr. Holmes, you are sentenced to death in which you will hang by the neck until dead. This punishment will be carried out immediately and without delay. That is my judgment.

Dr. Holmes." The judge paused, took a deep breath and then continued, "Do you have anything to say to this?"

Holmes stood, as the guards reached for their revolvers, turned and looked at the courtroom, "I was born with the devil in me. I could not help the fact that I was a murderer, no more than the poet can help the inspiration to sing. I was born with the "Evil One" standing as my sponsor, beside the bed, where I was ushered into the world and he has been with me, since."

"Take him away." The judge ordered.

As Holmes left the courthouse he spoke, as he was being led out of the courthouse. He confessed, following the conviction, "Twenty seven murders in Detroit, Chicago, Toronto and Indianapolis, and six attempted murders! He stopped before the officers led him out of the prisoner's entrance to the courtroom, "Judge, I request that I be buried in concrete so that no one can ever dig me up and dissect my body, as I had dissected so many others."

The judge ordered the last request, "Your request is granted, now take him away!"

H.H. Holmes was led into the courtyard just outside the courthouse. The noose had been prepared and hung from the tower. A large crowd had gathered around the platform where Holmes was to be hung. He was led to the gallows and a black hood placed over his head. Time stood still, as the crowd waited with anticipation. The trap door opened beneath him and Holmes quickly dropped. His head snapped to the side, but his fingers clenched and his feet jerked for several minutes afterward, causing many spectators to gasp and look away.

Although the force of the fall broke his neck and the rope had pulled so tight that it had literally imbedded itself in his flesh, his heart continued to beat for nearly fifteen minutes. A prison doctor approached the hanging body, checking for a pulse. Holmes was finally declared dead.

Colby Van Wagoner

ABOUT THE AUTHOR

Purchase the author's additional titles:

Massacre Cave
Crow Mountain
Return to Crow Mountain
Volume One
Compound
Dead in Love
Earth Mongers
and
The Jack and Jillian Children's Book Series

Visit the author @ www.colbyvanwagoner.com

CPSIA information can be obtained at www.ICGtesting.com
Printed in the USA
LVOW07s2034130815

450020LV00001B/3/P

9 781477 417614